Canadian Winters

Canadian Winters

S. G. Read

Stanley
George
Publishing

A CIP catalogue record for this book is available
from the British Library.

ISBN 0 9543267 1 7

Printed in Great Britain

First published 2003 by

Stanley
George
Publishing

Stanley George Publishing
39 Church Road, Pembury, Kent, England TN2 4BS

For my wife

CHAPTER 1

SARAH Talksloud sat watching television. She had the volume loud as she was all alone and it made her feel safer. The door was locked and had a chain on it to keep undesirables out. The chain was new, as was the television. Her mother, Willa, had worked two nights a week for some time to be able to buy the television for her. Now it was Sarah's pride and joy, even though it was small. For now when the other children at school were talking about a programme, she could join in with the conversation instead of keeping quiet because she had no idea what they were talking about. With her mother at work and her father in prison, two years into a life sentence for murder, and her being an only child, she had to be all alone when Willa was at work. Her mother could not afford a baby sitter.

Her father, Harry Talksloud, was a shaman away on tribal business but he ended up drunk in a bar and, after having an argument with a loud white man who was badmouthing a squaw, the same white man was found outside with Harry's knife in his belly. Harry could not even remember the argument, but the knife was enough for the Mounties, and enough for the jury as well!

The new chain on the door had been fitted because there was a serial killer on the loose who preyed on girls of about ten. Sarah was ten years old! Up to the start of this winter, five girls had been taken by this killer, four of them from their homes while their parents were at work. They had all been subjected to his intentions all night and all had been left in the middle of nowhere to die, naked, at the mercy of the cruel Canadian winter. Sarah had strict instructions not to open the door to anyone apart from her mother when she came home from work.

She did not hear the footsteps on the path outside. Normally the footsteps would have crunched the snow as the man walked up the path, but there was no snow as it was late this winter. She did not hear the first knock on the door. The second knock caught her attention and she turned the volume on the television down to listen. The third knock drew her to the door and she looked through the glass by the side of it. A man stood there and held up a gas can, as if to say, 'I'm out of gas'.

'Oh, it's you!' she called through the closed door. 'I think my Dad had some in the shed. I'll get you the key.' She was always willing to help someone she knew.

She took the key from its hook by the stairs, and walked back to the door. After taking off the deadlock she opened the door as far as the chain allowed and passed the key through the gap.

At the same time, Daniel Turner climbed off the greyhound in the middle of the square in Turnround. As he neared Turnround, he wondered how it had got its name, but when he saw the greyhound turn round in the square and drive back out the way it had come in, he wondered no more. He waited until the coach had gone, then surveyed his new home. On the other side of the square there were two clear paths leading into the trees. On his left was a store, still with its lights on. It was tucked up in the far corner with a side road to its left. Up the side road, Danny, as he liked to be called, could just make out a flag pole with the flag hanging limply on it. He toyed with the idea of looking in the store and visiting the office, but it had been a long journey and he needed refreshment. To his right was another side road, and on the other side of it stood a large house. Danny could just make out the sign as it hung by one of its chains. It read 'Maple Lodge', the very place he was lodging at. Still, he thought, in a place as small as this, a boarding house should be easy to find. He crossed the road and walked up the path. At the door, he hesitated. He had left his wife behind. When she found out that he was trying for a job in the Canadian wilderness, she told him there and then not to ask her to come out there if he got it. He did of course when he found out he had the job, but by then, Lucy, his wife, was living with her mother. She said, 'If you go out there, you go without me.' And that is just what he did. But he was wondering now whether he had jumped out of the frying pan and into the fire.

Sarah's shoulders dropped when she saw the key fall out of the man's fingers to the ground.

'Sorry, my hands are frozen. I've walked aways,' the man said as he bent to pick up the key.

'I'd let you warm them, but I'm not allowed to let anyone in when Ma isn't here,' Sarah replied apologetically.

9

'I should hope not! Not with all that's going on around here at the moment, and you being here all alone.' He stood up. 'The key has gone under the door. Can you reach it from your side?'

She squatted down. 'I can see it, but I can`t get it. Let me try with the door closed,' she answered.

'Yes, it went in the corner, I think.'

She closed the door, then reopened it. 'It's no good. I can't reach it,' she said, and, without thinking, unhooked the chain to retrieve the key. When she stood up with the key, the man had put his can down.

'Wrong move!' he said, grabbing her round the waist.

She struggled in vain. He threw her to the floor and held her there. She tried to bite his hand, and he had to move it out of reach.

'I was ready for that. You Indians are all the same. You never know when to give up.'

He pulled a piece of wood out of his pocket. It had string attached to both ends. He forced the wood into her mouth and tied the strings together behind her head.

'You won't try that again.' he said smugly. 'Now let's do the display.'

The display was what the parent, whichever one was first in, saw when they walked through the door. The clothes his victim was wearing were spread out in front of the fire, all of them! When the display was finished, with his victim tied hand and foot, he carried her to his vehicle. There was no hurry. Her mother worked all night, and her father was locked away. He dumped her in the back, and walked back to the house for his can.

'I'd better not forget you!' he said to the metal object.

'You are worth your weight in gold. Besides, you'll have my fingerprints all over you, and they can still ask for them.'

He closed the door and walked back to his vehicle where the girl was struggling to free herself.

'Be my guest, knock yourself out. I reckon I am an expert in tying up girls by now. You wait until I get to my little hidey hole, and I'll show you a few other knots before I let you go.'

Sarah stopped struggling when she heard him say that, but she could not say anything with the piece of wood in her mouth.

'Oh yes, I will let you go in the morning,' he said, looking out of the window at the lack of snow. 'Do you think it's going to snow, Sarah?' he asked as he drove away.

Danny looked for a bell, but could not see one. He knocked on the door and waited. After a few minutes, he knocked again and heard footsteps approaching. The door opened and a woman stood there. She had fiery red hair which looked out of control, a faded green dress and bottle green socks. She had a worn-down appearance which made her look older than she probably was.

'Good evening,' Danny said politely.

'You'll be the Englishman. The one who's taken Chief's job,' she replied acidly. 'You'd better come inside.'

'The fire,' Danny thought as he followed her inside.

She turned on her heels and walked away, veering slightly left to go up the stairs in front of her. He followed her.

'This is your room,' she said in a take-it-or-leave-it manner. 'Dinner is at eight o'clock.'

Danny closed the door after she had gone and tried the

bed. That at least was comfortable. He would stay here until he found something better.

At least she didn't call me limey, he thought, and stretched out on the bed.

The journey had been long and tiring, a boat from Liverpool, then a train from Quebec to end in a greyhound from Edmonton. His eyes closed and he knew no more until a hand shook his foot persistently. He opened his eyes to see a young girl he judged to be about ten years old. She had the same red hair as the woman but she wore a bib and brace, like jeans but with shoulder straps.

'Ma says to tell you your food is getting cold,' she said in what was obviously the local accent.

'Thank you, young lady. Where's the bathroom?' Danny replied.

'At the end of the hall,' she explained, and pointed the way. 'What's England like?'

Danny had to think about it for a moment before he spoke. How do you explain England quickly to a ten-year-old who has never seen it?

'It's sort of middle of the road really. It's a bit like Canada, but we rarely have extreme temperatures,' he replied.

'What's extreme?' the girl asked.

'That means it is rarely too hot for too long, and it is rarely too cold for too long, but we do have lots of rain.'

'You talk funny,' the girl said, and turned to go.

'Do you have a name?' Danny asked, trying to break the ice.

'Of course I do, silly!' the girl replied, and scampered down the stairs.

Danny scratched his head. 'Maybe I'll have to learn Canadian.'

By the time Danny reached the dining table, the three people who sat there had already finished their first course. There was no starter, just a plateful of something which resembled stew, and it was followed by more of the same if you wanted it. Danny sized each of the men up in turn, trying to decide which one was the red-haired woman's husband, but nothing visible told him the answer so he gave up and ate until he was full. At least you did not leave the table hungry here, he thought. The red-haired girl was there. It was she who brought his dinner, then sat between him and her mother, watching his every move with a child's fascination. A normal mother might have scolded her for her apparent rudeness, but Mrs Foy said nothing. As none of the others spoke to him while he ate, he found her attentions less of an annoyance and more of a pleasure. At least she recognised that he was there! As though Mrs Foy sensed that Danny did not mind the little girl staring at him, she stopped eating for a second.

'Stop staring, Annette,' she said with a voice to be obeyed.

Annette looked away immediately, but from then on glanced at him frequently, although what she hoped to see eluded him. After the meal, coffee was served, and Danny held his hand over his cup, hoping she did not pour the coffee on his hand.

'Is there any tea?' he asked naively.

Mrs Foy shook her head. 'Gracious no! No one drinks tea round here,' she answered.

'I do!' said Danny, a little irately. 'You do have hot water?'

'We can manage that,' Mrs Foy replied with a distinct iciness in her tone.

'Good, I have some teabags upstairs.' There was no way they were going to coerce him into drinking coffee, especially their coffee.

He collected some of the teabags from his room, not all of them as he had brought three large boxes with him to help him get established. He put twenty teabags in the tea caddy he had also brought with him from England, and took the caddy downstairs. He expected curiosity, and he was prepared to sacrifice that many to satisfy them. He found a mug in the kitchen, opposite the bottom of the stairs, so he made himself some tea and returned to the table. He ignored the others as he drank it and considered making a second but was curious about the store and the office.

'I think I'll take a stroll in the crisp night air,' he said, trying to sound normal.

'Well I hope you brought one of those with you as well!' Mrs Foy replied.

Danny laughed, assuming she had meant it to be funny, then stepped out into the cold night air. He threw his coat over his shoulders but, after a few steps, put it on. He had half-expected snow when he arrived but he could live without snow! He walked to the store to find out what type of store it was. As the lights were still on, and the sign read 'open', he tried the door which opened easily with a faint buzz. A man appeared from the back of the store.

'Good evening!' he said with a broad Scottish accent.

The storekeeper walked over and held out his hand. Danny took it gladly. This was the first pleasant greeting since he arrived.

'Yee'll be Daniel Turner, the new park ranger,' the storekeeper continued.

'None other, but Danny to my friends.'

'Danny it is then. I knew you were due in today so I stayed open to sell you a few things in case that Made Brickman lets you get acquainted with our lovely forest.'

'I was going to do that as tomorrow is Sunday, well, ask if I could anyway,' Danny replied.

'That's as maybe, but what yee don't know is that we are overdue for snow, and when we get overdue it comes down with a vengeance. My old bones tell me we will have snow tomoree, and lots of it,' the storekeeper replied. 'And Made Brickman knows it as well as I do, and he'll still let yee go.'

'I see you sell snow shoes, so sell me some, but what if it doesn`t snow?' Danny asked.

'If it doesn`t snow tomoree, I'll buy them back at twice the price,' the storekeeper replied.

'From a Scot, that is a powerful selling technique.'

'It is the truth, mon!'

Danny looked the Scot straight in the face.

'You know I have to go on this little walk?'

'That I do, now that I have met yee.'

'Then sell me what I need to survive in this wilderness of yours.'

'That I will, and on credit!'

'Are you sure you're a true Scot?' Danny asked.

The Scot laughed.

'Hamish McLaughland at yee're service,' he said with a mini bow. 'And when I have sold yee enough to keep yee alive tomoree, so that yee can come back and pay me,

15

I invite yee to join me in a wee dram.'

They made a pile of things for Danny to take, and then they sat and talked for a long time, supping whisky and swopping tales, some of which did nothing to help Danny feel at home there. Time came to part, and Danny left his new purchases in the store to collect on his way out of Turnround via one of the tracks he had seen from across the square. He walked back to the boarding house and, after negotiating the stairs, flopped on the bed and fell asleep. In the early hours, the cold made him pull the duvet over himself and that was how he stayed until morning.

As Danny slept, another man was enjoying himself to the cost of his victim but even he had a schedule to keep. At three in the morning, he looked out of his vehicle.

'No snow, Sarah,' he said to the now submissive girl. 'That is bad news. Bad news for both of us.'

He drove out of his hidey hole, back along the track until it met the Main Road. There he stopped. 'Be back in a while. Don't go anywhere,' he added, and slammed the door.

What the girl could not see was him taking a shovel from the back of his vehicle and crossing the road to the forest beyond. Had she seen that she might have tried to escape, but she believed him when he said he would let her go in the morning. She relaxed, and despite her position she fell asleep. It was an hour later when he returned, and it woke her. He wrapped her in his duvet to stop the moon highlighting her whiteness and carried her across the road. It was not until she saw the hole in the ground that she started to struggle, but by then it was too late. By now she was bound hand and foot, and he lowered her into the hole face down. She struggled and struggled, and when he took the piece of wood out of her mouth she screamed for help, but there was no one about to hear.

'Look, I don't want to hurt you, but I need to get away before you tell on me so I'll just bury half of you and go,' he said in between her screams.

'You mean it?' she asked.

'Cross my heart and hope to die,' he replied.

'Well okay, but I won't tell anyone about it if you take me home before Ma gets there,' Sarah replied, ever hopeful.

He did not answer, but just started to fill in the hole round her feet. Then it was her legs and back until only her head was visible and she was finding it hard to breathe.

'One thing, Sarah. I lied,' he admitted, and covered her head with soil.

He refilled the hole, stamped the ground down and walked away without looking back, carrying his duvet and his shovel.

Danny was awake by six in the morning despite it being Sunday and the fact that he had downed more whisky than he had had in three years, in one night. He found time for a hot bath and ventured down for breakfast. In the kitchen he checked on his teabags and found only five left. He smiled when the picture of one of the men chewing the teabag like tobacco popped into his head. Not a thing you would do twice. The breakfast table was laid out, and although there was no one else about, Danny helped himself. With the kettle which was simmering over the stove, Danny made himself a mug of tea and sat drinking it while the two men who sat at the table last night walked in. They both screwed up their faces in disgust at the sight, thus proving their guilt. Danny ignored them and enjoyed his tea before walking to the office, the building with the flagpole. He hesitated at the door for a second, then knocked. He was not due until Monday, but he thought he might get acquainted before then. A man in uniform sat behind one of the desks in the front office.

'What can I do for you?' he asked, not politely.

'Daniel Turner reporting in. I didn't realise it was a uniform job.'

'I'm not expecting you until tomorrow,' the man in the chair replied, as if it was a crime to be early. 'Would it have made any difference to you if you'd known it was a uniform job?'

'No, why?' Danny retorted.

'No reason. I'm Brickman, I run things round here.'

Brickman stood up and walked into the back room. When he returned, he had a flat box with him.

'This is your uniform. Try it on and get acquainted with the area for a couple of days.'

'How do you mean?' Danny asked, wanting Brickman to be the one to suggest he walked into the forest, not him.

'Have a look round where you are going to be working,' Brickman replied, without committing himself.

'What, have a walk round the forest?' Danny prompted.

'That sort of thing,' Brickman replied. 'This is our official map, which should stop you from getting lost.'

'I'll take a tent as well in case I go too far to get back before dark.'

'You'll need one of these,' Brickman said, holding up a radio. 'Just in case you have any problems.'

Danny detected a slight smile on Brickman's face when he spoke.

'Just remember to hold this button in when you talk, and let it go to listen,' Brickman explained. 'We are on channel one.'

Danny took the radio and uniform back to his room. The uniform fitted well, and he posed in front of the mirror, making sure the door to his room was shut. Happy with his appearance, he walked to the store. It was open when he reached it, and he stepped inside.

'Good morning Hamish,' he said as the Scot appeared from the rear of the store.

'Good morning, Ranger Turner, in all yee're finery. How's yee're head?'

'Could be better, but I'm sure a walk in the fresh air surrounded by trees will clear it for me.'

'Yee are as daft as the rest of them here!' Hamish snorted. 'Yee should fit in well. I suppose yee'll be wanting yee're gear then?'

Danny nodded. It was piled by the door, and Danny spread out the map Brickman had given him.

'Did he mention snow?' Hamish asked.

'No, but he did give me this in case I have any problems,' Danny replied, holding up the radio.

'Is it charged?' Hamish asked.

Danny turned it on and heard voices talking.

'Seems to be,' he replied.

'Noo as I was saying last night, keep the river on yee're right and stay near the river. If it comes down hard, just wait it out and follow the river back.'

The river was the right hand boundary of the park which

Danny was now helping to look after. It was a fairly new park compared to the others around, with good walks, horse riding, and fishing. You were advised to have a rifle with you at all times as there were bears and wolves about, but shooting was taboo unless it was in self-defence.

'I have a compass, so why do I need to stay near the river?' Danny asked.

'There will be less drifting out there, and yee can always catch yee're dinner out of the river as yee follow it back.'

'I did want a look at the river, so now is as good a time as any.'

'It'll strike a wee bit cold for swimming by now!' Hamish warned.

'I forgot to pack my cossy anyway,' Danny replied dryly.

'Just yee be careful oot there mon, and keep that rifle handy at all times. There are all kinds of beasties oot there. As the only other non-Canadian here, I have a vested interest in keeping yee alive, even if yee are a Sassenach!'

'I'll be back,' Danny said, as he threw the rucksack on his back. He was no weakling, and strode to the door as though nothing was in it. He turned in the doorway. 'I hope,' he added, and walked out.

He was soon in amongst the trees. This was what he had come for, trees, and more trees!

Willa Talksloud walked tiredly up the path. She stifled yet another yawn and walked round to Sarah's window. She could see she was not in bed.

'Slept on the sofa again in front of your new toy,' Willa said with a smile.

She walked back and tapped on the door. Nothing

happened. She repeated the knock, but still nothing. Willa fumbled for her key to let the door open as far as the chain and shout through the gap, but when she turned the key the door opened wide. She stepped in ready to tell Sarah off for not using the chain, and saw the clothes laid out in front of the fire. She did not know that was the killer's way of saying it was him. The police had not let that become public knowledge. She ran from room to room searching for Sarah, but she was nowhere to be seen. They had no telephone, so when Harry rang from prison she and Sarah had to walk up to the nearest public telephone and wait for his call. She ran to the same telephone now, as fast as she could, without stopping. Then, after calling the police, she could do nothing but wait for them to arrive, nothing but cry.

A car arrived and took her back to the house and, once they had established that it was their man, they waited for the forensic team to arrive. They started to organise a search but the police officers who had been involved in previous searches knew that time was precious. Soon it would snow and then they would not find her. Now at least they had a chance, thanks to the late snow.

Danny followed Hamish's instructions and found the track which lead down to the river. After an hour's walking and frequent checks with his map and compass, he heard the river gurgling nearby. Now he was on his way. He looked up at the clear morning sky and walked on happily. Hamish had quickly made modifications to the official map, to add on what he thought was important for this trip. They had been selling the same map to visitors for forty years according to Hamish, and in that time there had been a few changes. Even the river had changed direction at one point to go round a landslide. When he finally saw the river, he stood on the bank and watched the water as it rushed past, coming from his left as he faced the river and disappearing on his right into dense brush. He knew where it went, he had seen it from the coach as it passed behind the garage only to veer left and on into the forest again. He turned left and started to follow it up stream. The trail was easily walked at first until he reached the point where fishermen had detoured round brush. It was hard work but he kept right next to the river by cutting his way through the brush. He was determined to stay with the river, and he was in no hurry. After all, Brickman had said he should take a couple of days to look round, and he was not working today. Where he cut a path, it was his path and no one had walked it before. He liked that idea. The cutting was hard work but when he regained the trail he made up for the slow pace.

Two hours after starting to follow the river, he was conscious of a monolith in front of him. A large rocky outcrop sticking out of a small hill with the river running in front of it. It was hard to work out how tall it was from where he stood, but he did know it was in the way. Danny looked at his watch and decided to stop and eat when he reached the monolith. The lower section was hidden by brush until he was quite close. But then, from the angle he approached it, he could see two rocks which were apart at the top, touched halfway down and parted more and more as they neared the ground. It looked like a large bum, or ass as he thought the locals might say if anyone started talking to him who didn't have a thick Scottish accent. He smiled at the sight, and walked on. If he had had a camera, he might well have taken a photograph of it, but a camera was not a necessity and might have been the straw to break the camel's back. He was starting to feel the weight of the rucksack. As he neared the bum, it was too much when there was a shrub with dead brown leaves right at the bottom of the rocks and right in the middle of the crack.

'Disgusting mother nature,' he said and walked on. 'Come on, Canada! I'm here, show me what you can do!' he added, this time as a challenge.

It was the middle of the day when he finally planted his back against the rock and slid down. He sat resting, and ate the food Hamish had put in his pack, not prepackaged sandwiches but made by him this morning just before Danny arrived. The food was good, and normally he would have washed it down with tea but he wanted to get on. The bottled water would have to do until he made camp and boiled up some water to go with his flask of ice cold milk and the tea bags in his rucksack.

As he ate, he thought of Lucy, his wife in England. Rather than come with him, she had gone back home to her mother even though she and her mother fought like cats and dogs when she was there. She was welcome to that life. He was happy here. It was sheltered where he sat and he thought of making it his campsite, somewhere to return to when it started to get dark. He would take a full two days. If it snowed it could only drift in here if it came from the direction he had approached from. If it came from there, he could go to the other side for shelter. He looked at the bush with its covering of brown leaves and wondered if there was enough room to pitch a tent behind it using the

23

bush as extra cover? He pushed past it, rifle in hand, to find a hole with room for a person to crawl into. Was that a wise thing to do though? He bent and peered inside, it was big enough to crawl in comfortably, but it was dark further in and there could be danger from snakes or other creepy crawlies. To call and tell them he had been bitten by something and needed help was not going to happen.

He squeezed back past the shrub and took his torch from the rucksack. Just a look with the torch showed him there was enough room to settle there without having to erect a tent, but how far did it go in? He moved forward, checking very carefully with his torch all the nooks and crannies as he went to make sure there was nothing nasty there. He was not afraid of snakes or creepy crawlies but he was a long way from assistance, and a bite might prove fatal. He moved in further and further. The tunnel veered to his left then turned back to his right, and there it opened into a large cave. He was gobsmacked.

'Better than a tent any day,' he thought, 'But am I alone?'

He moved his rifle forward to be able to shoot anything which might come at him, and shone his torch slowly round the cave. There was nothing in the cave with him, and he relaxed. He crawled forward and stood up.

'Well, if it does chuck it down with snow, I know where I'll be,' he announced, and listened to the echo of his voice.

He turned to go back out and felt a draft on his face. Air coming in has to go out somewhere. He lit a match and it was blown out. He crawled back out and collected his rucksack. Inside it he had the wrapping paper from his sandwiches, and he wanted to see what happened if he lit a fire in there. The worst that could happen was that he would have to crawl out, choking on smoke fumes. As he passed the shrub, he took twigs and leaves to help his fire before he crawled back inside. He lit the pile close to the entrance but far enough away for the match to stay alight. He watched the paper light the leaves and the twigs, and saw the smoke drift for a few seconds, then it started to rise up and disappear through a crack in the ceiling. He sat and watched the fire die as it ran out of fuel. Mr Brickman was going to be disappointed if he wanted rookie Ranger Turner to call in for help. He left his rucksack inside and crawled out to collect the rest of his things. They would be safe in there. The glut of wood nearby persuaded him to cut firewood to store in the cave. It would be difficult to find fallen wood under two feet of snow, so he stored enough to keep him going for a couple of days and dragged in some longer lengths as a reserve supply.

'There,' he said, contentedly. 'Enough wood to keep me warm, provisions for a week if I'm frugal, and cover if it snows. Now, let's explore.'

He left anything he did not want to carry, inside, but covered it with the wood just in case. He crawled outside, ready for anything, or so he thought. He had two choices. Turn left and try to find a passage between the rock and the river, or turn right and leave the river. He chose left, walking down the hill to the river as it rushed by, and found a track past the rock. Even a rookie like him could read the signs here. Toilet paper was strewn about to show what the path was used for, and Danny had to look where he trod to make sure he kept his boots clean. Not a good advert for the park. He turned left at the bottom and started to follow the river again, but an excited shriek stopped him in his tracks. He was ready for anything apart from more Canadians. He listened. They were obviously young, and one of them had just caught a fish. After standing there for a few seconds, he retreated and started back up the hill. It was silly, and he knew it, especially as they were only young Canadians but he felt it would end up the same as when he walked into the boarding house for the first time. He passed the shrub which covered the cave entrance, and followed the slope until the rock stopped and was replaced with grass. He clawed his way up the grass and soon found himself on top of the rocks. Now he was able to get in a position to look down on the fisherboys. There were two of them, and he judged them to be twelve or thirteen years old. They had parked their bicycles on the rock near to where they were fishing, and there was a tent with rocks as tent pegs. He stepped back from the edge and took in the view, it was breathtaking.

'Now I know why I came,' he said, drinking in the view. 'I was beginning to wonder.'

He had a choice. If he wanted to follow the river, he had to go down and risk being seen by the boys, or he could follow the track the boys had ridden their bikes along to get there. It took him away from the river in a straight line. He chose anonymity and started to walk away from the river.

As he walked, the idea occurred to him that, as these were locals, someone around here did not think it was going to snow. Unless of course they lived close by, and their house was not on his map. He looked up at the clear blue sky, no sign of trouble there. When he came to the first junction, he unfolded the map to see if he could find the junction on it. He found it hard to see, and looked up. The blue sky had been replaced by ominous looking black clouds.

'Oh shit!' He grunted and, after two attempts to fold the map back as it had been, he gave up and stuffed it into his back pack as it was. Not something he would usually do, but there was no way he was going to give Brickman the satisfaction of calling for help. He hurried back toward the cave, and made the top of the rocks before it started to snow. When it started, it snowed as he had never seen snow before. It was a blizzard, and before he could make it down the slope it was covered in snow. He slid down on his back for speed, and when he was down he used his hand on the rock face to guide him to the cave.

Once inside, he relit the fire and built it up to make sure the heat kept the outlet at the top open. When it was burning brightly, he sat back contentedly, knowing a certain Mr Brickman was going to be disappointed that rookie ranger Turner did not call in for help. The word 'help' brought the two young fisherboys to mind, and he felt a little uncharitable. After all, they were on the park and it was his job now to make sure they were safe. They were probably at home now, in front of a log fire and eating their fish, but he thought he ought to check on them, just in case.

He crawled out of the cave and slithered down the slope to the river. The snow was already six inches deep and still coming down. At the bottom, he turned the corner very carefully, making sure he did not fall into the icy river. He made his way onto the flat rock the boys were fishing from, and stopped to listen. He could hear them arguing, and walked toward the sounds. They were in the tent which was now flat with the weight of snow, and they were struggling to get out. Each was blaming the other for their plight. Danny pulled the tent off, and saw them face to face for the first time. They were obviously frightened.

'Follow me, there's shelter on the other side of the rock,' he yelled over the noise of the river and the falling snow.

He walked back to the corner and found he was still alone. He went back thinking it was the snow that was holding them back.

'Come on, Marcus!' Danny heard one of them yell.

'I can't. If my Dad finds out I was here, he'll kill me!' the other boy replied.

'We might die if we don't,' the other boy yelled. 'I am freezing already.'

'But he's the limey,' the boy called Marcus replied.

'Is that a cardinal sin then, Marcus?' Danny asked when he was close enough. 'Now, I don't want to hear another word about it. You grab hold of my belt, and you, Marcus, hold on to his. It is my job to make sure you live through this, and that is just what I aim to do. Do you understand?'

'Yes!' they both answered, and did as he told them.

Danny walked to the corner, feeling the boy behind holding his belt, and started up the slope to the cave.

'Be careful, it is very slippery up here,' he warned as he started up the slope.

Half way up the slope, with the boy behind him still clinging to his belt, Danny heard a scream. He looked back in time to see the second boy, Marcus, sliding toward the water.

CHAPTER 2

DANNY could not believe his eyes when Marcus landed in the water. From where he stood he was powerless to help, but Marcus had the presence of mind to grab at a tree as he passed it, and when he hit the water he still had hold of a branch. Danny pulled the other boy to a nearby tree and wrapped his hands round the trunk.

'Stay here. I have to go and help Marcus,' Danny ordered, and slid down the bank aiming at the tree Marcus was holding on to.

He took a risk sliding down, but speed was essential as the cold water would soon weaken Marcus. He took in the scene as he hit the tree. Marcus had hold of a thin branch, and his hand was slowly slipping along it toward the end. Soon he would be adrift and at the mercy of the ice-cold river. The water tugged at Marcus relentlessly, trying to prise him loose but he was still there when Danny threw his weight against the tree to give him a solid anchor. He stretched out toward Marcus just as the boy's hand slipped off the branch. Marcus screamed as the water took him but Danny's powerful hand grabbed the flailing hand and, using the tree as an anchor, he pulled the boy onto the bank. Even for Danny it had been a superhuman effort, and he lay panting, both eyes on Marcus to make sure he did not fall back into the water. Marcus just lay there.

'I told you to keep hold of his belt.' Danny yelled over the noise of the river when he got his breath back.

Marcus, his face ashen, feebly held up the belt still firmly clenched in the fist of his other hand. Danny knew Marcus needed heat, and soon. He dragged him up the slope to where the other boy stood, one hand round the tree and the other hand holding up his jeans. Danny helped them both up the slope toward the cave mouth, making sure to keep between both of them and the river. He dragged Marcus past the shrub to the hole in the rock, with the second boy following him.

'You go in first,' Danny said to the other boy.

'What if there are snakes in there?' the boy argued.

'There aren't, I have already checked it, and there is a warm fire in there,' Danny replied.

The thought of a fire and warmth sent the boy scrambling into the tunnel. Danny half pushed and half dragged Marcus through the tunnel into the cave. By now he was shivering uncontrollably. As soon as it was stirred into life, the fire began to burn brightly, bathing them in its warm glow. The other boy was drawn to the fire like a moth to a candle. Danny lay Marcus on the floor and threw more wood on the fire, now really glad he had had the idea of cutting a supply earlier.

'Help me get his wet clothes off,' he ordered.

The other boy nodded, and Marcus was stripped of his wet clothes and wrapped in a blanket. Then they zipped him inside Danny's sleeping bag as well to try and warm him up. The long pieces of wood took on a new role as clothes horses, propped up to let the wet clothes drape over them to dry by the heat of the fire. When they had the clothes drying, the other boy knelt by his friend.

'Shouldn't we massage his hands and feet, Mr Turner?' he asked politely.

Danny was surprised at first when the boy knew his name, but when he thought about it, it was obvious that in a small place like Turnround everyone was going to know what everyone else was doing.

'Yes we should...' Danny started to reply, but stopped in mid-sentence as he did not know the boy's name. 'What's your name?'

'Robbie Johnstone.'

'You take one hand, Robbie, and I'll take the other.'

They massaged for some time with no sign of improvement.

'Did you have sleeping bags with you, Robbie?'

'Yes, they were in our tent,' Robbie answered morosely.

'I'll go and get them in a minute to start them drying. I think we might be here a while,' Danny replied. 'Are you hungry?'

'Yes.'

Danny stopped massaging, and walked over to the pile of wood. He pulled out his rucksack and rummaged inside it. The food was meant to last him a week, but with three mouths to feed it would not last long. His hand felt something solid in the gloom. He pulled it out and held it up in the light of the fire. It was the radio.

'Just the thing,' he said, a little relieved. He had forgotten about the radio. 'I'll get you a lift home. I think

31

Marcus should be in hospital.'

'Does that mean we get to ride in Greg's helicopter?' Robbie asked.

'How many rescue helicopters are there round here?' Danny asked in reply.

'Only Greg Pomeroy's, I think.'

'Well it seems likely then. Wait here while I call in.'

Danny stopped at the mouth of the tunnel.

'What am I supposed to say on one of these things anyway?' he asked.

'I'll tell you what to say, and when,' he offered, and followed Danny out.

Outside, Danny realised why snowshoes were necessary when his feet disappeared in the snow, but he was only going to radio in so he walked on to be clear of the rock.

'Someone giving, what you might call a greenhorn, instructions at this time could, if he so wanted, make said greenhorn sound like an idiot. On the other hand, the greenhorn, so treated, might just throw the other party into the river,' Danny warned.

Robbie smiled.

'Trust me, I know what I'm doing, I've got one of those things at home. Push the red button and say: 'What's your first name?' Robbie asked.

'Why should I say that?' Danny asked.

'No, I mean what is *your* first name?' Robbie explained.

'Oh I see. It's Daniel, Danny to my friends.'

'Right, push the red button and say, "Daniel Turner here, do you copy?" Then let the red button go, and listen.'

Danny did as he was told, but when he let the button go the radio crackled. Someone was talking, but not to him.

They all seemed to ignore him. He repeated his message in the middle of one man's reply but they just carried on talking. He tried again after the radio fell silent, but there was no reply.

'Do you think we might be out of range, Robbie?'

'No way! When we come out here camping, I have to bring mine and call in every hour or my Mum throws a wobbly.'

'In that case I think we have a duff radio here. Fantastic! Do you have yours with you?'

'No, we weren't supposed to come,' Robbie admitted.

'It's getting better as we go on. Come on, let's go back in. It's getting rather cold,' Danny complained.

They crawled back inside the cave and warmed themselves by the fire. Danny was thinking about his next move. This was like a chess game, and he did not want to lose any pieces!

'What did you do with the fish you caught, Robbie?' he asked as he warmed himself.

'They were in front of the tent.'

The word 'they' meant there was more than one.

'How many did you catch?'

'Two. Marcus caught one as well.'

'I'll go and get them. I'll get your sleeping bags as well while I am at it. Look after Marcus.'

'You will come back, won't you?' Robbie asked.

'Of course, unless I'm silly enough to fall into the river, and I will be trying very hard to avoid that!' Danny replied, and crawled out of the cave with his snowshoes. Hamish had shown him how to attach them to his boots, but he was not completely sober. Now came the real test. He walked down the hill slowly, not wanting to fall in. At the bottom, he looked at the racing cold water and realised he had to get help for Marcus as soon as possible; but how? He turned the corner and walked across the flat rock toward the only bulge there, which he assumed was their tent. In front, there were three small bulges, and he brushed off the snow to reveal the fish which he dropped into the deep pockets of his coat. He moved on to the tent and dragged out their sleeping bags. The tent had kept most of the snow off, and they would soon dry out, but he still had to get them back up the hill and into the cave. He wrapped them into a bundle, making it as small as he could, and struggled up the hill. Then he unclipped his snow shoes, put them on top of the bundle and pushed it before him into the cave.

As he hung one of the sleeping bags up, a Walkman dropped out onto the cave floor.

'At least we can have some music,' Danny said with a smile which was meant to be reassuring.

'What is going to happen to Marcus?' Robbie asked.

Danny finished hanging up the sleeping bag and walked over to where Marcus lay.

'He needs to go to hospital. I think he's going into shock.'

'That's bad, isn't it?' Robbie said. 'Have you got any string in your rucksack?'

Danny did not connect the two things.

'Why?' he asked.

'I'm tired of holding my pants up!' Robbie declared.

Danny sought out the broken belt. He had to force Marcus' hand open when they were in the cave and he remembered dropping it nearby. He stirred the fire to give more light, and found the belt where he had dropped it which reminded him of home. Not for finding it, but more for not being able to find things as Lucy had the habit of throwing away anything she did not want, which included anything Danny left laying about. The fire crackled and brought him back to the present. He took the belt back to the light of the fire and examined it. The loop of the belt passed through a D shaped hook which had an opening in the middle of the straight side of the D. The opening had been pulled wide open and the loop had pulled out.

'I can fix that,' Danny said, putting it down beside him.

'How?' Robbie asked.

'I'll show you as soon as I have one of these fish cooking,' Danny answered. 'Maybe some hot food will warm Marcus up.'

Danny pulled the fish out of his pocket, but there was no where clean to lay them so he squeezed them into his saucepan to keep them off the floor. He took his frying pan from the woodpile and unwrapped it. This was the first time he was going to use it. He gutted one of the fish, lay it in the frying pan and stood it on the ashes at the side of the fire to cook. It was all trial and error for him, but he did not want to cremate the first fish if he could help it.

When it was settled in the ashes, he picked the belt up and put the D back in the loop. A lump of wood served as a hammer, and he clubbed the D back into shape while it was in the loop. After a couple of tugs to see if it would hold, Danny gave Robbie his belt.

'Thanks, at least my pants will stay up now!' Robbie said gratefully, sliding the belt through the loops on his jeans. 'His Dad is going to hit the roof when he finds out about this.'

'Why?'

'Mr Brickman said we couldn't come out here today, but he didn't say why so Marcus decided to come anyway.'

'Are you telling me he is Brickman's son?'

'Yes.'

Danny laughed.

'Well, I'll be!' he said after a few seconds.

The frying pan started to sizzle loudly, and Danny pulled the frying pan away from the heat a little to stop the fish from burning. Afterwards, he sat staring into the flames, thinking of last night.

'Hamish was right,' he said, unconsciously turning his thoughts into words.

'About what?' Robbie asked.

'Sorry, I was thinking out loud,' Danny replied. 'He said we were in for snow, and lots of it!'

'Yes, he was right,' Robbie replied, morosely. 'I wish he'd told me, then I wouldn't be out here.'

As the fish cooked, he thought about how they could eat it. There was one plate, one frying pan which would be hot, and one saucepan with fish in it. He had an idea and crawled out of the cave with the saucepan containing the fish. By the shrub, he gutted the fish, made a pile of snow, laid the fish on the pile, and covered it with more snow. At least it would keep fresh! He wiped the saucepan out with more snow and, crawling back into the cave, began to realise how useful snow could be.

When the fish looked cooked, he broke it into three pieces with his fork and served it out. Robbie had his in the saucepan, while Danny tried to feed Marcus from the plate, but after the first mouthful he refused any more.

Danny ate the rest, then broke the last piece in two and shared it with Robbie.

'Well, if he won't eat the fish, maybe he'll drink some soup,' Danny declared. There was even more reason to get Marcus back in one piece now!

He crawled outside, wiped the saucepan out with snow again, then filled it with fresh snow. While the snow was melting on the fire, he pulled his rucksack over and found his Cup-a-Soup packet. He chose chicken - everyone likes chicken! When the snow had melted, he tipped the contents into the saucepan.

'Do you have anything to eat other than our fish?' Robbie asked.

'I have bacon and beans with me, and using the fish as well I reckon we could last a week, but I need to get Marcus to hospital.'

'What about the radio?'

'His Dad gave it to me when I set out. I hope he didn't know it was faulty. I'll try to fix it later.'

'Don't tell me you are an electronics engineer as well!' Robbie declared.

'I know my way around the circuits of a transceiver, if that's what you mean.'

'What's a transceiver?'

'One of these.' Danny held up the radio. 'It's just an old name for it,' he explained.

Danny pulled out the snow shoes to see if he could make a pair for Robbie. If the radio was completely defunct, he would have to drag Marcus back on a sledge, and Robbie would have to walk. Marcus started shivering again.

'I bet that water was cold!' Robbie declared. 'I'm glad

it was him who fell in, and not me!'

'Isn't he your friend?' Danny asked.

'Yes, but if anyone had to fall in, I'm glad it was him.'

The soup started to boil, and Danny pulled it away from the heat to let it cool off a little. He tipped the soup into his mug and checked the temperature before he lifted Marcus' head and spooned some into his mouth. A hand appeared from the sleeping bag, and he drank the soup from the mug but he still shivered. Danny rummaged in his rucksack again. One thing Hamish had insisted he brought was a bottle of whisky for medicinal purposes. He found it and tipped a drop in the mug. Marcus thought it was more soup and drank it in one gulp. His mouth opened wide as if he was choking, but then he relaxed.

'Wow, got any more of that?' he asked, shivering less than he had been.

'For medicinal purposes only!' Danny answered, and poured a drop more into the mug.

This time Marcus drank it slowly. More colour came into his face, and he stopped shivering.

'You're the limey who's taken over from Trailer Collins,' he said, almost normally.

'That's me, but I thought his name was Chief?' Danny replied.

'No, that is someone who was after Trailer's job as well, but he's a bit of an oddball,' Marcus explained.

'Oh. Nice country!' Danny grunted.

'It's okay if you know it,' Marcus replied.

'How come you're stuck out here as well then?' Danny asked.

'My Dad said we couldn't come fishing, but we came

anyway. If he told us it was gonna snow, we'd have come prepared,' Marcus answered.

'So your Dad thought it was going to snow?'

'He didn't mention snow at all,' Marcus declared.

'He didn't mention it to me either,' Danny said, then added, 'But then I would have still come if he had.'

'Why?' Marcus asked. 'That doesn't make sense.'

'I'm English, and we're like that!' Danny answered.

'Why?' Marcus repeated.

'I take it you are feeling better?' Danny concluded.

'A bit, but that water was cold. It sort of made me seize up,' Marcus explained. 'You must have had a shit belt on, Robbie!'

'I didn't know you were going to swing on it or I'd have put a super strength one on,' Robbie called from beside the fire.

By now, the light which filtered along the tunnel was disappearing as it was growing dark outside. Danny knew there was nothing more he could do tonight, but he needed something to sleep on. He carefully pulled the blanket out from around Marcus as he was planning to cover him with another sleeping bag. He could make do with the blanket. He unzipped and threw one of the dry sleeping bags over him.

'That one's mine!' Robbie declared. 'I don't want to sleep in his.'

Danny threw the sleeping bag across the cave to him, and repeated the operation with the other one.

'I'll leave that there all night if I can. I should be warm enough by the fire in the blanket,' Danny said quietly, but Marcus was asleep. 'I should get some sleep, Robbie. I want to be up early tomorrow.'

Robbie zipped up the sleeping bag, and slid into it fully clothed. Before Danny settled down to sleep, he checked the woodpile. Without cutting up the longer bits, he would need to cut some wood tomorrow to start it drying out. That was his first job in the morning, the second was to look at the radio and see if he could find out what was wrong with it. By the time he allowed himself to sleep, Robbie was fast asleep.

Danny woke and thought it was still night, but when he remembered he was in the cave he looked at the mouth of the tunnel and saw light filtering through again. He crawled outside into bright daylight, no clouds in sight but a deep layer of snow covered everything. He sniffed the fresh morning air.

'Good morning, Canada!' he said affectionately. 'You showed me alright.'

He crawled back inside and built up the fire. Both boys were still asleep, and Marcus was not shivering now, which he took as a good sign. He collected his axe and went searching for wood, and when he returned to the cave both were still asleep. He used his blanket to tow the wood into the cave, and stacked it up away from the fire to dry.

With his first task done, he put some snow in the saucepan to melt. The water soon boiled, and he made himself a mug of tea using some of the milk from his Thermos flask. This was his first mug of tea out in the forest. He liked a mug of tea first thing in the morning. This first mug of tea made him think of his home life in England with Lucy. They had tried for a family for twelve years until Danny had found out she was on the pill and had no intentions of ruining her figure by having his baby.

The row had been long and loud. It was a good thing they lived in the forest with no neighbours to hear them. Soon after, he was made redundant and was unable to find work amongst the trees he loved. He applied for this job and sat an exam. When he was offered it, he was over the moon but Lucy was less enthusiastic. She refused to come and 'live in a Godforsaken country like that', and moved in with her mother. Danny just said okay and came anyway.

The memory was driven from his mind when the fire crackled loudly, and he returned to the present. The mug was empty - now to look at the radio, but for that he needed light. He took the radio and crawled outside but soon returned for his blanket.

Robbie woke and looked around. There was now a big pile of logs in one corner, but there was no sign of Danny. He crawled outside to find Danny sitting in the mouth of the cave wrapped in the blanket.

'What's up?' he asked.

'Nothing,' Danny answered. 'I was just looking at this thing to see if I can work out what's wrong with it.'

Robbie watched as Danny used his pen knife to pare away the plastic around the screws which held the cover on. When he had pared enough away, he used the pen knife blade to undo the screws and remove the cover.

'What's wrong with it?' Robbie asked.

'I've only just got the cover off,' Danny replied.

He poked and prodded at the components and the circuit boards until he saw the problem.

'Can you see that?' he asked.

'What, that crack?' Robbie replied.

'That very one. I need to rejoin the circuit to make it

work. That must be the transmitting side. I need your Walkman.'

Robbie crawled into the cave, found his Walkman and crawled back out with it. When Danny cut a piece of wire out of the earphones, he was incensed.

'Hey, you've ruined them.'

'I reckon I have, but if it gets Marcus to hospital it will be worthwhile and I will buy you another one.'

'Oh, okay. Is there any coffee?'

'No, but you can have tea if you want it.'

'No thanks, what about some whisky?'

'I think not, unless you plan to take a dip.'

'No, I'll eat snow if I get thirsty.'

He watched as Danny stripped the wire and wound one end round the leg of a capacitor and twisted it up tight. He did the same with the other end to bypass the crack. Several times he stopped to blow on his hands as the temperature had dropped like a stone over night. With his bypass complete, he reconnected the battery while the cover was still off. When he pushed the red button in, the radio still crackled, which it did not do last night.

'So far, so good. Let's see if it still works when I put it back together.'

Danny replaced the screws, then crawled in to warm up before he tried to call for help. Marcus appeared to be running a temperature now.

'I'm going to climb up top for a better signal,' Danny said when he was ready to go.

'I'll come. I can tell you what to say,' Robbie replied.

'I only have one set of snowshoes,' Danny warned.

'That's okay, I can manage.'

'Okay, but remember what I said yesterday?'

'I know. Someone in my position could make someone in your position look an idiot, but I want a ride in Greg's helicopter,' Robbie answered.

They climbed the slope to the top of the rock, with Robbie struggling through the snow. Danny could see he would not be able to walk anywhere without snow shoes and was glad the radio was now working.

'Daniel Turner here, can you hear me?' Danny said, while Robbie tried to catch up.

'No! It's "do you copy?"' Robbie shouted.

Before Danny could say anything else, the radio crackled into life.

'Yes, I can hear you. This is Brickman here, and it is obvious that you are still alive. Are you in imminent danger or about to die? Over.'

'No, but...'

'Then stay off this channel, and that is an order. You do know what an order is? Over.'

'Yes, but...'

'No buts. I know it's cold, but I have other things which are a priority to me. I will contact you when I can. Over and out.'

'But I need a helicopter to pick up your son Marcus.'

There was no answer.

'He's probably switched off or changed channels,' Robbie said, standing knee deep in snow. 'That wasn't very nice. Doesn't Mr Brickman like you?'

'You get that impression, don't you? Maybe he has troubles back there, or he has found out that Marcus is missing.'

'What about me! Don't I count for anything?' Robbie retorted.

'You're probably in the frame for leading Marcus astray.'

'That's not fair. It was Marcus' idea.'

'Life is rarely fair, Robbie,' Danny replied, and he pictured Lucy with his son in her arms. He thrust the picture to one side and thought about the present. 'I'll see if I can get him on another channel - there are four on this thing. After all, he can't stop me talking when I have the red button pushed in!'

He tried the channels, one by one, without success.

'Maybe he turned to channel five,' Robbie offered. 'That one is like mine and only has four channels.'

'What do I do now then?'

'We could try to get a lorry on the Loggin Road - they are on channel four.'

'What good would that do?'

'You could ask them to phone the airport and get Greg Pomeroy to come out and get us.'

'Well, I am right out of ideas so we'll give it a go.'

Danny turned back to channel four and repeated his message over and over, waiting for a reply in between but without success. They were getting colder and colder as a biting wind was causing a very low windchill factor.

'Come on Robbie, we will try again later,' Danny said, when his fingers were nearly numb.

He could see Robbie was shivering and he was none too warm himself. Robbie did not argue and they slithered down to the cave entrance. Danny watched Robbie crawl inside, then tried one last time.

'Daniel Turner here, is anyone listening? Over.'

'Yee har,' a voice cried loudly, and when it was repeated Danny had to hold the radio away from his ear. 'This is the Big Bad Wolf here. Come on Daniel.'

'Hello, Big Bad Wolf. I have a sick boy out here who needs a lift to hospital, can you phone Greg Pomeroy and get him to come out with his helicopter? Over.'

'I will if you give me your ten twenty, Daniel. How do you like our Canadian winter? Come on.'

'Fine, just dandy, but what the hell is my ten twenty? Over.'

'Where you are. I have to tell him where to go. Over.'

'Hang on, I'll find out what they call this place. Don't go away.'

Danny crawled through the tunnel as fast as he could.

'Where are we? What do you call this place?' he yelled.

'Black Rock Flats,' Robbie answered. 'Did you get someone? Do you want it in French?'

But Danny was already halfway through the tunnel.

'Come on Big Bad Wolf, we are at Black Rock Flats. Do you copy? Over.'

'That's a big ten four, over.'

'What the hell does that mean? Over.'

'Well, if you want it in plain English it means yes! I've fished Black Rock Flats a few times with my Pa. Listen for Greg in about two hours, snow permitting. Over.'

'Okay and thanks. Over.'

'Any time, now this is the Big Bad Wolf signing off as your signal is starting to break up, over and out.'

Danny crawled back into the cave to soak up the heat from the fire. Help was on its way.

CHAPTER 3

DANNY sat quietly for a few moments, feeling the heat from the fire seeping into his cold body. He was very relieved that he had managed to make contact with someone from the outside world.

'Did you get through, Mr Turner?' Robbie asked.

'Yes, help is on the way. We will have to take turns listening for the helicopter when two hours are nearly up,' Danny replied. 'You can call me Danny if you like.'

'Okay, Danny. You saved Marcus` life, didn't you?'

'Not yet, but maybe when he's safe in hospital.'

'His Dad is going to kill him when he gets better. Is there any more food? I'm hungry.'

'Didn't you bring any with you at all?' Danny asked.

'No, he forgot.' Robbie pointed at the sleeping Marcus. 'Fish is okay now and then.'

'I reckon I can spare you some bacon and beans. I'll just have to head back when I run out,' Danny replied grudgingly.

'Aren't you going in the helicopter with us?'

'No, I came out here to get to know the place I will be working in, I can't do that in the hospital waiting room.'

When two hours were nearly up, Danny sat outside listening to the radio. There was a lot of chatter going on but none of it was about him. It was mainly about the two boys. He could have called in and told them, but orders is orders he thought with a wicked smile. He stayed out there until his fingers were numb, and then he let Robbie take over. When Danny took over the fourth time, the sky was clear and blue but the noise on the radio was growing faint. Before they changed again, the radio died completely. Danny crawled back inside.

'The battery's flat,' he announced.

'That's great! Now what do we do?' Robbie complained.

'We use these logs to make a signal for the helicopter to see from the air, just in case I can't get it going again.'

'Even you can't recharge batteries out here,' Robbie replied. Then added, 'Can you?'

'I can't do that. I'm no miracle worker, but my torch and the Walkman batteries might sort it for long enough.'

They crawled outside, dragging the long branches out with them one by one, and arranged them to make a large 'X' on top of the snow. As long as it did not snow before he arrived, he might see it and land without contacting them.

Danny sat in the mouth of the tunnel butchering the head phone wiring again. With the bulb removed from the torch he connected two wires to the contacts. The Walkman battery was easy - he unclipped it and wrapped the wires round the terminals. Then he joined them together, removed the radio battery, and held them on the contacts. Nothing happened!

'Maybe the radio battery still has some life in it?' Robbie suggested.

47

Danny tried to keep the wires on the terminals whilst clipping the battery back in. Nothing happened, but then he had no way of knowing if the wires were still there. He tried again and again. He was ready to give up when the radio spluttered and died when he tried to connect it.

'Nearly got it that time,' he said, with renewed hope.

Suddenly the radio was working again. They both held their breath.

'Greg Pomeroy calling, come on.'

'Good afternoon, Mr Pomeroy, nice of you to pop out to see us,' Danny said in his best British accent. 'Daniel Turner here, come on.'

'Good afternoon to you. Sorry the snow held me up. From the noise on the radio, they are looking for two boys. Is this one of them? Over.'

'Sure is, Mr P, I've got the full set here, over.'

'And they don't know? Over.'

'I was ordered to keep off the air by my new boss. I can't go against orders now, can I? Over.'

The pilot laughed.

'I won't tell if you won't. What's your ten twenty? Over,' he replied.

'The lower side of Black Rock Flats. We put out a marker. Land to the north of it, over.'

'Will do. ETA ten minutes, over and out.'

They both listened intently until they heard the helicopter.

'I can hear you, shall I bring him down? Over.'

'What is wrong with him? Over.'

'He fell in the river, over.'

'I'll bring a pod to you. Just wave when I land, over

and out.' As the pilot spoke, the helicopter swooped over, circled once and landed by the 'X'. The pilot unclipped what was obviously a pod and hurried toward where they were waving their arms, the blades still spinning above him. As he approached, Danny held out his hand and the pilot took it and shook it warmly.

'I'm Greg Pomeroy.'

'Daniel Turner, Danny to my friends.'

'Where's the sick one, Danny? Robbie here looks healthy enough.'

'In the cave. We'll have to throw some wood on the fire to give us light. I had to use my torch batteries to keep the radio going,' Danny replied, and lead him to the cave.

Greg saw the radio there with its jumble of wires.

'Very ingenious,' he admitted.

'Danny had to fix the radio as well. Mr Brickman gave him a bust one,' Robbie added. 'That battery came from my Walkman.'

'At least we'll be spared the heavy metal on the way back then!' Greg replied with a ready smile, and followed Danny into the cave. 'Seen any wolves since you've been out Danny?'

'Not one, but they might have seen me. You never know.'

Greg was a trained paramedic. He unzipped the sleeping back and examined Marcus before trying to move him. 'Just the water, was it?'

'Yep, but I reckon it was cold,' Danny replied.

'We lift him into the pod on three,' Greg announced, satisfied that it was safe to move Marcus. 'One, two, three.'

They laid him on the blanket which was already in the pod, and wrapped it round him. Then they slid the pod out of the cave and carried it to the helicopter. When it was secured inside the helicopter, Robbie climbed in but Danny kept his feet firmly on the ground.

'Aren't you coming?' Greg asked.

'No, I'm not one for flying, besides I'm supposed to be getting the lay of the land, and I can't do that from the fireside,' Danny answered.

'You'd better have this then.' Greg reached into the helicopter and brought out a package.

Danny opened it and found a new radio.

'It was ordered for you, but I thought you'd get an old one. This is the latest thing. If you choose channel six, it lights up on the office console. That way they always know when you want them. No one else has one of these yet.'

'I take it the old radio I was given belonged to Trailer Collins?'

'No, whoever shot him took it with them,' Greg answered.

'No one told me he was shot,' Danny complained.

'They think it was poachers. A lot of them still think of this place as their larder, and won't take no for an answer,' Greg explained.

Danny took the radio out of its box to examine it.

'It even has a switch so you can talk out without receiving if you want a bit of quiet,' Greg added, pointing to the switch. Then he climbed into the helicopter.

'I'll have a look at it later. I think it will be a bit quieter tonight,' Danny replied.

'You snored as well,' Robbie declared indignantly over the noise of the engine as Greg increased its speed.

'I was asleep then, so it didn't bother me.'

'It woke me up,' Robbie retorted as Danny moved away enough for the door to close. He remembered Lucy's complaints about his snoring.

'Brickman will be a bit upset when he finds out you've got the radio he was probably going to have,' Greg yelled, and closed his door.

Danny retreated to a safe distance and watched the helicopter lift off effortlessly. He watched it until it disappeared over the trees, then started to return the logs from the 'X' to the cave. Tonight he would sleep in the cave, and tomorrow he would head deeper into his forest. He took the wire from his torch and refitted the bulb. A quick flick of the switch cut a swathe through the gloom.

He returned to the warmth of the fire and thought things through. This was a good cave, and if he left enough wood here he would have somewhere to go when he was over this way, but it was lucky something else was not at home. A door of some sort to keep it private while he was away seemed a good idea, and he needed to collect the boys' tent and rods to keep them safe. He remembered the bike tracks. The bikes would have to be left outside under their tent to keep them from rusting. The boys' sleeping bags were still there, so at least he would not be cold tonight!

That night, he slept in his sleeping bag on top of the other two sleeping bags for comfort. The comfort and the fact that only a little light filtered into the cave from the outside made him oversleep by his standards. He raced about, putting things in the cave, carrying the bicycles past the bush and covering them with the boys' tent. He cut more wood and made a door to block the entrance. It had to slide into place but it would keep undesirables out. With all that done, he started walking up river again. He had been told to stay off the air and he was doing just that. The air he breathed out hung in front of him like a small cloud, and often lingered long enough for him to walk through it. Apart from the trees, there was snow, snow and more snow. No more brambles - they were covered in snow. The next time they would see the sun was when the snow thawed, and by then they would be flattened. He sniffed the cold air. It was clean and smelled fresh. He was glad he was here.

The trees were mainly firs with a sprinkling of rhododendrons or a near relative. He saw one lone oak tree on the edge of the fir forest growing where the rotting needles had not polluted the ground. The last time the tree fellers were here they had left it. Now it would stay until it died of old age, but its offspring, a lone sapling growing right on the river bank, would not be so lucky. Heavy rain, followed by high wind or even heavy snow, one day would send it falling into the river to be carried away by the current with little or nothing to show that it was ever there.

Back in England, there would have been a sprinkling of holly trees, but not here. When the firs were ready, they would be harvested, and with the oak being more trouble than it was worth, they would leave it to reign as king of the forest once more.

Every few miles, he took out his compass and his map to pinpoint where he was. At one point he looked at the map and found a cross drawn by Hamish. He looked down at Hamish's notes.

It read 'Suicide Falls'. Danny remembered Hamish making a joke about it.

'When they jumps, they falls.' By then, Hamish was well on the way to a hangover in the morning.

'I must remember to leave that off my tour,' he thought, and resumed his journey.

As he approached the turn-off which would take him past 'Suicide Falls', Danny saw a patch of red on the snow in front of him, and found a carcass. He took it to be a wolf, but it was hard to tell properly after it had been skinned. The skull had a bullet hole in it meaning it had definitely not died of old age. 'Poachers', Danny thought, and looked at the ground around the dead wolf for clues. He picked out three different snow shoe prints, and felt clever at doing so. He had heard no shot, and the wolf was cold but not frozen. He looked about him and listened for any sign of the poachers, but the forest was quiet, too quiet.

The news that Trailer Collins, his predecessor, had been shot and killed by poachers made him extra careful. Orders or no orders, he pulled out his new radio. There was no way he was ending up like Trailer Collins. He turned to channel six to make sure the console would flash, and to rub it in that he had the latest radio. He waited for an answer.

'Sorry I was so long. I didn't know what the flashing light was, and had to read the manual.' It was a woman's voice, and a woman who was not used to using a radio. Danny tried to sound professional.

'Daniel Turner here, come on.'

'How can I help?' the woman replied. 'And you can forget all that "over" and "come on" crap. I'm having a bad day. All our men are out looking for a lost girl, and Made is out looking for our son.'

'Well, he's wasting his time. I packed Marcus off to

hospital in Greg Pomeroy's helicopter yesterday,' Danny explained. 'As far as I know, his boy is safe and hopefully on the mend.'

'Our boy,' the woman corrected. 'I am Rosie Brickman. Why didn't you let us know he was safe? You must have known we were looking for him?'

'I did try, believe me, I did try. Robbie will tell you. I was told in no uncertain terms to get off the air. Didn't the hospital phone you?'

'They might have done, but I haven't been home yet today, and now I'm off to the hospital to see Marcus.'

'I'm on the track of some poachers - might be the same poachers who shot Trailer Collins,' Danny replied insistently. He wanted an idea as to what to do.

'I'll put you through to the Mounties before I go,' the woman said, and the radio went dead. 'There you are. I've put you through to the Mounties. Now I'm off.'

Danny waited.

'RCMP', a voice at the other end of the radio connection announced.

'Is that the Royal Canadian Mounted Police?' Danny asked naively.

'That's what I said. You must be the limey who's taken over Trailer's old job. Over,' the voice answered.

'That's me alright, and I`m on the trail of three poachers. They might be the ones who shot Trailer Collins. Over,' Danny replied.

'See what you can find out while I pull a couple of lads off the search to come and assist. They'll be glad of the change in routine. Remember, if it is them, they've already killed one ranger so they aren't likely to be worried about making it a pair. Over,' the Mountie advised.

Danny was trying to place the Mountie's accent.

'I'll be in touch when I know more, but don't call me. If this thing bleeps at the wrong time, I'll be deep in the mire, over.'

'Well, don't you be worried about shooting back if they shoot at you. Over,' the Mountie advised.

'I might be a limey, but stupid I'm not,' Danny replied tersely. 'Over and out.'

The man on the other end laughed. 'Good hunting, limey.'

Danny started to follow the trail left by the three men. It was easy. They had not bothered to try and cover their tracks. Either they thought they were alone, or they were planning an ambush. He chose the first. They obviously thought only mad dogs and Englishmen would be out here, and boy were they right!

The trail turned left away from the river. It was a fire break through the trees. He stopped to look at the map, and saw that it lead past Suicide Falls. The only road shown was the Loggin Road where he had managed to contact the Big Bad Wolf. He used his binoculars to study the area. There was no sign of the men, but there was another large red patch. Danny moved forward cautiously to the spot, and found another skinned wolf carcass. He followed the tracks doggedly but warily until the sound of a shot sent him sprawling in the snow. He had not been shot, but then again he didn't really want to be.

He lay there in the snow breathing as quietly as he could to be able to hear any noises nearby. He realised the shot was not aimed at him and climbed warily to his feet, picturing another skinned wolf. He started to follow the tracks again very cautiously. It was late in the day when he reached the patch of blood. This time, there were entrails as well but no carcass. They had taken it with them, obviously for food. There were signs that they had cut down a sapling to use to carry their kill, and the deep snow shoe prints told him it was heavy. That meant they would be moving slower. He looked at the map. Too far to carry a heavy load and make it before dark so they must make camp. The last thing he wanted to do was to accidentally walk into their camp.

He thought about it. There was no way he was going to stop, so overtaking was the other answer, but which side. The wind! He should have noted the wind before now. He held up a wet finger. It was blowing gently from left to right. He should use the trees on his right, but far enough in not to be heard. He moved into the trees and started to speed up. The sooner he was in front of them, the sooner he could move back to the fire break. He walked for half an hour before he realised what a pathetic idea it was. As soon as he moved to the fire break, they would find his tracks and know he was there.

'Come on Danny, start thinking straight,' he almost shouted at himself.

He used the compass to keep parallel with them and to make sure he did not find Suicide Falls the hard way. Moving fast, he could only imagine where they were and, when it started to grow dark, he shook the snow from the lower branches of a fir tree, dragged the snow out from under it, cut some branches from another tree as bedding and made a hasty shelter. No fire tonight, just cold biscuits and sleep, tucked snugly in his sleeping bag. At first light, he stood up and sniffed the clean air. He was where he wanted to be, and loving every moment of it. Even the cold and deep snow could not detract from his pleasure.

Soon he was on his way again, after a breakfast of cold beans straight from the tin. An hour later, a smell stopped him in his tracks; it was tobacco smoke. He knew now that he was level with the poachers and, with their load, he would soon be in front of them. Amazingly, as he walked off, the only thought he had was about Trailer Collins - would he have known who it was by the brand of tobacco? For two hours he walked at speed until he was sure he was well in front of the poachers.

'Daniel Turner calling, any Mounties listening? Come on.' He used channel six because the missing radio the poachers had was not new enough to have that channel.

'Only me! Will I do? Come on.' It was the same voice with the accent Danny could not place.

'Sounds like you'll have to,' Danny replied. 'There are three in the party, and I have managed to get in front of them. I hope to spot their transport soon, and will call in then. Over.'

'I have managed to free up three men and myself to come out to wherever you say. Where are you? Over.'

'Travelling south with my back to the river and Suicide Falls to my right. Over and out.'

Danny walked on, cold and hungry but with a point to prove. Suddenly the ground in front of him dropped away, and Danny was sent sprawling down a bank. At the bottom, he looked around for signs of the poachers but everything was quiet. No one had seen him and that was a relief. In front of him was a snow covered road. He checked his map and found it was not shown. He stood on the road which did not exist and looked around. He did not know how long he had before the poachers arrived, but he needed to be ready when they did. To his left was a large bridge, covering what appeared to be a small stream. 'At some point in the year, it must get bigger to rate a bridge that size,' he thought.

To his left, there was an opening through the rock, probably man-made, to a flat area beyond. Opposite him, there was an upward slope leading to more trees. He tried to flatten out the mess he had made of the snow, and while he was doing it something under the bridge glinted. He moved to see more, making sure he made as few tracks as possible. It was the bumper of a vehicle. He crossed to the other side of the road and carefully climbed up into the trees, then travelled in a circle to view the vehicle from downstream. It was a pick-up truck. Was this their wheels? He thought the answer was a definite yes, but how to disable it to allow the Mounties time to get there. Should he stop and call in, or try to make sure it stayed put? He stuck his snowshoes in the snow and radioed in.

'Daniel Turner calling, over.'

'Good day to you, Daniel, what news have you? We are ready to come when you give us your ten/twenty. Over.' It was the same accent.

'There is a pick-up truck parked under a bridge, but the road isn't on my map. I've walked a day and a half from the river in a straight line parallel with the fire break which runs past Suicide Falls. Over.'

The pick-up on Danny's receiver was good enough to

hear the papers rustling at the Mounties' H.Q. as they looked at maps.

'We think it's the Mine Road. If it is, you should see it was cut right through the side of a hill. It used to be a quarry. Over,' the accent replied.

'I've seen the cut, so I think you're right. It's a big bridge for the stream it spans.'

'That seals it - it must be the Mine Road. We are on our way. E.T.A., one hour. Over.'

While he was talking, Danny was looking about him and saw tyre tracks in the stream bed.

'I don`t know if it helps, but I think they drove up the stream to get here and they are facing back the way they came. Over,' he advised.

The paper rustling resumed, and it told Danny they were looking to see where the stream went.

'That could take them anywhere. No wonder we never catch them. If they get to drive off we'll lose them again, over.'

'I'll try to find a way of delaying them if they return before you arrive, but let's not dawdle, over and out,' Danny replied, and turned the radio off.

Now, how to walk up to the pick-up truck, disable it, and walk away without letting the poachers know anyone was there? He remembered a film where a car was disabled by blocking the exhaust, but when they realised that he would be found out. He walked through the shallow water in the stream as far as the pick-up and quietly lifted the bonnet. The key was in the ignition, and he turned it to get the ignition lights on. Then he worked his way through the fuses, pulling them out and replacing them until the ignition lights went out. All he had to do now was to blow the fuse! He used a screw driver to hold the fuse across the battery until it blew, then replaced it. He did the same with the spare, then as an extra he stuffed snow up the exhaust to block it whilst making sure it could not be seen by anyone approaching the pick-up.

When they found the snow in the exhaust, he hoped he would no longer be alone. He retraced his steps down the stream as far as his snow shoes, and hid in the trees. Still there was no sign of the poachers, but they would soon be here and he looked about for a vantage point where he could watch everything that went on. He chose to cross the road to the bank where he had fallen, and keep watch from there. He cut branches to lay on, and placed the blanket on top for comfort. Then he wriggled into his sleeping bag for warmth and settled down to wait. Even with the thought of three possible killers approaching, he was happy. This was far better than the sham life he had been leading.

Half an hour passed without incident. There was no sign of anybody, and no tobacco smoke either. The hour was almost up, when Danny smelled the same tobacco smoke. They were there. He peered cautiously over the snow he had piled in front of him, to see a man, rifle in hand, crouching at the start of the fire break. The man looked all round before he signalled the other two forward. They were carrying the carcass on the sapling when they appeared. It looked like some kind of deer, but Danny was not into animals, just trees. The three walked under the bridge and dumped their illegal gains in the pick-up. Danny waited for the worst as there was still no sign of the

Mounties. After a few minutes, he heard a raised voice, so raised that he could hear every word.

'It's your bloody pick-up. Why don't you look after it!' He spoke English with a French accent.

'It was okay when we came weren't it?' The second man spoke English with very little accent. 'Someone must have done something to it.'

'Who was it then? Big Foot? A flying Big Foot who doesn't leave any tracks? Just get it going before someone comes along.'

Danny smiled as he listened.

The third man joined the conversation. He was shouting, not for any other reason than to be heard above the others.

'The ignition fuse has blown,' he explained. Then, after a pause, said, 'The spare is fucked too.'

'Why do you keep a fuse which is no good?' the first voice asked.

'I tell you they were both okay. Someone's been here,' the second poacher hissed.

The first man to arrive stepped out from under the bridge and looked around, Danny was sure he must see him.

'Well, I can't see anyone. If Trailer Collins was still alive it might have been him, but we know he's dead don't we! I taught him not to mess with a Dupont! Anything that side?'

'No!' the poacher with the French accent answered.

'Then use another fuse and let's get out of here. We won't be needing the horn with what we've got on board.'

Danny heard the engine turn over and over without starting. He also felt a presence beside him.

'I hope you are a Mountie!' he said quietly.

'Lucky for you, I am,' the Mountie replied at the same volume, but with the same accent Danny could not place. 'Give a man a bit of room.' The Mountie bellied down on the blanket beside Danny. 'What's going down?'

'I disabled the pick-up parked under the bridge but they used another fuse to try to get it going. When they find the snow up the exhaust, they will know they aren't alone!' Danny replied. 'Are you it?'

'No, there are four of us. We have been after this lot for a while, so we came in numbers. I have two on the other side of the bridge, and one other on this side.'

'Well, that's something,' Danny scoffed.

'You do know how to use that rifle?' the man with the accent responded.

Danny looked at the Mountie. The first thing he noticed were the stripes on his arm. He was obviously a sergeant but it was hard to see much more where they lay. Danny was given the impression that the sergeant was shorter than Danny and with an excess of stomach.

'The bullet comes out of this end,' Danny replied, pointing to the barrel.

'Well, don't think twice about using it!' the sergeant replied.

'I thought you were here to arrest them?' Danny said.

'If they killed Trailer Collins, then I don't think they will want to come quietly. I don't think you will hear the words, 'Okay, it's a fair cop!'

'What do I do then?' Danny asked.

'Nothing until one comes this way. Then if you think he is going to shoot at you, don't be afraid to blow the sod into the middle of next week,' the sergeant replied.

This was new to Danny, but if it came to a choice between them and him, he had a good idea which one he would choose.

'You make it sound easy, but how do I know when they are going to shoot at me?' Danny asked.

'Pointing their gun in your direction is the usual sign.'

'Is that a good enough reason to shoot them?' Danny asked.

'Hell, it is for me. But I'll let you make up your own mind.' The sergeant looked at his watch.

'Well, my men should be in position by now, and it sounds like they just found the snow you stuffed up their exhaust.'

The sergeant picked up a megaphone from beside him.

'You under the bridge, this is the Royal Canadian Mounted Police, come out with your hands held high and toss out any weapons before you do,' he ordered.

'No way, Mountie. Come and get us if you want!' a voice replied from under the bridge.

Danny recognised it as the voice of the first poacher he had heard speak.

'One of you is suspected of killing a ranger. Do you others want to go down with him?' the sergeant asked.

One of the poachers fired at them, and they were showered in snow.

'If you want to shout at them through that thing, can you do it from somewhere else?' Danny asked dryly.

The sergeant laughed, and held his radio to his mouth.

'Okay Hiram, shoot out the tyres,' he ordered. 'Over.'

There was no reply, but two rifle shots rang out in quick succession.

'That will stir things up a mite,' the sergeant whispered, and aimed at the bridge in readiness.

The men under the bridge started firing, and more snow was showered over them.

'Now, that is what I call just cause,' the sergeant said, and started firing at anything he could see under the bridge. The other Mounties started firing, but Danny waited. His father had taught him to fire only at what he could see. The sergeant signalled a ceasefire by holding up his rifle and the firing stopped.

'To hell with this,' one of the men under the bridge shouted. Danny recognised it as the second poacher. 'I weren't with Abe when he shot Trailer. I'm coming out, don't shoot!'

A rifle was thrown from under the bridge on the side Danny could see, and a man appeared with his hands high in the air. He walked down the stream away from the bridge.

'One down!' the sergeant chuckled.

'Come back here, Walters, you coward,' they heard one of the others cry.

'No, Abe. I only shoot game. It was you who shot Trai...'

The sentence was cut short by a shot from under the bridge. The walking man crumpled to the ground and landed with his face in the snow.

'Hell of a thing to do,' the sergeant yelled, and started firing again.

Over the noise of the shooting, a man's voice shouted.

'For God's sake, don't shoot. I'm coming out, and in a hurry!'

A rifle flew out on the other side of the bridge, followed by a man zig-zagging to avoid the same punishment for deserting. Before the Mounties on that side could react, a shot sent the man flying but they could tell he was still alive and fired at the bridge to keep him that way. Such was the ferocity of their onslaught, it forced the suspected murderer out on Danny's side, running, zig-zagging, and firing as he ran. The other Mountie on their side stood up and fired at the running man but he fired back, and the Mountie dropped out of sight with a yell. The sergeant fired, and the running man fired back, spraying snow in Danny's face yet again.

'Do you get the idea yet?' the sergeant asked.

'I get it,' Danny replied, and fired one shot at the running man.

The man was thrown sideways and did not move again.

'Well, it takes a hell of a lot to get your dander up, but when it's up you don't waste much time, do you?' the sergeant said, with a hint of admiration.

'I was taught not to do in two shots what you could do in one,' Danny explained. 'My father was very thrifty.'

One of the Mounties from the far side appeared cautiously from the bridge to see what was going on. He saw two bodies, and moved to investigate.

'This one's dead, shot in the back,' he called up, after checking the nearest to him. He moved on to the next one. 'Dead too, shot plumb through the heart.'

'Damn!' Danny muttered.

'What's the problem? He was firing at us. He had just shot two people, and you got the bastard with one shot through the heart. What more do you want?' the sergeant asked, a little confused.

'I was aiming at his leg!' Danny grunted.

The sergeant laughed.

'Well Daniel, I'd sure keep that under your hat for a while if I were you!' the sergeant replied.

Danny wriggled out of the sleeping bag, climbed to his feet and held out his hand.

'It's Danny to my friends.'

The two shook hands, and a friendship was formed out of adversity.

They walked down to the two bodies in time to see the Mountie who had been shot by the running man, appear over the mound of snow he had used as cover.

'I thought you'd been shot,' Danny said, surprised to see him on his feet.

'Only a nick, but it bloody hurt!' He pointed to his bleeding earlobe. 'A bit to the left, and I'd be even less intelligent than I am now.'

'God forbid,' the sergeant retorted.

The bleeding Mountie held out his hand.

'Chuck Petrie at your service. You must be the limey I've been hearing about.'

'Danny Turner,' he replied as they shook hands. 'Limey, born and bred.'

'And a crack shot,' the sergeant replied with a grin.

'So I see,' Chuck replied. He turned over the man Danny had shot. 'Abe Dupont, as I live and breath.'

'Well, he ain't,' the first Mountie on the scene quipped.

'This is Hiram K Charterhouse,' the sergeant said to introduce the speaker. 'That's why we just call him Hiram K. The one up there on the bridge, who should be fetching the Jeep, is John Lodge.'

'On my way, Sergeant Mulroon.' He nodded to Danny. 'I

think the other one's going to make it. Shall I call Greg in?'

'Have to, I suppose,' the sergeant conceded.

'Sergeant Mulroon. Now there's a good old Canadian name,' Danny said, with a hint of a smile.

'Hiram K, pick up that bastard's gun. I want ballistics to run some tests on it to see if it was used to kill Trailer Collins,' the sergeant said, ignoring Danny's comment. 'Chuck, are you fit enough to collect wood? We are likely to be here a while waiting for the meat wagon.'

'I can do that,' Danny offered, before Chuck could answer. 'I need to do something to warm myself up.'

Danny collected wood and lit a fire while the others arranged for the bodies to be collected by the meat wagon as they called it. They also attended to the wounded, and arranged for the helicopter to collect them.

'What happens now?' Danny asked when the sergeant stopped to warm himself by the blazing fire.

'Well, we've had the fun. Now comes the paperwork! As soon as the meat wagon arrives and takes the bodies away, we'll drive back to your office and you can type out your report while I get some food at Hester's. Let's see what they died for.'

Danny left the fire and followed the sergeant to the pick-up under the bridge. This was the second time he had visited the pick-up, but the first time he had had no inclination to browse. Now the pick-up had flat tyres, but its load was still under a tarpaulin in the back. The sergeant pulled the tarpaulin back.

'One stag, and a big one too, two wolf pelts, one female by the looks of it, and assorted other pelts. Not a lot to die for,' the sergeant exclaimed.

'What happens to the meat?' Danny asked.

'It goes down in the book as burnt!' the sergeant replied.

'And in reality?' Danny asked.

'In this case, it will be sold in Hamish's store and the money will go to Trailer Collins' widow and children.'

'Sounds fair to me. What about the wolf pelts?'

'We have to hand them over to the government.'

'A politician's wife will be well on the way to a wolf skin coat.'

'More than likely,' the sergeant grunted, and they walked back to the fire.

The other three Mounties were there warming their hands. Chuck offered Danny a cigarette.

'No thanks, those things are lethal. Look at those two over there for proof. One of them was smoking, and I don't.'

'Are you sure you're not that Sherlock Holmes?' Hiram K asked.

'No. He'd have known which brand of tobacco it was, and I could never wear a hat like that.'

The Jeep radio burped. 'Greg Pomeroy on his way, E.T.A. ten minutes, over.'

The sergeant walked over to the Jeep and picked up the handset.

'About time too! We are freezing our balls off down here! Over.'

'Don't worry, I'm good with a needle and thread!' Greg replied. 'How many injured? Over.'

'One bad one, and one pretend one, over.'

'Mind you don't find out what it's like, Sarge,' Chuck warned.

'You should have kept your head down and let Hawkeye

there deal with him,' Hiram K said with heavy sarcasm.

'Okay, let's get ready for the chopper,' the sergeant said, interrupting the banter.

Danny watched Greg land for the second time, and was impressed with the ease of his landing. The trees hampered him, but he dropped it just where he wanted it.

'I think you might want to do some shooting practice before long,' John Mulroon said when the others were out of earshot.

Danny nodded. He could see how things were heading. He walked out to meet Greg with the others.

'Not you again!' Greg said as a greeting. 'Just how long have you been in this country?'

'Seems like years,' Danny replied.

'You've met then?' Sergeant Mulroon concluded.

'Yeah, Danny called me out to take Made Brickman's boy to hospital.'

Sergeant Mulroon gave a low whistle.

'You found him as well?' he asked.

'Yep.' Danny did not elaborate. 'Anything else you want sorting while I'm out here?'

Greg slapped Danny on the shoulder. 'At least let me give you a lift this time.'

'No way! Not in that thing! I can't see what keeps it up. I'll go back in the Jeep in Chuck's place if that's alright with John.'

'We're not afraid of flying, are we?' Hiram K asked. 'Not Hawkeye!'

'Hawkeye!' What have you been up to now, Daniel?' Greg asked, a little like a mother chastising a child.

'He shot Abe Dupont stone dead from the ridge up

there,' Hiram K replied, not letting Danny answer, and pointing up the slope. 'Right through the heart.'

'I didn't think he had one,' Greg snorted. 'I heard a whisper that Dupont might have been the one who shot Trailer Collins.'

'We'll know when you take the gun to ballistics instead of standing here gassing,' Sergeant Mulroon retorted.

The two injured were loaded on board, ready to be airlifted to hospital.

'You are welcome to travel back with us, but we have to wait for the meat wagon. The chopper would be quicker,' Sergeant Mulroon added.

'No, I'll wait with you, but as I'm going back I might as well cook the food I'm carrying. Anyone up for bacon, beans or fish?'

'What sort of fish?' Hiram K asked.

'I don't know, I'm not up on fish. The type that swims in the water.'

'Good, just the type I like!' Hiram K replied with heavy sarcasm.

Danny pulled the fish out of his rucksack. It had frozen on the journey.

'Looks like a yellow perch to me,' John Mulroon said, on seeing the stiff fish.

'At least it hasn't gone off,' Danny said as he dropped it into the skillet with a clang. 'I think I should have cut it in half before it froze.'

The rotor on the chopper picked up speed and, as he lifted off, Greg gave them a wave. Seconds later, he was gone. As the food was cooked, it was eaten, with Hiram K taking charge of cooking the fish.

'So how come this road isn't on my map?' Danny asked when his plate was empty.

'It's just a copy of an old map sold as the latest thing,' Hiram K explained.

'Isn't that illegal?' Danny asked.

'Might be, but unless you go somewhere that has actually changed, you wouldn't know any better.'

'That's not the point. Doesn't the mine owner mind?'

'No one's seen Wilson the mine owner since fall. Well he ain't strictly the owner, it was repossessed for back taxes. We thought he'd left the area, but now we aren't so sure.'

'Why not?' Danny asked, not knowing he was delving too deep.

Hiram K looked at Sergeant Mulroon before answering.

'Can't discuss it really, it's an on-going investigation.'

'Fair enough. That means the mine isn't being worked at the moment?' Danny asked.

'It's played out,' Sergeant Mulroon explained. 'Wilson was losing money, and it was only a matter of time before he lost it. They took everything of value, even the mobile he used as an office. All they left was the boarded-up mine, the power shed, and a shed full of wood with a lock that won't open. It's up for sale if you're looking for somewhere off the beaten track.'

'The whole place is off the beaten track!' Danny retorted.

'Digging out the quarry made Suicide Falls,' John Lodge said as he wiped out his plate with snow. 'If you drive about a kilometre down the road, you'll come to the mine, and if you drive through the cut and turn right and drive to the end, you'll be in position to catch anyone who jumps.'

'Do they all die?'

'Usually, it's quite a drop,' Sergeant Mulroon said as he accepted his food from John Lodge. 'If it's summer and they get snagged in the roots, we can save them, but the only one I know who survived is in the nut house. The others just find another way.'

An ambulance appeared from the trees and made its way slowly down the road toward them. John Mulroon looked at his plate.

'This always happens. I'll learn to be first to eat, one day!'

'I'll deal with it,' Hiram K said. 'It's about time you actually eat the food when we cook out.'

CHAPTER 4

IT WAS dark by the time they reached Turnround. Danny opened up the office and typed out his statement. Hamish wandered in when he saw the Jeep arrive, and showed him how to turn off the direct connection to the Mounties. Then Danny and John Mulroon walked to Hester Foy's for a meal. Danny was not looking forward to it, but his reception this time was very different from when he first arrived. As soon as he had finished his meal, a mug of tea was placed on a coaster in front of him, and a raffia mat appeared with a teapot on it. It was covered by a tea cosy with a robin on it. Back in England it would have gone unnoticed, but here it was like a pat on the back.

After the Mounties had left, he settled in front of the log fire and during the evening Annette found her way on to his lap. She fell asleep there, and Hester, seemingly with no effort, picked her up and carried her off to bed. Danny started to nod off and soon went upstairs himself. He lay in bed thinking about his two-day adventure and decided to drive out to the mine just to see what it was like.

After a good breakfast he walked down to the office, but it was deserted so he walked back to the store. Hamish was behind the counter when he walked in.

'Good morning, Hamish.'

'Good day to yee, Danny, yee've certainly made yee're mark!'

'All in a day's work. Where's the nearest estate agent?'

'They're land agents over here yee Sassenach, and yee are talking to one.'

'Is there anything you don't do?'

'In a place as small as this, yee either do a little of everything or yee go out of business. How can I help? Is it that bad at Hester's that yee want to buy a house already?'

'No, not really. Why didn't you mark the Wilson mine and the quarry on the map? The map must have been made in the nineteenth century!'

'Yee were supposed to stay near the river. It's three days on foot to the quarry.'

'Not if you are in a hurry. I hear the mine is for sale.'

'The whole shebang is for sale. Come into the office and I'll get the details oot.'

Hamish produced a layout of the quarry with the mine in it. The quarried area was an oblong with a road cut through the left hand corner of one of the longer sides. From there the mine was straight ahead, tucked near the other corner on the same end of the quarry. It showed three buildings and the actual mine. Hamish drew a cross over one of the buildings.

'The government took that to pay off outstanding taxes and the like,' he explained.

'Are the other two still there?'

'Yes, although the power shed roof blew off in a storm. That's the smaller one on the left of the road. The bigger one is full of wood, and the lock won't open.'

'Do I need keys?'

Hamish produced a bunch of keys.

'Yee go and have a look. We'll talk about money later.'

'I can't really leave the office, because there is no one there to take over.'

'No, now that Rosie and Made are in Lower Superior hospital with Marcus, and the other two are out with the search party.'

'What search party? What are they searching for?'

'A young lass is missing, poor thing. Come on, I'll show you how to transfer incoming calls to your Jeep, then you can go.'

'That'd be okay if I had a Jeep.'

'There's one parked in the back of my garage. It's the Jeep Trailer drove. As yee took over his job, it seems only right yee should have his Jeep.'

They walked to the office together, chatting as they went. When Danny opened the door, he heard Brickman's voice over the radio.

'Brickman here, do you copy?'

Danny picked up the handset.

'Turner here, over.'

'That was a dirty trick. Over.'

'What was? Over.'

'Saving my boy's life. I suppose you want to be treated like one of the family now? Over.'

'Heaven forbid. Like a human being might help. Over.'

'You have our thanks, over.'

'I was just in the right place at the right time, over.'

'Lucky for Marcus. I hear you also killed the skunk

who killed Trailer. Over.'

'We won't know that for sure until they have the ballistic report, over.'

'Rosie sends her thanks and her apologies for giving you a hard time. She was worried about Marcus, in fact we both were. Over.'

'Gimmee that thing,' Hamish insisted, and took the handset. 'Since when have yee worried about Marcus, Made Brickman? Over.'

'And good morning to you, Hamish. As you asked so nicely, it's since we found out he is as pig-headed as I am! Over.'

'Is he going to be okay? Over.'

'He's going to make it, but we'll both be staying until we are sure. Daniel can run the office while I'm gone. Over.'

'Daniel, is it noo? What happened to the limey bastard?' Hamish inquired.

'That is when he isn't listening. Enough of this idle chatter. This channel is for official business only. I'll see you when I get back. Put Daniel back on. Over.'

'The limey bastard here. Over,' Danny quipped. When you get them on the run, keep them on the run!

'The office is all yours until I get back, in fact you are all there is at the moment! Phil and Carrick are helping the Mounties, and I'm stuck here but it is usually quiet at this time of year. Any problems, either deal with them or pass them on to the Mounties and let them deal with it, over.'

'It will give me something to do, over.'

'I'd have thought you could do with a rest! Over.'

'You never know when Super Limey is going to be needed! Over and out.'

Danny replaced the handset.

'Noo, all yee have to do is plug this wee thing into this wee socket, then turn this switch off and the Jeep is the office. Here are the keys, but look after them as they are officially the property of the government. Pop them in later tomoree and we'll discuss it over a wee dram. I have to send a fax and find out some details.'

Danny drove out of Turnround, reversing the route Sergeant Mulroon had taken to get to Turnround. He followed the road until it met the Loggin Road, turned right and waited for the first right turn which lead to the mine. He drove across the bridge slowly, remembering the gun fight, then headed for the mine through the opening the quarry workers had made.

He had his copy of the layout and drove up to the first shed. This was the power shed, and it had no roof as expected, but when he went to unlock it he saw there was no door either. Three boxes were fixed to the wall but there was no sign of wiring. Danny scrabbled in the snow and found three cables laying loosely on the floor. The power had been disconnected and Danny wondered how much it would cost to have it reconnected. He made a note on the pad he had with him - things to find out. There was no way a generator would fit in the shed, so was it mains or was there a generator shed which was not shown? He made another note.

Then he drove a further twenty metres until the boarded up mine entrance was on his left, and the long shed on his right, ten metres on. There was another shed marked on the map, but it was long gone. He stepped up on to the flat ground where the shed should have been, and scraped away some snow to reveal a concrete base. 'That might be useful,' he thought, and made another note.

Danny was no slouch when it came to paperwork, which his many qualifications attested to. It was they that had helped him land the job, and the fact that Barry Jaimeson, the man who offered it to him, found his age, and therefore compound knowledge, a plus instead of a minus. Being first in the exam also helped, but Barry chose him the day he met him, even though he had to let the system run its course until he told him.

Deep in thought, Danny tripped as he walked across the base and fell flat on his face. His first reaction was to look round to see if anyone was watching, and his second was to laugh at himself for doing it. His third was to see what he had tripped on. A black cable - obviously the other end of one of those in the power shed. Another bulge proved to be a water pipe.

He finished his walk to the mine, and unlocked the door in the boarding. The darkness in side gave way to the daylight, and he walked into the mine as far as he could see; at least it was dry in there, a place to shelter if close by. He switched on his torch and walked in further, but the light soon dwindled to nothing and he stopped in fear of finding a vertical shaft the hard way! If nothing else, he had a shelter either side of the territory he was looking after, and this would make a good home.

HOME, he had thought of it as home! This place made him feel good, and he wanted it. He turned his attention to the long shed and, after a hard struggle with the lock, he gave up. There were two windows, so he rubbed the snow and ice clear to peer in. The shed looked to be full of off-cuts, bits of wood no one wanted except as firewood, but then he'd need firewood for his huge fireplace. The floor of the quarry was sparsely covered by saplings, so any logs would have to be brought in to be cut up, or the off-cuts could be brought here. The back of the shed was piled high with railway sleepers, very useful. The ground looked as if it dipped towards the middle, but he would only find out when the snow thawed.

He drove back to Turnround, intent on moving things forward as soon as possible. The store was open but there was no sign of Hamish. He called out, and waited. No one came so, dispirited, he walked to Hester Foy's.

Hamish sat at the table, playing cards with the two men he had first met there. He knew now, after talking to Hamish, that neither was her husband, although the one named Gaston had designs on her.

'Your store's wide open. You'll lose half your stock!' Danny warned.

'I used to think that as well, but it doesn't happen round here. If they can't pay me, I get it later when I'm aboot,' Hamish replied. 'I've given up worrying. Everyone knows what everyone else is doing round here soon after they've done it, bar one that is, and if I could lay my hands on him he'd know it!'

'I take it you're referring to the missing girl no one will talk about?' Danny prompted.

'Aye. This time it's Sarah Talksloud. When we find her, she'll be what they used to call a good Indian!' Hamish responded. He had been drinking, and it showed.

'Take no notice of him, Mr Turner. It's the whisky talking,' Hester Foy said in a matter-of-fact way which rather nonplussed him.

'The name is Danny. I take it there is no sign of the girl, then?'

'She'll turn up, come thaw, God rest her little soul!'

Annette appeared in the doorway wiping her eyes. Hester gave her a big cuddle.

'I had a bad dream, Mummy,' Annette said, sleepily.

'Don't you worry. I'll chase all the bad dreams away. Come on, I'll run you a bath. The men can look after themselves for a while.' She picked her up and carried her to the bathroom.

Danny put the keys to the mine on the table next to Hamish and watched the cards. They were playing nine card brag. He knew the game; a small stake each time built to a good win when someone managed to win the pot.

'Match a third of the pot, and you can sit in,' the man with a distinct French accent offered.

Danny looked at the other man, who nodded. He put in his money and sat down. Playing was far better than watching. It was better than three card brag, as a lot of money could be lost in a very short time in three card brag. He sat and played impassively, as an Englishman should, although some of his hands made him despair, and it was only the intervention of the others which saved the pot. It was more a game of enjoyment than a way to get rich. Really it was a cheap form of recreation, with Hamish getting more drunk as each round passed.

When Hamish lurched out to the toilet, Gaston, who introduced himself as Gaston Wolfe, informed Danny that this was an annual event since the death of Hamish's wife. Hamish sat, played cards, and drank all day until he passed out. Usually then, his son, Callum, was on hand to help put him to bed.

The game was in full swing when Danny's radio screeched. He grabbed it quickly.

'John Mulroon here, are you about Danny? Over.'

'I'm here John. What's up now? Over.' Danny was expecting to be called out again.

'We've just had the results back from ballistics. Abe Dupont's weapon killed Trailer Collins. The other man killed was Seth Walters. He leaves a wife and three kids. I'm just going out there to tell them. Over.'

'Rather you than me, over.'

'Comes with the stripes, I'm afraid. Over and out.'

Danny put the radio back where it had lain, and picked up his cards. Outside a lorry stopped, a big lorry. The slamming of the lorry door was followed by the stamping of boots in the hallway to dislodge the snow.

'That'll be Callum now,' Gaston advised, and a man with a bushy black beard walked in. Danny judged him to be in his twenties, but it was hard to tell behind the beard.

'I take it it's snowing oot Callum,' Hamish said as if he were stone cold sober.

'Yep Pa, as always on Mum's day,' Callum replied. 'You're still in the chair, then?'

'It'll be a while yet, laddie. Yee haven't met Danny here yet, have yee? This is my son Callum, Danny.'

'We've talked on the radio,' Callum replied.

'We have?' Danny asked.

'Yee har,' Callum cried, but not as loud as he had done when he answered Danny's distress call.

'You're the howling wolf,' Danny said, remembering

81

the cry over the radio when he was trying to get help for Marcus Brickman.

'Big Bad Wolf, actually, but you were close. Did Greg sort things out for you okay?'

Danny was surprised by the lack of Scottish accent.

'Yes. Thanks for your help. He took the two boys to hospital in his helicopter.'

'But Danny dinna go with them. He went on to track down some nasty murdering poachers. He shot Abe Dupont through the heart, as dead as a dodo, he did,' Hamish added.

'I didn't think the Duponts had hearts,' Callum replied. 'I don't think he'll be missed, except by his brother, maybe.'

'A murdering family,' Hamish complained. 'They should have been drowned at birth. His brother is in prison in Dakota for killing a man. They should have given him the chair or whatever they do down there, not life in prison.'

Hester Foy walked in and placed a bottle of Vodka on the table in front of Callum.

'Thanks, Hester,' Callum said, as he sat in the vacant chair.

'Just make sure he doesn't hurt himself when he finally goes, like he did last year!'

The card game continued through the day and into the evening, with everyone waiting for Hamish to slide under the table, which Danny was told was the outcome every year since Hamish's wife had died. The level of the whisky bottle next to Hamish diminished gradually, as did his sobriety until he finally slid under the table. That was the end of the card game, and Hester gathered the pot. She put it in a tin on the mantlepiece over the fireplace.

'That will stay put until the next game,' she explained, as Danny had some money in the pot.

Danny and Callum carried Hamish back to the store and put him to bed.

'Thanks, Danny,' Callum said as he closed his father's bedroom door. 'He still misses her. It came as a shock when she died because she was always so strong.'

'What happened?' Danny asked, not sure whether he should have done.

'She had a heart attack. We called Doctor Shoesmith, but she was gone by the time he got here.'

'I didn't know you had a doctor here.'

'He has an office in the school building.'

'You have a school?'

'Yep, fairly big one too. A lot of children who live out in the sticks come to it. The next school is way down in Timberline.'

'It just goes to show, you shouldn't go on first impressions,' Danny replied.

'Looked that bad, did it?'

'I thought this was all there was!'

'If you turn left out of Hester's, then left again and walk down the road, you'll find the school, the local pub, and a fire station. We even have a clinic. In the summer, a quack from the hospital in Lower Superior comes round every once in a while and de-wrinkles a lot of old folk. For a price, of course!'

'You mean he comes all the way out here just to smooth out a few wrinkles?'

'Yep, and there's enough rich, vain old ladies to make it worth his while. Do you remember the garage you passed on the way into Turnround?'

'Yes, it looks a bit big for a small place like this.'

'Well, it earns Margaret Joliff a small fortune, and she spends some of it at the clinic. Chief has to chauffeur her eight times a year. Vain old cow!'

'Chief? Wasn't he the one who was after my job?'

'Yes, but Barry turned him down. I don't know why, but they seem to have made a good choice.'

'Thanks for the vote of confidence. Why do they call him Chief?'

'His given name is Jeremy Julian Joliff! Do I have to say more?'

'No, I get the picture. Can I buy you a drink for your help earlier?'

'The help was free, but you can buy me a drink, after all I was born a Scot!'

CHAPTER 5

DANNY woke early the next morning and walked to the store. The sign said 'Open', and the door opened when he tried it, but there was no one about and he assumed they were sleeping off their hangovers as Callum's lorry was still parked outside Maple Lodge.

He wanted to find out what he could do to his piece of land if he bought it. He needed a place to live in, and the mine was not high on his hotel guide. The store had an array of books for hire, so he searched through them until he found one on building regulations. He was one of a few men who would read regulations right through to find loop holes or anything to steer clear of. He took it to the office and sat reading. The radio remained silent, as did the phone. He made notes on a pad as he read, until he'd found what he wanted. He developed a distinct 'go for it' feeling.

He walked back to the store when he was ready to eat at Hester Foy's. Hamish and Callum were sitting either side of the counter talking when he walked in.

'You're up then,' Danny observed.

'Only just. Is that good reading?' Callum asked.

'Not bad if you like that sort of thing. How much is the

hire charge?' he asked.

'One day, one dollar, no half days,' Hamish replied.

'You certainly woke up feeling Scottish, but still cheap at half the price. It says in here that I can build a log cabin without applying for any sort of permission as long as it doesn't obstruct the highway.'

'Callum will soon haul yee some logs, Danny. I take it yee are interested in the Wilson mine?'

Danny put his dollar down on the counter and nodded. 'If I can afford it.'

'Come into the office. I put the papers on the desk, just in case.'

They sat in the office a long time, thrashing out the details. Danny was a thorough man, and asked about everything he had made a note of. When they emerged from the office, he had a smile on his face. This was the first time he had bought a place of his own.

'Yee are noo looking at the new owner of the Wilson mine and surrounding property,' Hamish announced.

Callum was pouring a cup of coffee.

'I hope he's not going to be landed with any outstanding bills or taxes?' Callum said.

'There are a few he'll need to pay to get supplies and such. Me for one!' Hamish replied.

'You wily old goat!' Callum retorted.

'Noo is that any way for a bairn to speak to his poor old father?' Hamish complained.

'Your poor old father did save me a lot of money, so I feel it is only right he isn't out of pocket over the deal,' Danny interceded.

'Where do you plan to erect this log cabin?' Callum asked.

'On the base they put in for the mobile they repossessed. According to the plans, it was designed so a house could be built on it eventually. He put deep enough footings but he was only able to get permission for a portable building as it is on the park. I can put logs round the base and know they won't move.'

Hamish looked at his watch. 'Time for a feed, I think.'

As Danny stood up, Hamish held out a bunch of keys.

'I think these are yours,' he said, and tossed them to Danny.

They walked to Hester Foy's for something to eat, which was followed by another session of cards, with the accompanying drink.

Danny was roused from a deep sleep in the morning by a persistent tugging at his arm. He opened his eyes to see Annette Foy's red hair.

'Mr Mclaughland says you're wanted at the office,' she said, when she saw his eyes were open.

Danny looked at his watch. It was eight o'clock. 'Damn!' he grunted.

Annette giggled.

'Sorry! Thank you for waking me,' Danny said.

'That's okay, Red's a friend of mine.' And without explaining what she meant, she ran downstairs.

Danny washed and shaved before he called in at the office, to find Hamish waiting for him.

'Do yee remember the man Abe Dupont shot at the bridge the other day?' he asked.

'Which one? He shot two.'

'The one that died. His name was Seth Walters.'

'What about him? He hasn't come back to life, has he?'

'His boy's run off, went yesterday. His mother is sick with worry.'

'I doubt if me arriving to look for him is going to make her feel any better,' Danny retorted.

'I know it's not a job yee are thrilled with, but yee is all there is, or I wouldn`t ask yee.'

'What about the Mounties?'

'They are still searching. John Mulroon asked me to ask yee. The boy's name is Redman, he's eleven, took a fishing pole but no rifle.'

'If I'm going to be walking through the forest, there doesn't seem any point linking the Jeep up to the office. How will I call for help if I need it?'

'I'll be in the office until I'm not needed.'

'Thanks. I'll need some supplies.'

'There be two boxes on the counter, one for yee and one with a few oot of date things for Kate Walters. She's no a bad lass.'

Danny drove to the store and threw the boxes on board, then sped away, giving Hamish a wave of his hand as he went. He was not going to be greeted with open arms where he was going - where was he going? He slammed on the brakes and slithered to a stop.

'Where am I going?' he called, standing half out of the Jeep.

'Drive past the turning to your mine, and it's the next hoos. It has a green tin roof.'

Danny drove on as fast as he could. Finding the house proved very easy, the green tin roof clearly visible, showing how much heat was being lost through the roof. Danny made a mental note to insulate his roof well. A woman came out to meet him, and Danny assumed she was Kate Walters. He judged her to be in her mid-thirties and, although she was dressed in what Danny thought was drab clothing, a cotton dress and a sweater, he thought she looked quite pretty.

'When did he go?' Danny asked, trying to sound official.

'Some time yesterday afternoon. When are the others coming?'

'They're not. I'm it!' Danny replied.

'That gives me a great deal of confidence, I don't think!' She was upset and it showed.

Danny ignored the remarks, and took the box Hamish had sent from the Jeep.

'Hamish sent you a few things.' He stood them on the ground next to her, and loaded his rucksack with food. 'Don`t worry, I'll find him.' He left out a packet of biscuits. They would have to be breakfast, not quite the same as the breakfasts Hester served up. 'Are these his tracks?'

'Yes, but as soon as it snows, they'll be gone!' She had no confidence in him whatsoever.

'There is a radio in the Jeep, I'll let you know when I've found him.'

'Well, I won't hold my breath!' the woman replied, and Danny thought enough was enough.

He started to follow the tracks made by the boy's snow shoes. They led to the fence, and Danny could see deep impressions on the other side meaning the boy had dropped down wearing his snow shoes. Danny took his snow shoes off and dropped them into the snow the other side, making sure one end stuck into the snow. The sight of him chasing his snow shoes into the forest would not help either of them at the moment. He jumped over the fence, put his snow shoes back on and, after wiping the snow off his boots, he started after the boy as fast as his legs would carry him. He knew that if it snowed before he caught up with the boy, his tracks would be erased, although he knew a good tracker might find them under the snow. The tracks were easy to follow, and Danny judged them to be walking parallel with the Loggin Road.

When he came to a bank and saw the Mine Road below, he knew where he was. He made it down the bank without falling, and followed the tracks to the bridge. Here the boy had lingered, possibly looking for some sign of his father. Danny tried to imagine the thoughts going through the boy's mind. Surely he was in there somewhere and not in a good light. Did he blame Danny for his Dad's death? It spurred him on. He had to save this boy at all costs, and take him back to his mother, although he was dreading the first meeting with the boy.

The tracks led into the fire break toward the river. The boy had his fishing pole, according to Hamish, so it was a fair assumption that he was going to fish the river, but it was a long river with lots of fishing pegs. He came to the boy's first camp site. The ashes were cold and, although it was getting late in the day, Danny walked on, eating another pack of biscuits to sustain himself.

He kept going until dark, then slept under the boughs of a fir tree, a fire close by to give him a little warmth, and he was able to cook some hot food. He needed it by now. If it snowed overnight, he would have to search the river bank, assuming the boy beat him there.

As soon as it was light enough to travel, Danny was off. The tracks were still there, showing it had not snowed. He had cooked his breakfast by the light of his fire while it was still dark, to save time. Catching up with this boy had become very important to him. It seemed like a make-or-break situation. Besides this was no place for an eleven-year-old on his own without a gun.

By midday, Danny had found the boy's second camp, but the built fire was unburnt, and the wet broken matches strewn about, told a tale. Danny did not stop but walked on faster. Two hours later he found a snow shoe with a broken strap. He tucked it into the straps of his ruck sack and walked on. He could see by the tracks in front of him who the snow shoe belonged to and he would need to mend it so the boy could walk home. The tracks stopped under the low branches of a spruce, and the snow had been built up to stop the wind blowing through.

Danny was more than a little apprehensive. If he had not come to Canada, the boy's father might still be alive. He found himself unable to pull back the branches or even to call to the boy. Instead he chose the cowardly way. He walked up wind and cleared a patch of snow. He made camp and lit a fire. Soon the smell of cooking bacon was drifting past the boy's hiding place. He crawled out and limped over to the fire where Danny sat repairing the damaged snow shoe.

'Hi, you must be Redman,' Danny said, as though they had just met in a local park.

'Yes,' the boy replied, and warmed himself by the fire. As the only place to sit was the blanket Danny was sitting on, the boy remained standing. 'Who are you?'

The boy must have known who Danny was, with his accent, but he still asked the question as if to make sure.

'My name is Daniel Turner.'

The boy took a step back.

'You killed my Dad!' he said accusingly with venom in his voice.

'No I didn't. It was Abe Dupont who shot your father in the back,' Danny explained, choosing his words carefully.

'My Dad didn't do anything wrong.'

'No, the only thing he was doing was trying to get away from Dupont. It was Dupont who killed the ranger I replaced, and your father knew it.'

'Mr Dupont shot Trailer?'

'Yes, we ran some tests on his rifle to prove it.'

'But you did shoot someone?'

'Yes, I shot Abe Dupont.'

'Is Mr Dupont dead?'

'As a Dodo! He won't shoot anyone else.' Danny held out the repaired snow shoe and the boy took it.

'Thanks,' he said politely, and put it on, but he still remained standing.

Danny put hot food on his plate and held it out to him. Redman took it but ate it standing up. He did not speak again until the plate was empty.

'Thanks, I needed that.'

Danny looked at his watch.

'We can reach the river before dark if we move now.' It was an offer.

'You're not taking me back, then?'

'Not yet! You came to catch fish didn't you. I'll let your mother know you are safe when we reach the river. I could do with a rest and a few hot meals before we start back. Why didn't you bring a rifle?'

'My Dad told me never to touch his rifle.'

'Well it's time you learnt how to use one...'

'I know how to shoot,' he interrupted., 'My Dad showed me before he...' Redman stopped talking and looked away.

'Come on, help me break camp or we won't reach the river before dark.'

Redman walked away toward the tree he had been sheltering under. Danny watched him go and wondered if he would come back. If he ran off again, it was going to be an interesting journey home. He had the urge to follow, but it was better to show trust so he started to break camp.

Redman did return with his things, but not until Danny had stood waiting anxiously, wondering if the boy had gone out the other side of the tree and walked away. They started for the river, side by side. It was getting dark when they reached the river.

They had walked hard, and the boy was tired but he still helped Danny pitch the tent. Then he collected wood for the fire, but although the river was close he made no move to start fishing.

'Where were you planning to fish, Redman?'

'At Black Rock Flats, if I can find it. My Dad took me there a couple of times. They call me Red, not Redman.'

Danny remembered Annette Foy saying Red was her friend, now he knew what she meant.

'Well Red, let's cook some food. I'll take you to Black Rock Flats tomorrow.'

'You know where they are?' Red asked in surprise.

'Yes. I'm a quick learner.' Danny winked as he replied.

He was toying with the idea of not calling in until they reached Black Rock Flats, but relented as the woman would be worrying. He picked up his radio.

'Daniel Turner here for Mrs Walters, over.'

He repeated the message until the woman answered.

'Kate Walters here. Have you found him?'

Danny held the radio out for Red.

'You push the red button to sp...'

'I have used one of these things before. Trailer was a friend of mine,' Red said, interrupting. 'Hi Mum, I'm fine. We're at the river. Over.'

'Well, you just come straight back home. I want a few words with you that the whole world can't hear.'

'It's dark, Mum, and Mr Turner is tired. He needs to rest, over.'

'Thanks a bunch,' Danny grunted. 'Now she'll think I'm a cripple as well.'

'Don't ever go off like that again. I've been worried sick,' Kate Walters continued, either not hearing Danny, or just ignoring what he said.

'But we didn't have any food. Dad would have gone out and got some.' Red started to cry and to get angry at the same time.

'I'll get some more wood,' Danny said, and walked out into the darkness with his torch. He did not like arguments or family squabbles, and he had had enough of them when he was living with Lucy. Some over petty things, some over more important things, like the time she had been deceiving him by taking the pill to make sure there were no children. When he returned, Red was cooking the bacon. Danny picked up the radio.

'Danny here, are you there, Hamish? Over.'

'I am Danny. I was just giving up on yee for tonight when I heard the Canadian version of the Waltons. Yee found him alright? Over.'

'Yes, we'll rest for a day, then head back on Friday. The boy's worn out. Over.'

'Good luck with the fishing. Over and oot.'

Danny put the radio down and saw that Red was staring at him.

'What's up? Have I grown another head?' he asked.

'Why did you come to Canada?' Red asked in return.

'It's the only job I could get. Over in England, they reckon I am past it as I'm approaching forty.'

'If you hadn't come, my Dad would still be alive.' Red did not say it as an accusation but more as a fact.

'Possibly. I didn't want him to die, you know.'

'What happened?'

Danny thought for a few minutes, whether to tell him exactly what happened or not, but decided not to keep anything back and be caught in a lie later. He explained the events leading up to Red's father's death, starting from his finding the first carcass up to his father trying to surrender to the Mounties and being shot in the back by Dupont. Red squirmed into his sleeping bag in the tent, and Danny heard him crying. He cried for a while, and then he drifted into a deep sleep. Danny sat outside, annoyed that his father was the one to die. He liked this boy. It was something that would not go away, and he was still thinking about it when he eventually fell asleep.

First light found Danny stirring the fire into life and putting on more wood. He started cooking the breakfast.

The noises and smell of cooking bacon drew Red from his sleep. Danny had had his first bad night's sleep in Canada, mainly because of what had happened to Red and his family. If he had taken the fencing job, Red's father might still be alive and what hurt most was that there was nothing he could do about it.

They ate in silence, packed up the tent, and walked on to Black Rock Flats. It took them two hours to reach the Flats, and Danny followed the path which Robbie and Marcus had used. They lay their packs down away from the water.

'You start fishing, Red. I'll be back in a minute,' Danny said, and waited for approval.

'Okay,' Red replied.

Danny walked round the corner and up to the cave. He collected the two fishing rods, not poles as Red had. These were good rods. He took the fishing equipment as well, to make it a good session, and started back. As he approached the corner, he heard Red shout and he hurried round the corner as fast as his snow shoes would allow, fearing the worst. Red was pointing at the river.

'There's something out there,' he shouted excitedly.

Danny dropped the fishing equipment and moved to where he could see. Something furry was floating by, trying to swim and making pitiful squeaky noises. He hurried back to the equipment, picked up the landing net and ran to the tree he had used to throw Marcus to safety. Leaning out as far as he dare, he deftly scooped up the furry bundle and swung it on to the bank. Red had dropped his rod and followed Danny.

'It's a wolf cub,' he cried excitedly.

Danny stood up and lifted the cub out of the net by the scruff of its neck.

'Well, this is the first wolf I've seen since I arrived here, apart from the two dead ones.'

'Do you think they were its Mum and Dad?' Red asked.

'Could be, I suppose. Let's hope it's weaned.' The wolf cub was shivering with cold, so Danny tucked it inside his coat for warmth. 'Have you caught anything yet, Red? We have an extra mouth to feed.'

'No, not yet, give me a chance.'

Danny picked up the two extra rods as they went, making sure the cub did not fall out as he stooped.

'These two rods should help.'

'Wow, they're expensive rods. Where did you get them?' Red asked.

'I'm looking after them for friends of mine.'

With three rods, they were soon catching fish, well Danny was. Danny could see Red was getting annoyed, as he was catching nothing, and offered him a rod. At first, Red refused but he soon relented and, once he was catching fish, he was happy. Danny gutted all they caught, and dropped them in Red's bag. Red wanted to empty the river, and Danny had to point out that they would have to carry all the fish back to his home, before he would stop fishing.

'Let's build a fire and cook some fish for our guest,' Danny suggested, and started to walk away with the rods.

'We usually cook the fish here and sleep here as well,' Red replied.

'We can do that if you like, but first let me show you something,' Danny replied, and led the way to the cave.

'Wow, a cave!' Red cried, and it echoed round them,

so he repeated it for effect.

Danny lit a fire using some of the wood he had stored there, and Red was soon sitting in front of the fire on his sleeping bag with the cub wrapped in Danny's blanket on his lap.

'We'll have to think of a name for him,' Red said as he sat stroking the cub.

'Any ideas?' Danny asked.

Red thought for a moment.

'No, but I will think of a good one.'

When the fish was ready to eat, he mashed some up using a little of his precious milk from the flask, and offered it to the cub.

'Well, we can assume it's weaned,' he said when the plate was licked clean.

'And hungry!' Red added.

They slept in the cave that night, with Red keeping the wolf close to him.

CHAPTER 6

THE darkness of the cave caused them to oversleep, and it was late morning when they eventually started back. The weight of the fish and the wolf cub slowed them down and, after their third night together, Danny knew they would not make it back to Red's house before dark the next day. They travelled as fast as they could, but as dark approached Danny made a decision.

'If we hurry we might make my place.'

'Do you have a house then?' Red asked.

'Not really a house. I bought the Wilson Mine.'

'Oh! My Dad used to work there now and then before Mike went away,' Red replied.

Danny stopped walking when he noticed tracks in front of them.

'Are those horse tracks?'

'They look like it. Must be from old Peterson's place. He's the only one with horses round here. People ride them in the summer.'

Danny followed the tracks with his eyes.

'Do they lead to where I think they do, Red?'

'What, the edge of the quarry? Yes, it's a good view.

My Dad took me there once.'

There was that 'my Dad' again, making Danny's stomach churn.

'The tracks go in, but none come out,' Danny said.

'There is another track out further on. That's where they'll come out, I think.'

They reached the mine as it was getting dark, but they had seen no more hoof prints.

When Danny tried to call in, his radio was dead. He would have to wait and call in from the Jeep in the morning. They ate more fish, then slept in the mine. Before Red woke in the morning, Danny walked over to the long shed and tried to unlock it for the second time. After ten minutes of wiggling the key and a lot of cursing, the padlock clicked open. The door creaked as he pulled it, mainly due to the length of time since it was last used. Someone had pushed sawdust into the lock to make it hard to open. It had worked well, and Danny wondered why it had been done. What was Wilson hiding in here? He clambered over the wood for a better view and found a large sawbench skilfully hidden under the wood.

'Very clever, Mr Wilson,' Danny whispered softly. 'If you had it all planned to beat the bailiffs, why do a runner? Are you killing little girls? Where are you?'

He assumed he would never know the answer, and locked the shed again. It was time to wake the sleeping Red, much to Red's annoyance.

Kate Walters saw them coming, and reached the fence in time to pull Red over it and hold him to her.

'Don't you ever do that again. I thought I'd lost you as

well as your father.'

'I'm sorry, Mum, but we didn't have any food. We caught loads of fish for you,' Red replied, not resisting the embrace.

The word 'we' caused her to look at Danny.

'Thank you,' she said almost humbly. 'There's a message for you inside.'

He followed her into the house, after plugging his dead radio into the recharge socket.

'You, into the shower, you smell!' she said, pushing Red towards what Danny assumed was the bathroom.

This made his two sisters giggle.

'It's not me! It's this!' Red replied, holding up the cub.

The two girls were beside him in an instant.

'Isn't it lovely?' the bigger of the two girls whispered.

Danny estimated her to be nine or ten. The other girl looked to be five or six at the most.

'Where did you get that?' Kate asked.

'Mr Turner saved it from being drowned in the river,' Red answered.

Danny was surprised by the 'Mr Turner', as Red had got used to calling him Danny, but he said nothing.

'Sit down, Mr Turner, while I make you a drink,' Kate ordered. 'Tea, isn't it?'

'Yes, thank you,' Danny replied, and sat down. He was looking at Kate Walters in a new light, and parts of him which had not stirred in a long time, were stirring!

A few minutes later, she returned with a mug of tea. Danny took a sip and liked it enough not to spit it out.

'Can I offer you something to eat? I have stew in the pot,' Kate offered.

S G Read

'Thank you, I am hungry.' This was a totally different reception from the one he had received before.

'Can I have some, Mum?' Red asked.

'I thought I told you to have a shower?'

'But it wasn't me you could smell.'

'Well it is now.'

'But I have to look after the cub.'

Kate looked at the cub. The two girls had it in their pram and were tucking it in.

'It looks okay to me. Scram, or I'll wash you!'

Red fled from the room. That was out of the question at his age.

Danny finished the mug of tea. It had been better than he expected. Kate put a plate of stew on the table in front of him, and he started to eat. It made a change from fish, and he did not have to cook it. Before he finished the stew, Red returned wearing a towel and sat next to Danny, waiting for his food.

'I hope you are clean, Redman,' Kate warned.

'Of course I am, Mum. Can I have some stew?'

'I thought you didn't like my stew?'

'I can change my mind, can't I. Anyway you only make stew, so I have to have it.'

'I cook other things when I have the makings. I'm not a magician you know.' She slid a plate of stew in front of Red. It was then she remembered the message from Hamish. 'Mr McLaughland asked me to tell you to call in when you got back as he couldn't get you on the radio.'

'No peace for the wicked,' Danny moaned, and stood up.

'Do you want me to make you another mug of tea?' Kate asked.

'That would go down a treat, thank you. I'll just see what Hamish wants.' He walked out and sat in the Jeep. 'Danny calling Hamish, come on.'

'Hello Danny. This is John Mulroon here. Are you still at the Walters place? Over.'

'Yes, over.'

'A pony has been stolen from Chester Petersen's stables. As all my men are tied up and you are in the area, I want you to look into it for me. Hold up your right hand. Over.'

'Why? Over.'

'Have you got your right hand up? Over.'

'Yes. Over.'

'Good, you're deputised. You're working for me until you solve this case. Where do you plan to start? Over.'

'Suicide Falls. I saw tracks leading up there. Over.'

'Oh shit, that's all I need, a jumper. Keep me informed. If you do recover the horse alive, leave it at Kate's for collection. They have an empty stable there. Good luck. Over and out.'

Kate stood at the table when Danny returned, a mug of tea stood in front of her.

'How can you drink that stuff?' Red complained. He had obviously tasted it.

'With great pleasure, thank you very much,' Danny replied, and started to drink. He needed to get going.

'Was it about the horse?' Red asked.

'Yes, it's been taken from the Petersen ranch. If I get it back, I have been told to bring it here. I understand you have an empty stable.'

'We have. No horse to put in it any more but the stable is still sound,' Kate replied.

'Can I help you?' Red asked, a pleading look on his face.

'What about the cub?' Danny replied.

Red looked at the cub tucked up in a dolls' pram and covered with a little blanket.

'Marie and Isobel are all over it. They think it`s a doll! So can I help?'

'Sure, you can groom the horse when I bring it back.'

'That`s not what I meant.'

Danny smiled.

'I know,' he replied.

'I know the way, and I can save you time by riding the horse back here when you find it,' Red continued, wearing Danny down.

'Can you ride a horse, then?'

'Yes, I used to have a pony. Can I come? Please!'

Danny looked at Kate Walters, partly for help and partly for her opinion.

'Don't involve me,' Kate said, holding her hand up as if to ward off any involvement. 'As you know, he's got a mind of his own and he uses it.'

'Go on, Mr Turner. I can help.'

'If you come, you call me Danny.'

A big smile appeared on Red's face.

'Yes Danny!'

'Why Danny?' Kate asked. 'Why not Dan?'

'There are lots of names that sound like Dan. I was always answering people who weren't talking to me, and it was a bit embarrassing so I started to answer only to Danny, and it seems to work.'

'Do you want me to cook some fish for you to take with you?' Kate asked.

Out of sight of his mother, Red pretended to be sick. Fish three day's running was enough.

'No thanks, I have some supplies at my place if we need them,' Danny replied. 'But thanks for the offer.'

After the initial ice cube meeting, Danny was seeing a different person - a caring mother and a pretty woman. Under other circumstances he would have been tempted to ask her out for a meal, his first step toward a relationship.

'It won't take me long,' Kate argued, wanting to help.

'We'll be okay, Mum. I'll look after Danny,' Red replied.

'You won't get far dressed like that!' she retorted.

Red scurried away to dress.

'Are you sure this is okay?' Danny asked.

'You saved him out there, so I don't think I'll worry when he is with you,' Kate answered.

To Danny it was like a pat on the back. He headed out to the Loggin Road and drove as far as the turning for the Mine Road. He followed the road and parked by the bridge. The radio battery was still charging, so he would have to return to the Jeep to call for help if he needed it, but he was not worried. If someone had jumped, it would be a case of sweeping up the remains. It was the main reason for coming to the top of the Falls. He did not want Red to see the remains of a jumper.

'Do you want to wait here, Red?' Danny asked.

'No way! I can ride the horse back when we find it, and I want to see you arrest whoever took it.'

'It might get a bit ugly,' Danny warned.

'How do you mean?'

Danny's first thought was to pretend to dive into a swimming pool as a clue, but resisted the idea.

'The person or persons we are chasing have stolen a horse. In the old days, they would have been hanged as soon as they were caught,' he explained.

'What lynched, like in the westerns?'

'Yes, and no we can't lynch them when we catch them.'

'Did I say anything?' Red complained.

'No, but I sensed you were about to. Now I want the quickest way to the falls. Which way do we go?'

'Shouldn't we walk up to where the tracks were to see if they came back that way after we passed by?' Red asked.

'You could wait here for me,' Danny replied.

'Come on, it's this way.'

They walked into the trees, Red leading as he had been there before. They walked for half an hour before they came to a low fence which had notices above it warning of a steep drop. The fence was not a barrier, as it was only a metre high, so anyone who wanted to pass it could do so without any trouble. They started to follow the fence round, with the fence on their left. It was staked in position and looked quite sturdy. After a hundred metres, Danny noticed that the fence was now loose and resting against the vegetation. The next section was leaning back even more, and there was a pony tied to a nearby tree. Danny looked at the tracks, hoof prints lead to the edge and then returned to stop at the tree the pony was tied to, then they were replaced by small footprints which lead past the fence. They did not return, and there was no one in sight.

'Stay with the horse, Red,' Danny ordered.

'Why? It's tied up!'

'Because I say so! Okay?' Danny replied.

'But...'

'Look, do you want to help me or not?'

'Okay, I'll stay with the pony but don't blame me if you slip and I'm not there to help you.'

'I'll risk it,' Danny replied dryly.

He walked to the low fence. It was a picket fence, and its backward slope and the nearness to the edge made it difficult to climb over. As it was loose, Danny pulled it forward and lay it on its face, treading it down to make it lay flat, and crushing the vegetation underneath. Now he was able to lay down and peer over the edge. He expected to see a red stain below, but instead he could see someone hanging upside down half way down. The right leg was hooked in the protruding roots, the right arm was hooked in them lower down. Danny could not see much, just a pair of jeans and long blonde hair.

'Are you okay?' he called, and almost laughed at the stupidity of the question. There was no reply from below, and it was possible that she - the hair led Danny to believe it was a woman - had frozen to death as she hung there.

A head appeared next to Danny's on his right.

'Who is it?' Red asked.

'You tell me! I think it's a girl.'

Red moved forward for a better look, and Danny grabbed hold of his arm.

'That's far enough,' he ordered.

'But I can't see who it is.'

'You'll have to wait until I rescue her then.'

'How can you get her back up here?' Red asked.

'I can't, but I know a man who can. I need you to ride to the Jeep and bring back the hand radio. I hope it has charged enough to use. Can you use the Jeep radio?'

'Yes, Trailer used to let me use it for him.'

'Then ride to the Jeep on the horse...'

'It's a pony,' Red corrected.

'Pony, then! Call Greg Pomeroy and tell him what's going on and where, then come back with the radio, a blanket, and the rope. Can you do that?'

'No trouble. Are you going to go down there then?'

'It's the only way I can think of to find out if she is still alive, unless you can think of another way?'

'We could shout!'

They tried shouting several times without response.

'If she is still alive, I need to get the blanket round her.'

'Wow! Part of a real rescue. This is better than riding round with Trailer. Do I tell the Mounties?'

'Yes, but they're still busy at the moment, so they might not be able to spare anyone.'

'Oh yes, they're still looking for Sarah,' Red said, remembering something he'd rather forget. 'Can you ride a horse, Danny?' he asked, changing the subject.

'Why would I want to ride a horse?'

'To get from the river to my place in one day.'

'With a sore backside!' Danny added.

'No, it's easy,' Red replied, and tried to mount the pony, but failed.

'So I see.'

He tried again, but this time Danny helped him up. Once settled, he rode off in the direction of the Jeep.

Danny waited patiently. There was nothing else he could do. He tried shouting down several times without response. Red would get back quicker than if he had walked, and speed was of the essence. He lit a fire to warm himself up.

He would need all his faculties working when he climbed down on the rope. Not something he was looking forward to. He opened his pack and took out what he thought he might need, including his sharp pocket knife which would make short work of any roots he found in the way.

Finally, Red appeared from the trees on the pony. Danny took the rope, tied it to a tree, and lowered the loose end over slowly so that he didn't dislodge the girl and send her plunging to her death. When the rope was in place, Danny tucked the radio into his pocket, threw the blanket over his shoulder, gave Red a wave, and slid over the edge. He could think of a lot better things to be doing, like sitting in his new log cabin in front of a blazing fire, but if the girl was alive she needed help as fast as he could get it to her. The blanket might just keep her alive.

When Danny reached her, he could see that the leg in the roots was broken, but the arm looked okay. He assumed that she had tried to take some of the weight off her broken leg by tucking her arm into the roots before she passed out. Danny felt for a pulse and found one. She was still alive, very cold, but alive. At least his climb had not been in vain. Danny wrapped the blanket round her as best he could, and by hooking his leg and arm into the roots moved close enough to try and warm her up with his body.

'Is she alive?' Red called from above.

'Yes, but she is very cold and her leg is broken,' Danny shouted back. 'Did Greg give you an E.T.A.?'

'What's one of them?'

'Estimated time of arrival.'

'No, but he said he'd be here in about forty minutes.'

Danny smiled. There was nothing more he could do

until help arrived. Hanging there, he thought more about his log cabin. Now that he had a sawbench, he could trim the insides of the logs to give a flat wall inside. In fact, if he cut three sides flat leaving only the outer side looking like a tree trunk there would be very little filling in of gaps, and it would be easier to heat. He ran through how he would set it out several times, then thought about the wolf cub. What was he going to do about that?

'I can hear the helicopter,' Red shouted down, and brought Danny from his daydreams.

He carefully lifted the radio out of his pocket as his hands were cold and stiff, and slipped the wrist strap on. He would need it to talk to Greg.

'Is that you I can see half way down Suicide Falls, Danny?' a familiar voiced asked.

'Who else would it be, Greg? I've got a girl here, around eighteen I'd guess, hanging upside down with one well-broken leg tangled in the roots. She's still alive, but very cold and unconscious. Over.'

'Let's hope she stays unconscious. It's better that way. I'll get Hiram K to lower the harness. When I have her weight, you will have to cut away the roots. Got a knife? Over.'

'Yes, I think my knife is sharp enough. How's it going, Hiram K? Over,' Danny asked.

'Well, I reckon I'm feeling a lot chipper than you at the moment, good buddy, over,' Hiram K replied.

Danny dropped the blanket and put the harness round the girl, not easy as she was upside down. When it was on, he pulled out his pen knife but his hands were cold and it slipped from his fingers. He instinctively tried to stop it with his free boot but merely sent it spinning through the air to the bottom of the falls.

'Damn!' he cursed. 'You can rule out cutting the roots unless you have something suitable up there. Over,' Danny reported, annoyed at himself for his stupidity.

'You're the lumberjack, Danny. We're just the transport,' Greg replied. 'Try to steer her leg clear as I lift her then lower her. Keep her upside down until her leg is free. Over.'

'I'll do my best,' Danny replied. 'But I can't give directions and hold her, over.'

'Hiram K will call it as he sees it. Signal to him if you want anything. Over.'

The helicopter did not stray from where Greg held it, and they slowly freed the girl. Danny kept her upside down until her leg was free, and then he let her swing slowly up the right way until he could no longer reach her.

'She's clear, Greg. What now? Over,' he called up.

'I'll move away in case she spins back into the roots. That leg looks bad. The sooner I get her to hospital, the better. What about you? Can you get up again? Over.'

'No, I'll climb down. How far does the rope reach? Over.'

'Two metres short of the ground. Over.'

'I can do that all right. Safe journey. Over and out.'

'Be careful, Danny,' Hiram K called, but Danny was already climbing down, his fingers getting more and more numb. He wanted to be near the ground before they gave up altogether. At first he was able to use the roots as he climbed but when they ended it was a sheer drop to the snow covered ground below. He gritted his teeth and climbed down inch by inch, the rope wrapped round one leg to slow his progress. He lowered himself, one hand dropping to be below the other hand, with the steadying influence of the rope round his leg, until the rope was no longer wrapped round his leg.

It was a shock when it happened, as he had no thoughts of looking down and he nearly fell. He steadied himself and, with the last of his energy, he climbed down to the end of the rope. There was no going back, even if he wanted to. It was only a short drop to the ground but it was filled with emotion. First the relief of not having to hold onto the rope any more, followed by the impending impact. He let go and landed on his feet, his knees and the snow cushioning the fall. He took deep breaths to get his wind back, at the same time blowing on his fingers.

'Red! Can you hear me?' he called up. When there was no reply, he repeated the call louder.

'Yes, are you down yet?' Red's young voice sounded squeaky and it was obvious he never doubted that Danny would reach the bottom.

'Yes! Can you pull the rope up and lower my snow shoes on the end of it?'

There was no reply, but the rope started to snake its way back up the cliff face until it was no longer visible. When it returned, the snow shoes were attached to the bottom but there was no way Danny could reach them.

'Let the rope fall. I can't reach my snow shoes,' Danny shouted. Nothing happened. 'Let the rope fall. I can't reach my snow shoes,' he repeated even louder.

This time, he moved out of the way to make sure the falling rope did not hit him when it came down, and as he did so he saw his penknife. He walked over to where it lay, his feet sinking into the soft snow. The knife lay on a layer of ice where the snow had obviously melted. Beneath the ice he could clearly see a hand. From the size and condition of it, he thought it to be a man's hand. Could this be Wilson? The rope hitting the ground broke the fascination which held his eyes to the hand below the ice.

'Meet me at the Jeep,' Danny called up. The shouting brought back memories of a fight he had had with Lucy. He had just received the results of tests which he had done to try and find out why they had no children yet. He was fine, and she had refused point blank to go in for tests. The row had been long and noisy.

'Okay, I'm on my way,' Red shouted down, and sent the memory spinning back to where it had come from.

Danny strapped on his snow shoes, coiled up the rope and, with that over one shoulder, picked up the blanket and headed for the road. He could not see the road but he knew it was there!

CHAPTER 7

RED was sitting in the Jeep, pretending to steer it by the time Danny arrived. The pony was tied to the rear bumper. Once again it stirred a memory, this time a nice one. He could remember his father letting him drive their car in the forest when he was not much older than Red.

Danny's father had been a forester all his life, living in the house which Danny had taken on after his father's smoking had caught up with him. Lung cancer, Danny decided, was not a nice way to go. He had never wanted to smoke after that, and never had. He was tempted to give Red a driving lesson, probably his first, but the horse needed looking after, and he wanted Red home long before it was dark. Travelling through the forest after dark was risky enough without being a little boy.

'Take the pony home and make sure it is looked after,' he said a little sadly.

'Do I get paid?' Red asked. That made Danny smile.

'Of course, if you do a good job. I'll get the money back from the owner,' he replied.

'What about you? Are you coming to collect the wolf cub?' Red asked.

Danny smiled again. He had forgotten about the wolf cub. He'd have to go there again, and he was looking forward to it!

'I'll be along later. I have some loose ends to tie up first, you know, paperwork and bits and pieces.'

The loose end was the hand under the ice but, as Red had just lost his Dad, the loss of a friend might not help him too much, so he was going to call in after Red was gone.

'I'll see you soon, Red.'

Danny watched Red climb on the pony and ride off, without help this time. He used the Jeep as a step. Danny waited until Red was out of sight before he picked up the hand piece.

'Daniel Turner here, do you copy?'

'It depends on what you want Danny. Over,' a voice replied.

'That sounds suspiciously like John Mulroon. Over.'

'You got that right. What's the problem? Over.'

'Why should there be a problem? Over.'

'Because it's you! Tell me everything is hunky dory and I'll believe you. I know you didn't drop her because she just arrived at hospital. So what's up? Over.'

'I found a body at the bottom when I climbed down. White male, might be the missing Wilson, over.'

'What makes you think it is Wilson? Over.'

'I can't see a stranger coming all the way out here just to top himself, over.'

'You'd be surprised. That place has made a name for itself. They come from all over just to see it, besides it doesn't fit our thinking on the missing girls, over.'

Danny noted that he said 'girls' but did not say anything.

'I just bought the place! Over,' he moaned.

'I know! Over,' John replied with a chuckle.

Danny laughed.

'Very funny, but what do we do about the body? Over.'

'Wait there. We'll be out, but keep away from the scene. We have to treat it as suspicious until we know otherwise. Over.'

'Okay, I'll be at the mine. Over and out.'

Danny drove to the mine. He had no tools but he could unload the wood from the shed with the saw hidden in it, and find out what else was in there. Once more he struggled with the obstinate lock but he knew its secret now and persevered until it yielded. The pile of wood was big. This was going to be a herculean task and, after his recent adventure, it was not very appealing, but he wanted the wood out. He carried the first log over to the mine. His first thought of dumping it outside had been superseded by the thought of keeping it dry by putting it in the mine. There would still be room for him to sleep there tonight. He unlocked the mine and started stacking the wood neatly to one side, but by the time John Mulroon arrived he had hardly made a dent in it.

'Where are the rest of them?' Danny asked when he saw John was on his own.

'On their way along the bottom of the cliff. They know the way, they've been there before. No fire? I expected a warm fire, at least!'

'Try shifting this lot over there, John, you'll soon be warm!'

John took off his coat and did just that. After half an hour, John's radio burped.

'We can't find anything. Over,' a voice informed him, and waited for further instructions.

John looked across at Danny.

'This isn't an English joke, is it?' he asked.

'No! Where are they looking? The body is in a frozen puddle about ten metres from the base of the cliff.'

'No wonder they can't find it, they're usually right next to the base of the cliff. He must have jumped, and how!'

John relayed the message, and then they continued to move the wood. The radio burped again.

'He must have taken a running jump. Maybe he was learning to fly!' the same voice said. 'It could be Wilson but we'll need to run some tests, over.'

'Damnation!' John almost spat the word out. 'If it is, it means we are no nearer catching the killer of these girls.'

Danny did not press for information, and they both increased their efforts to move the wood until the saw bench was visible.

'Did you know this was here?' John asked.

Danny nodded.

'He knew they were going to foreclose, and made sure they didn't find this. That way he could still earn a living. It doesn't point to a man about to jump off a cliff.'

'Who knows what tips the balance and makes someone do something like that. He might have done it in a fit of depression. They will be able to tell us if it was murder.'

They unloaded all the wood. Underneath the sawbench there were other tools, and a winch used to pull the heavy logs onto the saw bench.

'You won't have to buy any snow shovels,' John said, holding three of them aloft.

'I won't use them. I take it we will have more snow?'

John nodded.

'We will that,' he replied.

'Then it can lay where it falls as far as I'm concerned, unless it drifts and blocks a door or the road. I can't see the point of moving something which is likely to be replaced as fast as I clear it,' Danny declared.

'You ought to talk to my wife about that,' John suggested.

'No thanks, it didn't work on my wife so I can't see it working on yours.'

'I didn't realise you were married, Danny. Where is the good woman?'

'Back home in England. She didn't want to come out into the wilds of Canada. No spirit of adventure.'

'And you have?'

'Obviously, but I didn't realise just how much of an adventure it was going to be.'

The radio burped again.

'This is going to take some time, Sarge. He's encased in ice. Over,' the voice advised.

John walked over to the radio.

'Just make sure you do it right. This is an important one. Over.'

'Will do Sarge, over,' the voice replied wearily.

'Sounds like they need some hot food,' Danny said with a smile. He was glad it was them doing it instead of him. 'I'll light a fire. I think we have enough wood.'

'Have you any food, though?' John asked.

'Of course! Only bacon and beans though. Oh, and some eggs.'

They cleared the snow off the concrete base, and lit a

fire on it. Then two improvised benches were rigged up out of the longer off-cuts. They built the fire up for heat, and later on six people sat round the fire, talking and eating.

They loaded the remains onto the meat wagon, but were in no hurry as the body was still encased in ice and showing no disposition to melt.

When the food was gone, they still sat talking. Danny asked about Canada, and the others about England. Later when everyone decided to go, Danny toyed with the idea of sleeping in the mine, but when it started to snow the bed at Hester Foy's grew more and more appealing. He drove back to Turnround.

He woke early as usual, and after a large breakfast he walked to the office. All was quiet and, after sitting there for half an hour, he phoned the hospital to ask about the girl they had saved. The only information they would give was her name, Constance Jonson, and the fact that they had saved both her leg and her baby. The news that she was pregnant might explain her reason for jumping.

Danny drove to the hospital to talk to her if he could. Having wanted a baby since he had married Lucy, he was damned if he was going to see one killed with its mother in some other pointless way. He drove out of Turnround as far as the Loggin Road, turned left and headed for Lower Superior. Then he followed the signs for the hospital and parked in the large car park.

It was many miles away from Lake Superior but they had still named the place Lower Superior! As he travelled, the scenery had not seemed to change. There were trees, more trees, and even more trees, and Danny liked every inch of them.

The nurse at reception directed him to the girl's ward. She had not asked who he was but merely reacted to the uniform. This was only his second visit to a hospital in his life, once in England and now once in Canada. The desk in the ward was empty and he waited there to ask where the girl was until a commotion drew him down to the source of the noise. He recognised the girl who was refusing an injection. Without hesitation, he pinned the girl's arms to the bed while the nurse quickly took advantage and gave her the injection. The girl glared at Danny.

'Thank you, Mr...?' one of the nurses said.

'Turner, Daniel Turner,' Danny replied.

'You!' the girl hissed. 'You were the one who caused all this.'

'I didn't make you pregnant,' Danny retorted. 'He's the one you should be sorting out.'

The girl calmed down.

'You don't understand,' she sighed.

'Explain it to me so I can understand then, Constance.' Danny pulled over a chair and sat down by the bed and waited.

'You will never understand.'

'Try me.'

By now they were alone, the nurses going about their business, glad of a respite from the girl's constant complaining.

'Well, here goes then. I fell in love with someone, or at least I thought I had. We were lovers. I was on the pill - he was supplying them. I thought if I got pregnant he would have to leave his wife and marry me. How wrong can you be? His wife has all the money. He was just living with her and screwing me on the side. When I told him I was pregnant he gave me the money for an abortion so that we could carry on as before. The bastard!' She was starting to get louder.

Danny put his finger to his lips.

'It's only me who wants to hear you,' he whispered.

'I threw the money back into his face and ran off. When I got home, the doctor had phoned for me to come and see him. My father was suspicious and gave me the third degree. They guessed what it was and when I wouldn't tell them who the father was they threw me out. Clothes and all. What would you do?'

'Tell the wife of the man who did it. Drop him in the shit, for one.'

'She's a witch. If she knew about it, she'd want the baby to bring up as her own and I'd be left without anything. I know her.'

'What if you had lost the baby when you jumped? Would you have gone back to the way things were once your leg was better?' Danny asked.

'No way!'

'Then there is hope for you yet.'

The girl smiled for the first time.

'They say you climbed down Suicide Falls on a rope to rescue me?'

'Just doing my job. This visit however is overtime. You know you are likely to be charged with stealing the pony?'

'Yes, it's a bit of a bummer. I was going to jump Harry over the edge and die with him but I couldn't do it. He hadn't done anything wrong, had he? If I'd have done it that way I wouldn't be here talking to you now.'

'But Harry would be dead as well.'

'I know. What was it like climbing down to get me?'

'Not my favourite thing since arriving - a bit like bungy jumping with a rope, I suppose.'

'Have you been bungy jumping, Mr Turner?'

'No, but I have a good imagination, and the name is Danny, by the way.'

'How did you get me down? I can remember my leg getting hooked in the roots and trying to free it, but then I must have passed out.'

'I called out Greg Pomeroy in his helicopter, well, Red did. I was halfway down the cliff feeling foolish.'

'You know Red? Redman Walters?'

'Yes, we met.'

'I taught him to ride.'

'Well, when you are fit you can teach me as well.'

'That might be hard from prison.'

'Well, you are not in prison yet. When they let you out of here you can stay with me until the trial.'

'Do I get a choice?'

'Yes. Me or prison.'

'Some choice!' The girl moved her leg and grimaced as she did so. There was a cage round it with bars protruding from her leg, obviously to hold her broken bones in the right place. 'Where do you live then?'

'The Wilson mine.' This was the second lie Danny had told in his life. It was a lie to him as he had no idea if he could build his cabin before she was released from hospital. He hoped his new friends might know a way of speeding things up.

'Isn't that where I would have landed? It's in the middle

of nowhere! Still at least people won't be walking past pointing at me and my bastard.'

'If I were a free man, I'd marry you, then it wouldn't be a bastard. I've wanted a baby for years only to find out my wife was living on the bloody pill.'

'Divorce her and we'll get married. Then you'll have the baby you want.'

Danny leant over and kissed her on the forehead.

'I want one of my own. Can you face another one?'

She kissed him on the cheek.

'I'll let you know after this one is born.'

Danny stood up.

'Don't go giving the nurses a hard time,' he ordered.

'No Dad,' Constance answered cheekily.

She felt better now, but how long would it last?

Danny drove back to Turnround feeling happy. He knew there was no chance of him marrying Constance. Lucy would block it until well after the baby was born, but Constance felt better and he wanted to keep it that way. She was at least looking forward now. He skidded to a stop in front of the store and sought out Callum whose lorry was parked in front.

'I want enough logs to build me a log cabin,' Danny announced.

'You'll have them. What's the plan?'

'The girl I helped to rescue is pregnant. She has been thrown out by her parents, and the father of her baby is a married man who doesn't want to know. By the time she gets out of hospital, I want to have somewhere warm for her to live.'

'You don't ask for much, but when you do it's a

challenge,' Callum replied. He looked at his watch. 'First delivery in about two hours, if that's okay with you?'

'Fine. I'll be there waiting.'

'So will I!' Hamish added from the doorway. 'And I might be able to drum up a few friends, but yee pay for the refreshments or they'll be thinking I'm a soft touch.'

Danny smiled. 'I think you're a soft touch already. I need more supplies. The Mounties ate all I had.'

Callum walked to the door and Danny waved. He assumed he was off to get the first load of logs, but Callum knew he would need the generator from the garage and was about to load it.

'I'll bring a few things oot with me, but what about tools?' Hamish replied.

Danny wrote out a list, and as he did so he explained his idea of trimming the logs on three sides to make them fit snugly.

'I have some resin to seal them together. I'll bring a few barrels of the stuff.'

'Where can I get a generator to run a sawbench?'

'The McLaughland garage of course. It'll run anything you want it to.'

'You haven't seen the size of the sawbench.'

'I don't have to, laddie. I sold it to the man, and the generator to go with it. But I had to take it back before the tax man appeared.'

Callum appeared from the back of the shop.

'I've loaded the generator, so I'll drop it off on my way to get the first logs. I managed to get Pierre out of bed, and he said just help yourself to the logs.'

'Who's Pierre?' Danny asked.

'The man in charge of the logging,' Callum answered.

'Are you ready to go?'

'I have to collect a few things from Hester, and then I'll catch you up.'

'You'll be lucky!' Callum said with a laugh. 'Not many people can catch the Big Bad Wolf.'

'I'll be Red Riding Hood. Talking of wolves, I should collect the cub I saved at Black Rock Flats from the Walters' place. The girls are treating it like a doll.'

'Yee saved a wolf?' Hamish interjected. 'I didn't hear aboot that.'

'It was in the river. I used one of the boys' landing nets to fish it out.'

'Yee'll have to take it away from the girls or you won't be able to loose it back into the wild.'

'I know. I'll collect it on the way.'

'I'll see yee oot there. I think Bob and Gaston will come as well.'

Danny drove to Hester's, collected what he needed, and drove to the Walters' house. Red ran out to greet him as he turned into the driveway.

'How's the pony?' Danny asked.

'Fine. I exercised him today. Have you come for the wolf cub?'

'Yes, I have to make sure it isn't too friendly with humans so I can set it free when it's big enough.'

Kate Walters appeared, this time in a pretty dress.

'I made them put it in a shed in a box when it was dry and warmed,' she said knowingly. 'You can take the box if you like.'

'Thank you. I will need something to keep it in.'

Red ran off to fetch the cub.

'Will you stay and eat? It's only meat loaf,' she said, almost apologetically.

'I can't, I'm afraid, or I'd have loved to. I have to meet Callum. He's dropping off a generator for me.'

'Are you going to be working out there?'

'Yes, I need somewhere to live and look after the wolf until I can set it free.'

'I think you might get some help, or hindrance, out there,' Kate warned, nodding at the approaching Red.

'Out where?' Red asked.

'Big ears!' Kate replied.

'What, at the mine? Are you going to start on your log cabin?' Red asked.

It had been one of their topics of conversation to keep other thoughts away as they walked through the forest.

'I'm starting today. Hamish is bringing out some help, but until the cabin has a roof on it, I'll have to stay in the mine with the cub.'

'Captain Webb!' Red said, holding the cub up. 'As he was in the river, and you're English, I named him after an English swimmer from one of my Dad's cigarette cards.'

Danny took the cub from Red.

'Captain Webb it is then. Hello Captain Webb! Now I really must go, but thanks for the offer of the food.'

'Call in any time. I'll always find something for you.'

Danny looked at her in the pretty dress, and thought of more than food. Then he remembered the approaching funeral, and pushed the thought away.

'Thank you,' he said, climbing into the Jeep. He made sure that Captain Webb was safely in, and drove off with a cheery wave.

CHAPTER 8

WHEN Danny left the Walters' house, he saw Callum on the road. Callum had obviously dropped off the generator, and was on his way for the logs. Danny waved, and Callum honked his loud horn as he passed. Danny found the generator sitting outside the long shed where the sawbench was hidden, and he wondered if they knew all about it. He fought with the lock once more, and decided to replace it with one that worked.

He looked at the wiring inside to figure out where to connect the feed from the generator to make it safe to use the saw bench, and was still working on it when a lorry pulled up. It was Hamish, and with him were Bob Trueman, who drove the school bus, and Gaston Wolfe, the man who was the closest thing to Hester's husband.

They cleared the fresh snow from the concrete base, ready to put the logs on when they were cut, and lit a fire for warmth. When Danny had connected the generator, Hamish showed him how to start it, and Danny was pleased to hear the saw whine into life. They were all ready to start. The four of them manhandled the barrels of resin and the damp-proof membrane from Gaston's lorry, then put a pot on the fire for coffee. The heat melted what snow remained, and they swept it off the concrete to give an almost snow-free base to build on. They heard Callum's lorry approaching, and walked out to meet him. Callum expertly lifted the logs from the lorry with his mechanical grab, and piled them on the far side of the long shed, ready for winching. He laid the last log down with one end on the sawbench, all ready to go. He stayed while they cut the first one, following Danny's plan, mainly to see if it would work. With the three sides cut, the log was sawn to length and manhandled into place. All that remained was to cut the ends to accept the end of the next log. They chose to half-butt it for ease, which they did with a chain saw.

Satisfied the system would work, Callum left to collect more logs. The next three logs were cut and put in place, making a giant square, with the damp-proof membrane underneath. Danny cut the next log in half lengthways after it was trimmed, to be put in place where he wanted the doors. They were his door liners, all they had to do now was to build the logs up, making sure each one was painted with resin and pinned by a wooden dowel to the log below.

His first idea of having just one door had been poo-pood by the other three in case he was snowed in on one side. They said a door on the other side was essential. He saw the wisdom of this and put one in. With precision cutting, there were no gaps to bung up with mixed clay and straw. The resin was enough.

Callum made three more journeys to the logging camp, and then parked his lorry close by. As the height of the walls rose, so did the effort of getting the logs up there. He used the grab when it was getting too high to do by hand, even though it tore into the wood in places. As they were working, Red arrived on the pony to give it some exercise, but mainly he stayed with Captain Webb, walking him like a dog. The cub seemed happy enough to go with him, and Danny thought it did no harm to exercise the cub.

When the end of a hard day came, the shell of the cabin was up to door height, with two door and two window openings. The shell was as solid as a rock. The resin and the pinning on the corners helping to give it even more strength. Gaston took two tarpaulins from his lorry, and they stretched them over the building to save clearing snow next time. The fire under the tarpaulin was allowed to go out.

After seeing off his new friends, Danny lit another fire near the mine entrance and sat by it watching the flames. Red had also gone in time to be home before dark, so it was just him and Captain Webb, who was well fed and sound asleep in his box. This would make a good home, he thought, as he carried the cub into the mine and closed the door.

In the morning, Danny walked out with his rifle to find something for Captain Webb to eat and, as he walked back carrying two jack rabbits, he heard Callum's lorry approaching.

'Tired of bacon, Danny?' he called.

'No, I thought you might be hungry,' Danny replied.

Callum unloaded the logs while Danny cooked breakfast for the two of them.

'No help today?' Callum asked, when the logs were stacked and he was ready to eat.

'No, Gaston had to go into Lower Superior. I'll winch the logs in to trim them but after that I'll have to stack them. There's no way I can fit them by myself.'

'I'd like to stay and help, but I have deliveries to make.'

'Don't worry about it. I'm just grateful for the help yesterday. Look at what we did on a day of rest. Isn't it beautiful?'

'Some rest! But it does look okay. That was a good idea about cutting the logs like that.'

'When do I pay for the logs?'

'I'll let you know how much when Pierre tells me. Prices tend to vary.'

They ate, and Callum drove off again. Danny fed Captain Webb, and then started on the first log. His Jeep was the office for as long as this would take. After a struggle and a lot of cursing, Danny winched in the first log, trimmed it and let it slide off the bench. He repeated the action, but added to the cursing until all the logs were trimmed. He looked long and hard at the cabin, but there was no way he could get a log up that high on his own. He would have to wait for help, and waiting was not his strong point. He took Captain Webb for a walk with a length of rope round his neck. The day passed without incident and without help. As darkness approached, he decided to go and visit Constance. No one would come here to work in the dark. He drove to the hospital, made sure Captain Webb was warm and comfortable, and went in to see Constance. When she saw him, her face lit up and it made him feel good.

'How do you feel today?' he asked.

'Better than yesterday, but I'm sure they are trying to kill me.'

'Well, they haven't succeeded unless you're a ghost.'

'There aren't such things as ghosts. When you are dead,

you are dead, and that's what I should be: Dead!'

'Not that trip again. If you're going to be all melancholic, I'm out of here.'

'There's no such word as melancholic.'

'Of course there is. I thought you went to college?'

'I did, but not for long. My Dad thought I should pay my way so I had to leave and get a job. I thought by working and saving hard I could put myself through college, but look where it got me. A broken leg, a stomach which will soon balloon into some horrible shape. I'll look grotesque.'

'There's no such word.'

'Very funny. Where's the fruit and the flowers then? I thought when you visited people in hospital, you took them fruit and flowers and stuff like that?'

Danny held out a box of chocolates he had bought in the hospital foyer.

'Thanks, there's no point in worrying about my figure, is there?' she said, and ate several chocolates before closing the box. 'I'll save the rest for the nurses. I've been a real pain in the bum.'

'If you know you're being a pain, why not stop?'

'That's easy for you to say. You're not the one lying in a hospital bed with your leg in a cage. It does hurt you know, I'm not making it up.'

'I'm sure it does. That leg went through quite a rough time, but they say it will get better and, when it does, you can come and stay with me.'

'I won't be able to climb stairs.'

'I'm working on it. When I have finished, it will be all on one floor and you will have your own room. By the time they let you out of here, it should be finished.'

'The doctor said four to six weeks before they think I can walk on it properly.'

A nurse arrived with a bunch of flowers in a vase.

'Who sent them?' Constance asked.

'Who do you think?' Danny replied.

Constance picked up the chocolates and held them out in front of the nurse.

'Do you want a chocolate, nurse?' she asked.

'Thank you,' she replied, and took one.

'Take the box and share them. It's the least I can do.'

Danny watched the nurse walk away with the chocolates.

'I wonder what they tasted like?' he said slyly.

Constance put her hand to her mouth.

'Sorry, I thought... I mean, I didn't think... Did you want one?' she spluttered.

'No, but it would have been nice to be asked.'

Constance picked up the vase of flowers.

'Do you want a flower?' she asked.

Danny laughed, and so did she. He liked it when she laughed.

When Danny returned to the Jeep, Captain Webb was pawing the window. He took him for a walk round the car park, drawing several comments from the people they met. They returned to the Jeep, and Captain Webb settled down for more sleep.

After two weeks, the walls were complete and Danny was busy making roof timbers when he had the time, to be ready when help was available. The two tarpaulins still covered it, and Danny considered it his home, albeit a very cold home! The next project he could do on his own, was the fireplace, and he wanted this fireplace to be very big and very special. A fireplace fit for a palace! He designed the fireplace he had always wanted, and built it with stones from his own quarry. He bought a brazier to warm the area where he was going to lay the bricks - he wanted no cracking or sagging. And he had to buy special bricks and cement to withstand the heat of his log fires. Bales of hay were stored in the mine to cover the fresh-laid bricks to keep the relentless cold out.

Whilst he was working late one evening, someone else was on the prowl.

Helen Richter sat on the sofa watching television. Although her younger sister was upstairs asleep, she had the volume of the television up high. It made her feel safer, in light of recent events, while she waited for her mother to come home from work. She knew that she mustn't go near the door if anyone came, and to phone for help if she thought there was trouble. Her grandfather had drummed that into her. He was a prison warder. Because of the television, she did not hear the snow crunching as the man approached the house. She did not hear him take the spare key from the flower pot by the front door. She knew nothing until a hand was clamped over her mouth.

'If you wake your sister, I'll have to kill her,' he hissed in her ear. 'Do you understand?'

Helen nodded. He took his hand away from her mouth, but kept a firm grip on her with his other hand.

'Kneel down!' he ordered.

She did as he said, and he gagged her.

'Stand up!'

Again she obeyed, and he removed her nightdress before

tying her hands and feet. Now he relaxed and walked upstairs. He knew he had half an hour because the little girl upstairs had told him when her mother came home. He opened the bedroom door and watched her as she slept.

'Soon little one, soon,' he whispered, then walked to Helen's bed and made it look like someone was asleep in there. He took a last look at the sleeping six-year-old, then hurried down the stairs. This was a new M.O. for him. He usually spread the nightdress, or what ever they were wearing, in front of the fire, but he had a long way to go and did not want to be interrupted. This time, he hid her nightdress under the sofa before throwing Helen over his shoulder. He dumped her in his vehicle, before quickly returning to lock the house and put the key back where it came from. A sprint down the path in his snow shoes and he was driving away. The falling snow would cover his tracks and make the mother hurry indoors.

In the morning, he carried her naked into the trees and stood her down in the snow.

'You thought I was going to hurt you, didn't you? I'm not like that. You can go now. Bye.'

Helen turned and ran into the trees to get away from this man she thought was her friend.

Danny spent his time working in the office, working on the cabin, or visiting Constance in hospital. He was alone in the office as there was now a fresh search going on. It annoyed him that he was not asked to help, but someone had to man the office although it was very quiet after the brief flurry of activity when he first arrived. Hamish, Bob, Callum, and Gaston were regular visitors, stopping for an hour here and there, making sure there were enough of them to work on the roof, and it was eventually finished with authentic bark tiles. This left only the inside to do, and that was Danny's homework. The firewood in the mine was used to light the fire in the fireplace as soon as it was complete, and the cabin started to warm up. Now Danny had his home.

It was one big room with a fire at one end, but it was a start. Danny covered the wooden face inside with plasterboard, not because the wood was ugly but for fire protection. He made a bedroom and a bathroom. Only one bedroom, as he had no idea how long Constance would be there. She might go home, go to prison, or even leave for the city. While she was there, he would sleep in the dining room near the fire. If she was not sent to prison, and it became obvious she was going to be there for a while, he would build an extension, but not hurriedly like this.

Constance rang him in the office to say she was coming out after only four weeks. They had had enough of her. While she was there, her parents had not come to visit her, but they did send her belongings along, and Danny put them in her room. He collected her from hospital in his Jeep.

Captain Webb was left in the cabin as she had yet to meet him. He wheeled her through the front door to a blazing log fire, and a wolf cub who raised his head, smelt someone new, and walked over to where she sat. Constance was very nervous despite Danny's assurances, but when she was sitting in his new armchair, and Captain Webb laid his head on her lap and fell asleep, all her nervousness disappeared.

When it was time for bed, Danny put Captain Webb

into his basket. He was too big now for the box Kate had given him. Then he helped Constance to bed. The cage on her leg was a problem but she was over the worst. Now at least she had someone who loved her for what she was.

The second day she was there, Callum arrived with more logs to repair the outhouses. Danny invited him in for coffee which Constance had made. This was their first meeting, but from that moment Callum found reasons to visit almost every day. Danny watched like a worried father but he knew Callum, and nothing really bad could happen, not now. He realised that only good could come out of his visits, and found things to do outside while Callum was there. He did not know if it was the right thing to do because he had never been a father figure before and would probably never be again.

The one thing that stood between Callum and Constance was the name of the baby's father, but she stood firm, and Callum, now in love with Constance, learnt to live with it. It was the only subject which put her into a bad mood. The two men discussed it but they never came to any conclusion or got any nearer to finding out. Danny wanted to confront the man and, at the very least, punch his lights out, but when he realised how deep the bond between Callum and Constance was getting, he decided to let sleeping dogs lie.

Everyone was happy until the court papers arrived. With John Mulroon's help, Danny had managed to keep Constance at home with him until the trial, but now she was upset. He phoned Callum, who came running to comfort her. Hamish rang and gave him the telephone number of a good lawyer, and after that he could do no more than leave it to the expert. He knew she was guilty of breaking into the stables and stealing a horse. If she had told them the name of the father, the lawyer could have had extenuating circumstances taken into account, but the owner was pushing for a maximum sentence.

Danny sat in the court listening to the proceedings, and thinking. Even though things looked black, then blacker, for Constance, he was still thinking. Why did she go and steal a horse from Petersen? He was a married man, a lay preacher, a pillar of the community, or was he? Was this Constance's personal attack against her denigrator?

'I must be going dim in my old age,' he said, and Hamish gave him a quizzical look. 'Just thinking aloud, Hamish,' he assured him.

Petersen was Constance's employer. He sat in the back of the court with his wife. Was this the witch? She certainly looked the part! The verdict was a foregone conclusion, and the only glimmer of hope was the clemency of the judge. Unfortunately it was a woman judge, the horsey type. Danny watched the Petersens until Mrs Petersen left. Mr Petersen stayed to hear the verdict, so he was obviously interested in the sentence. Danny changed seats and sat next to him.

'Mr Petersen, isn't it?' Danny asked.

'Yes, and you must be Turner, the man who recovered my property.'

He did not even call it a horse, and there was no Mr Turner or Ranger Turner. Danny did not like this man at all.

'And the girl.'

'A waste of time that was,' Petersen remarked, and Danny could have hit him.

He remembered just in time what his father had once

said: 'A poor man respects being hit. You hurt a rich man through his pocket.'

'That was uncharitable for a lay preacher,' he replied.

'But true. Her parents have thrown her out. She has nowhere to go and, as soon as she can, she'll do it again, you mark my words.'

Danny wanted to mark more than his words, but his father prevailed.

'You sending her to prison won't help. At the moment she has a good home with me, and I am going to find the father of the baby and make it known throughout the country what sort of bastard he is. She won't tell me his name, but I'm taking out a paternity suit against the man I think is responsible so that he can pay for the baby's keep.'

'So you know who it is?' Petersen asked.

'I have a good idea.'

'Good ideas count for nothing.'

'We'll see. I happen to know his wife is outside. I'll go out and ask her about it.' Danny stood up and moved toward the door.

Petersen grabbed his arm.

'Let's not be hasty. Maybe I could put in a good word for her?'

'It would have to be a VERY GOOD WORD!' Danny replied, emphatically.

Petersen released his arm and stood ready to go to the front of the court, but Danny grabbed his arm.

Once more his father's words rang in his ears.

'When you get them on the ropes, make it worthwhile!'

'She really likes that pony, and Christmas is approaching. Sorry, I suppose you call it Thanksgiving?'

Petersen tore his arm free and walked to the front of the court. There was a short argument between the prosecutor and Petersen, then the prosecutor stood up.

'Your Honour, in light of fresh evidence the prosecution has decided not to continue, for the sake of justice.'

The expression on the horsey judge's face barely changed, but it was several seconds before she said, 'Case dismissed,' and banged her gavel on the top of her desk.

Petersen turned and walked out, but on the way he gave Danny a handwritten note. It read: *'I hereby give to Constance Jonson the pony named Harry as long as it is collected from my stable by someone other than the aforementioned person.'*

Danny watched Petersen walk out then walked up to where Callum was helping Constance to stand.

'That was a turn up,' Callum said, a broad smile on his face. 'I saw you talking to him. What did you say?'

Constance looked straight at Danny, but said nothing.

'I just said that Constance was a nice girl, and as a lay preacher he should look for the good in people, not strike them when they were down.' It was all lies, of course, but Danny thought it was up to Constance to tell Callum when she was ready.

He held out the note. Constance read it and her eyes lit up. It was worth more than money to Danny, especially when she kissed him full on the lips.

'Thank you, Danny. I wish you were my father.'

Callum looked put out.

'Am I missing out on something?' he asked defensively.

Constance limped up close to him and gave him a long loving kiss.

'You know what you asked me earlier, Callum. Well the answer is yes!' she said, when she caught her breath.

Callum lifted her off her feet and spun to face Danny.

'I'm getting married!' he yelled.

'We are getting married!' Constance corrected. 'You will give me away, Danny, won't you? My father isn't exactly flavour of the month.'

'I'll be glad to, and I don't think you'll find a better man, apart from me of course. Where's the church?'

'The nearest one is Timberline,' Callum answered. 'But I reckon we'll be using the office in the school.'

'I could always get Greg Pomeroy to fly a priest out and hold it at my cabin?' Danny offered.

Constance looked at Callum and nodded. She liked the idea that only her friends would see her like this.

'I'll have to check my calendar to make sure it isn't already booked though,' Danny added with a smile.

'It will be the day after I get this thing off my leg!' Constance retorted. 'I am not getting married while I am still bolted to this thing.'

'Come on, let's tell Pa,' Callum said, and steered her toward the rear of the court.

Danny followed. His business here was finished, and Captain Webb would be getting restless. Last time that happened, it cost him a coat, chewed beyond recognition! Once outside, he saw them all congratulating her.

'You are all invited to an engagement party at my place on Saturday. Bring a few friends,' he called over the noise.

'We'll be there, Danny,' Callum answered. 'You've never been to one of our parties, have you?'

'No!'

'When we party, we party!' he continued.

When Danny arrived at the cabin, Red was there with Captain Webb.

'Hi, Danny. I'm never going fishing again,' he groaned.

'Fish again tonight, is it?' Danny guessed.

'Yes! This time it's fish pie.'

Danny walked out the back door and into the adjoining room which he had built between the mine and the cabin. He still had his back door but now he could walk to the mine without getting wet or snowed on. It also meant he could get at his large pile of logs even if he was totally snowed in. The door out of the new room was on the right as he walked to the mine, giving a good chance that one would be free of snow. He walked to the mine and unlocked the door. There hung a wild turkey, which he unhooked and carried through to the cabin.

'I found this on the road yesterday. It's too big for me so you might as well take it home with you.' The 'found it on the road' tale was a complete lie. He had seen the turkey cross the road out of the park and stalked it with Captain Webb. Three times he had cornered it, shot and missed. The last time he crept very close and aimed at the large body only to shoot it in the head.

'Wow! That's a monster! Is it for Christmas?' Red squealed.

'Do you think it will do for Thanksgiving?' Danny asked.

'No, that's gone, but it will be fine for Christmas,' Red replied.

'I thought Christmas was Thanksgiving?' Danny responded.

'No, that's in October. Where's Connie? Is she in jail?'

'No, the case was dismissed, and now she owns Harry.'

'You're kidding. My Dad said that Petersen was a mean old bastard!'

Danny looked sharply at Red, and Red knew he had spoken out of place.

'But I'm meaner, and if you say something like that again, you will find out just how mean.' It was all bluff, but it worked.

'Sorry. Why isn't she here, then?'

'She is with Callum. They are engaged.'

'What does that mean?'

'They are going to get hitched.'

'What, married?'

'That's what I said.'

Red punched the air like a footballer.

'Yes-s-s!' he cried.

Danny was confused.

'There is going to be an engagement party here next Saturday, and all are welcome.'

'What, not my sisters as well?'

'Them an' all! Even your Mum.' Danny reflected on that. Why mention her. He knew why but he was just not admitting it.

'Can I have a beer, then?'

'You'll be lucky! Now scoot, and thank you for feeding Captain Webb.'

'I can't scoot, as you call it, the old... Mr Petersen collected Harry today, so I had to walk here.'

The turkey was nearly as big as Red. There was no way he could walk home with it.

'Come on, I'll drive you home.'

He drove Red home, expecting to be invited in, but it was a cold climate there. He dropped Red off and drove away leaving him to struggle in with the turkey and the news.

When he had returned to the cabin, he sat in front of the fire with a glass of whisky.

'Now why on earth don't they tell you that Christmas Day and Thanksgiving are two different things. Petersen must think I am stupid.'

With the door shut against the cold, and the blazing fire in front of him, Danny was soon asleep. It would be early in the morning before he would wake and go to bed, now that it was available.

CHAPTER 9

W HEN Red struggled in with the turkey and told Kate about the party, she knew she had overreacted to Connie being there. Connie was about to marry someone else, and Kate was all the time thinking that Danny and Connie were... She clenched her fists. Being stuck with a no-good husband the first time, she had no plans to do the same again. Danny was different, a man to be taken at face value and that was what she would do from now on.

She watched Danny drive away and regretted it, but it was an opportunity lost, never to be repeated unless she acted. When Red and the girls were asleep, she sat thinking and came up with a plan. She wanted a man, and boy was he a man!

News of the party spread. In a small place like Turnround, a party was not to be missed, and people were getting ready for it. The day of the engagement party arrived. With it came Hester Foy in Gaston's lorry, with Annette, Kate Walters and her two girls. Gaston had taken Red to collect Harry for Connie, and he was going to ride Harry to the party.

'Good day, ladies,' Danny greeted them, doffing an

imaginary hat.

'Just show us where the kitchen is, and leave us to it. If there's going to be a party, then it might as well be done right,' Hester answered in her usual brusque way, and walked past Danny into the cabin.

'Good morning, Mr Turner,' Kate said as she followed Hester inside.

'Don't I get a say in this?' Danny asked Gaston, as he dropped the side of his lorry.

'Don't be silly! Of course you don't! Look at all the food they have cooked ready for today. Do you think they would let a mere man get in the way of it running smoothly? We party well, not often, but well!'

The food was neatly wrapped in clingfilm and it covered the floor of the lorry.

'How many are coming, for God's sake?'

'Enough to eat this lot and more.'

They carried the food into the cabin, tarried awhile in the warm, but were soon ejected by the women.

Red was there on Harry when they were ejected.

'Just too late to help, I see,' Danny commented.

'Amazing that as you left before we did,' Gaston added.

'I got lost,' Red remonstrated.

Danny picked up a handful of snow and started to make a snowball. Gaston saw what he was doing and followed suit.

'You wouldn't?' Red asked, as he slid off Harry to be less of a target.

But they would. Red ducked under the first snowballs, and started to make his own. Soon a snowball fight was in full swing. Danny had his own method with snowballs, distraction then throw. He waited until Red was looking at him and threw a snowball high, trying to get it to land on his head. Red watched it as it arced, and it was then that Danny threw his second snowball on a low flat trajectory. It hit Red on the chest, and Danny threw an arm in the air as a footballer would. Now other people were joining in, Annette, Isobel and Marie on Red's side; Marcus and Robbie on Danny's side.

'You wouldn't think they were grown men, would you?' Hester said, watching from the doorway.

'Oh I would,' Kate replied.

Constance and Hester exchanged meaningful glances, but Kate was oblivious to them. She was watching Danny. She stood there for a while, then walked over to him, avoiding snowballs as she walked.

'Mr Turner, I am going to have to send that lovely turkey back. It would be a waste. We'd never eat it all before it went off, and I'd hate to throw half of it away,' she said.

Danny looked at her in her best dress. She was better than ten Lucys.

'The name is Danny. And you could send Red down with some so it did not go to waste.'

'You could come up and share it,' Kate retorted, not in the ladylike fashion she had aimed for.

'I could if I was asked,' Danny replied.

'Then I'm asking,' Kate almost shouted.

'Then I'm coming,' Danny replied at a more genteel volume.

'That's settled then,' Kate said, and turned to walk back to the cabin. As she walked, she reproached herself. 'You handled that really well, Catherine.'

Little did she know that Danny was doing the same as

he threw his snowballs. As darkness fell, the snowball fight ended with both sides declaring they had won, and the partying started in earnest.

The main room in the cabin had been decorated with flowers by Constance, 'for something to do', and Danny had only enough time to cut long planks as tables which were set up in the room between the back door and the mine. The generator was humming away in the distance as he still had no power supply. The room only had a dirt floor, and Danny made a mental note to put in a wooden floor before the wedding. A heater in the room with the food kept it just warm enough as it was well insulated against the cold.

The cabin filled to overflowing, but at least Danny met people he had never seen before. He met Url Jensen for the first time. She came with Hamish and Callum. The party stopped just long enough for the announcement of Constance and Callum's engagement, with Constance's announcement that from now on she was Connie. She no longer wanted to be called Constance as her father had named her.

Then the party continued well into the night. Made Brickman appeared with Rosie, and Made introduced his wife to Danny. He was not planning to come as they had not long returned with Marcus from the hospital. When Marcus went missing, he guessed where he would find him, with Robbie at the party.

They stayed until midnight, then took Marcus home, where he should have been.

Morning came too soon for Danny. He stood up, holding his head. Nothing stopped the pain and it did not help having to pick his way across the room avoiding sleeping revellers. The bathroom was at least empty, if not clean. He took some pain killers and flopped back into the armchair he had slept in. One by one, the revellers woke, washed, and left after a coffee to help sober them up. They all thanked Danny for a good party before they left, if Danny was awake.

The hangover lasted all day, and he went to bed at eight o'clock. Connie never appeared from her room apart from limping to the bathroom and back. If she felt like Danny, he could understand it.

As he was going to have Christmas dinner with the Walters, he wanted to buy a present for each of them. He drove to Lower superior early the next morning, as he thought he ought to at least make an appearance at work. He was surprised by the number of people already about. He walked around, looking in the shops for inspiration. For Red, he bought a watch, for the girls, a doll each, both different so that there were no arguments later. He saw a dress for Kate Walters, but had no idea what size she was.

'Can you tell by the manikins?' the woman behind the counter asked. She was a very large woman.

'No, not really, but she's smaller than you.'

'Gracious, I'd hope she is! Is there anyone you can ask?'

Danny thought for a moment. He could ask Hester Foy, but what would she think about him buying presents for Kate Walters so soon after her husband was killed? 'What the hell, it's only a Christmas present!' he thought.

'Yes, there is. Where is the nearest phone?' he replied.

The woman lifted a phone on to the counter.

'You can use this one.'

'Do you have a phone book or something

She picked up a large book and dro
counter. He looked up Hester Foy's numbe

'Maple Lodge. Hester Foy speaking. How can I help?'

'It's Danny Turner, Hester. Do you know what size dress Mrs Walters takes?' he asked.

He heard Hester chuckle on the other end of the phone.

'I do. She takes a twelve, and don't make it too low below the knee. Red is her favourite colour.'

'Thanks.'

'You're welcome. Now if you don't mind, I do have a Christmas to prepare for. I take it I no longer need to invite you to our Christmas dinner?'

'No, I have already been invited, but thank you anyway. Bye.' Danny replaced the receiver and looked up. The woman stood there with a red dress, size twelve.

'Do you want it gift wrapped?' she asked.

'No thanks!' Danny replied. He liked to wrap the presents. He also enjoyed the look on children's faces when they liked the presents. Lucy had never understood why he had bought John Pope, another forestry worker, and his children a Christmas present each. It was the pleasure of wrapping the presents and the look on their faces when they opened them. Christmas at home had been dull and lifeless. This year in Canada, he was looking forward to it.

As he put the dress in the Jeep, he thought of Connie. He needed to make sure she was invited to the Walters, as there was no way he was going to leave her alone on Christmas Day. Connie! He needed a present for her. She still had a cage round her leg although she was now getting quite mobile on it, and the baby was starting to show. What

⌐ get her? In front of his Jeep, barely two metres away was a shop window with a saddle in it on a wooden horse. It was not the saddle for Connie, but they were sure to have one better suited for her. He walked in and looked around. One saddle said to him, 'Buy me for Connie', and he did just that. Now he could go home and wrap the presents. Not Connie's though, that was going too far. He would hide it in the mine until it was time to give it to her.

As he was wrapping the last present, Kate's dress, the radio burped.

'Brickman here. Are you up and about, Danny?'

Made sounded a little worse for wear.

Danny walked over and lifted the handset.

'I'm here, Mr Brickman, over.'

'The name is Made, Danny. The search has been officially called off. We'll not see her until the thaw. As we are all back in the office, and this is officially the last day of work before Christmas, we are having a party. Are you busy? Over.'

'Sounds like you've already started. Over.'

'Just a few drams to keep the cold out. Over.'

'I can still feel the last hangover. Over.'

'You can always drink club soda. Over.'

'You can see that happening! I'll be there in half an hour. Do I need to bring anything? There's a few things left over from the party. Over.'

'Bring it all! Over and out.'

Danny did just that, but not until he had hidden the wrapped presents from prying eyes, and fed Captain Webb. Now that Red was looking after the pony again, he was a regular visitor, whether Danny was there or not. The fire was never allowed to go out, and Captain Webb was taken out for a walk when Red was there. Danny drove to Turnround for another hangover, but it was the festive season after all and he had at least twenty years of not enjoying Christmas to make up for. This was his first Christmas in Canada and he wanted it to be good.

He awoke the next morning, in the bed he had first slept in at Hester's, to an insistent tugging at his arm.

He opened his eyes to see Annette standing next to him.

'Mum says that breakfast is ready and has been for some time,' she said.

'How did I end up here?' he asked.

'I don't know, do I? I was asleep,' she replied.

Danny smiled at her. She didn't change.

'I'll be down in ten minutes.'

'Mum says not to have a bath as there is someone asleep in it.' With all information passed on, she ran back down the stairs.

Danny settled for a wash next to the snoring man. It was Carrick, one of the other park rangers. Carrick was the only name he knew him by. After breakfast and several mugs of tea, he headed home. It was Christmas eve, and he thought he would take the Walters their presents so they could open them in the morning. True he would not get to see their eyes light up when they opened them, but he thought presents should be opened first thing on Christmas morning. Callum's lorry was parked outside the cabin when he arrived.

'Good morning, Danny!' he greeted, too loud for Danny even though he had tried to keep his drinking to a minimum the night before.

'It would be if you didn't talk so loud, you're up bright and early.'

'I take it you made it to the office party last night?'

'I couldn't really say no, now could I?'

'I suppose not. Hester has invited Dad and me to her place for Christmas, and she wrote an invite especially for Connie, by hand!'

'Has she accepted?'

They heard Connie walk to the door of her room. It was an unmistakable sound.

'I don't want to do anything that would ruin your Christmas. If you don't want to go to Hester's, then I'll spend Christmas here with you. No one should be alone at Christmas,' she said, using the door for support.

'I have had an invite for Christmas, and I was going to ask you about it, so if you want to go to Hester's, do so by all means.'

'So who has invited you then?' Callum asked.

'Kate Walters. The turkey I found is too big for them, and I am going to help them eat it.'

'You sly old goat!' Callum replied, with a wink.

'Less of the old! You two have a good Christmas now.'

'We will,' Connie replied, now using Callum for support.

'As I won't see you in the morning, you might as well have your present now, Connie. I haven't wrapped it, and you'll see why,' he added, and walked out the back door.

When he walked in carrying the saddle, her reaction made Danny's Christmas. Her eyes opened wide. She was lost for words, but the smile said all. Callum took the saddle, and Connie walked over and gave Danny a big hug and a big kiss.

'I take it I don't have to send it back?' Danny asked.

He looked at her face, tears were flowing freely. She still couldn't speak, so she just hugged him. No one had ever bought her such a nice present before, apart from the ring Callum had given her at the party.

'It must have cost a fortune,' she eventually managed to say.

'It has already been worth every penny,' Danny replied. 'Now get along and have a good time you two.'

He waved goodbye as Callum drove away. Then he collected the presents for the Walters from the mine. He woke Captain Webb from a sound sleep and led him to the Jeep, where he jumped in and curled up again. Sleeping was something he did well! He loaded the presents, a box of groceries, and a box of Christmas crackers. With the makings, Kate should be able to have a good Christmas, and Danny was actually looking forward to it. He found himself nervous on the short drive to the Walters' house, so much so that he almost stopped and turned round. Red heard the Jeep arrive, and came running out to greet him.

'Hi Danny, come in,' he cried, and led Captain Webb in, making it impossible for him not to follow.

'I won't stop,' Danny said, when he was inside. 'I just brought a few things over for tomorrow to make it a special Christmas, as it is my first in this country.'

'You'll stay and drink a cup of tea,' Kate ordered. 'I'll set an extra place for you at the table.'

Red pretended to put his finger down his throat and be sick.

'It must be fish again,' Danny thought to himself, but sat down anyway.

The tea was served and it was good. Kate was obviously trying to impress him, and it was working. A plate was slid in front of him by Red, and Marie brought him a knife and fork. When it was served, there were sausages and mash, with peas and carrots.

'What happened to the fish you were cooking, Mum?' Red asked in surprise.

'That was for the animals. We were going to have these sausages tomorrow, but now that we have Mr Turner's magnificent turkey...'

Danny stood up before she could finish.

'It is either Danny, or I am going home now,' he announced.

'I'm sorry,' Kate said quickly. 'Danny's magnificent turkey. So I thought we'd have the sausages today. Now stop talking and eat.'

Danny sat down again and ate. The rest of the day flew by, and it was late when Danny stood up to go home. He had enjoyed himself just being there.

'It's not worth going home, Danny,' Red insisted. 'You might as well stay here tonight. You can have my bed.'

Danny looked at Kate for confirmation of the offer.

'We would be pleased if you stayed,' Kate said, then added, 'I would be pleased if you stayed.'

'Captain Webb is comfortable. It would be a shame to disturb him,' Red continued.

The girls joined in with cries of 'please stay', repeated numerous times.

'Okay! Enough! I'm staying,' Danny cried, and sat back down.

The girls were excited as it was Christmas eve, but they

were still tired, so Kate put them to bed. Red stayed up as he was going to sleep on the sofa. Kate and Danny talked about things in general, with Red piping up when he had an opinion on something they were talking about. Later he fell asleep, and they stood outside in the cold night air looking at the stars.

'No clouds means no snow on Christmas day,' Kate said with a shiver.

Danny took off his jacket and put it round her shoulders.

'I think we have enough to be going on with,' he said with a rueful smile which was lost in the darkness.

'You'd think so, but I like a white Christmas. It makes up for a lot of bad times the rest of the year,' Kate replied.

'In that case, I hope we get snowed in tomorrow,' Danny declared.

'The only problem with that is that the children are here,' Kate retorted.

Danny was lost for words. If she meant what he thought she meant, he needed to visit a chemists.

'But they do sleep sometime,' Danny answered carefully.

'Not on Christmas eve, they don't. I take it you have never been around children on Christmas eve?'

'No! My wife was making sure I never endured the burden of being a father. Chemists have a lot to answer for in my book.'

'You didn't know?'

'I was thick. What can I say? I even had tests done, and passed with flying colours.'

'I could stand a fourth!' Kate replied. 'But now I think it is bed time, and you are in Red's bed!'

Danny watched her disappear into her bedroom. Well it was hers and the two girls. Danny waited until the light went out, then walked into Red's bedroom. He stripped to his underpants, slipped into the bed and fell asleep instantly. To him it seemed like seconds later when an insistent tugging at his arm woke him. He expected to see Annette, instead it was Isobel.

'Wake up, Mr Turner, it's Christmas day!' she cried.

Danny looked at Red's clock. It was six thirty in the morning. He had never been around young children on Christmas morning, but even being woken at six thirty did not throw him.

'I know that, but does your mother?' he replied when he had gathered his thoughts.

'She told us to go back to bed,' Marie replied. She was the elder of the two.

'It sounds like a good idea to me,' Danny admitted.

The girls looked at each other, then jumped into bed with Danny, one on either side. Danny put his arms round them and cuddled them until they fell asleep. He did not know what else to do. He had never dealt with young girls before. When they were sound asleep, he slipped on his trousers and crept into the living room where Red was asleep on the sofa. He could have gone and slept on one of their beds, but they slept in the same room as their mother, and to him that was too presumptuous. He was left with the only armchair. The other one had been moved to make way for the Christmas tree, which stood by the end of the sofa. He shivered and stirred the fire into life, piled on some more wood and sat watching the flames.

He was startled when Kate said, 'I'm sorry about that,

Danny. Have you been out here long?'

Danny looked at his watch.

'Only an hour. I didn't know what to do. I've had no dealings with young girls.'

She gave him a mug of tea, but Red chose that moment to wake up as if an inbuilt alarm clock had chimed.

'It's Christmas day!' he almost shouted, and jumped off the sofa. 'Happy Christmas, Mum!' he said more sedately, and gave her a big cuddle.

The girls woke again, and came running out of Red's bedroom to cuddle their Mum. Danny saw a chance to go out to the Jeep and get their presents.

He returned with them, and waited until the noise had died down.

'I have something for Isobel Walters,' he announced.

Isobel ran forward to collect her present from Danny.

'Now a Miss Marie Walters.'

Marie came for hers.

'And now for a Master Redman Walters!'

Red walked up for his.

'Last but not least, Mrs Seth Walters!' Kate walked up for her present.

She opened her present and was suitably impressed! Red walked up and gave him their present. He knew whatever it was, it had cost them dear, and he was all prepared. He had undergone many Christmasses where it had been only Lucy and him, and they were the worst Christmasses of the lot. How could this be worse?

'This is from us all!' Red declared.

Danny knew that his reaction to their present would show, even if he was trying to hide it, but he had no need to hide it. It was a compass that looked like a wristwatch. He strapped it on his wrist above his watch.

'Thank you. At least I won't get lost now.'

He knew how much it cost as he had thought of buying Red the same present, and that made it extra special.

Christmas day passed. They ate well, and the turkey was perfect. In fact they ate too well as usual, and spent an afternoon feeling less than comfortable. To ease their bloated stomachs and to give Captain Webb some exercise, they went for a walk in the forest.

When darkness fell, all Danny's efforts to leave were thwarted by the pleas of the children, and Danny spent a second night there. Not that Danny had fought too hard to leave. Boxing day was much the same as Christmas day but without the presents. Danny was starting to like it.

He was getting to know Kate quite well, and parts which had been dormant since he had arrived were starting to stir. Even though he was still a married man, and had never once thought to cheat on Lucy, he decided that if the chance came he would at least consider it. A major step forward for him and his upbringing. He made a mental note to contact Lucy and start divorce proceedings. She was no good to him in England. He was saved from having to decide, by the radio.

'Brickman calling Danny, come on.'

Danny picked up the radio grudgingly.

'Danny here, and if you want me to go hanging over a cliff, the answer is no. I'd shower them in carrots! Over.'

'No, you can do this one standing up. Some clown has just hit a bear on the Loggin Road. It's hurt bad according to him, but still moving. Go out there and stop it moving, permanent like. Oh, and the carcass has to be brought in. Watch yourself though, they get mighty ornery when they've been wounded. Over.'

'Thanks a bunch, just what I need! Over.'

'You're nearest, but don't wait until you can see the whites of its eyes,' Made added with a chuckle. 'Over and out.'

'Duty calls I'm afraid, and before you ask, Red, there is no way you can come on this one. I can't even be sure of looking out for me let alone worry about you as well.'

Red looked suitably dejected, but brightened suddenly.

'Does that mean you are going to leave Captain Webb here?' he asked.

'No, on the contrary. I am hoping he will find the bear for me.' He turned to face Kate. 'Thanks for a lovely Christmas. Will you see the New Year in with me?' The question came out of the blue. His mouth seemed to take on a life of its own for a few seconds.

Kate showed no surprise, but looked down at Red then back to Danny.

'We'd love to, but I have no more food to cook apart from fish,' she replied, feeling a warm glow inside.

Danny and Captain Webb walked to the Jeep.

'I'll find something, even if it is bear!' he called back, as Captain Webb jumped in and settled down. Danny jumped in the Jeep and, with a wave of his hand, drove off.

CHAPTER 10

THE spot where the collision had occurred was easy to find. It was not snowing, and the telltale broken glass and displaced front grille from the vehicle were still plain to see. He followed the bear's tracks, with Captain Webb at his side and his rifle cocked ready. As they walked, the wolf cub started to take the lead, and the distance between them grew as he gained in confidence. Falling in the river and nearly drowning had left a lasting impression on him, but life had to go on. The cub loped along in front, making Danny walk faster to keep up with him until he suddenly froze in his tracks! Danny lifted the rifle to his shoulder and crept forward. He was very nervous. This was the first time he had come face to face with a bear, and he wanted to survive to tell someone about it.

He inched forward ready for anything and, through the branches, he could see what he thought was a bear. He considered shooting from where he was, but his father had drummed into him many times, 'Never shoot at something you can't see.' He circled round the tree until the bear came into sight. It was in a heap in the snow. He moved forward carefully, but the bear did not move. It was dead.

'What an undignified way to go for such a magnificent creature,' Danny thought. 'Well old feller, you aren't going to trouble anyone any more. I bet the person who hit you was as drunk as a skunk,' he said, relieved that he did not need to shoot it.

'How the hell am I supposed to get something this big back to the office? Over,' Danny yelled into his radio.

'You got it then. Is there nothing you can't handle? Apart from flying that is! Over.' Made laughed at his own joke, and he was obviously still celebrating.

'Women probably come second on the list! Over.' Danny replied at a lower volume.

'You got that right. If`n the bear's dead, it ain't going to bother anyone so mark where it is and I'll get it picked up tomorrow, over.'

'Will do. By the way, I'm coming in singing tomorrow, very loudly! Over.'

'You would do that, wouldn't you?'

'You bet. Over and out.'

Danny had sat in the Jeep by the side of the road thinking of going back to Kate's, but he didn't want to do anything to damage the relationship which was growing, and Seth was not long in the ground! He decided against it and drove to his cabin. Captain Webb sniffed the cold grate, and curled up by it waiting for Danny to light a fire. Once it was blazing, Danny sat in his armchair and fell asleep.

In the morning, he started to tidy up. He had a New Year's eve party to prepare for, so he needed to go into the store and buy a few things. Outside, a lorry pulled up, and he looked out of the window to see Callum's lorry without the trailer attached.

Connie limped in.

'And where have you been for the past two days?' she scolded.

'Who are you? My Mum?' Danny replied.

'I bought you a present,' she announced. 'I'm sorry it's a bit late.'

She pointed to the present Callum was carrying.

'Well we bought it together. I chose it and he paid for it as I haven't any money. It was Callum's idea.'

Danny looked at the present, and was relieved when it was much larger than a wrist compass. He opened the present and found it was a book. It was entitled, *The Complete Book of Trees,* and he flipped through the pages.

'Thanks! I had to leave some of my books behind.'

He kissed Connie, and shook Callum's hand.

'Can I offer you a drink? There's coffee on the stove,' Danny said, waving his hand in the direction of the stove.

'Coffee will do,' Callum replied. 'Black with a hint of sugar.'

'Guess what?' Connie said, as Danny poured the coffee.

'Don't tell me you've already had your baby?' Danny replied.

'No! Don't be silly!' Connie scolded. 'Try again.'

'Your Dad's coming to the wedding.'

'That's even worse. They are going to take this monstrosity off my leg on the fifth of January,' she declared.

'So when is the wedding?' Danny asked.

'The tenth, if that is okay with you?' Connie asked.

'I'll get in touch with Greg Pomeroy and see if we can get a priest out here then.'

He gave Callum his coffee.

'I'm having a New Year's party here if you want to come?' he continued.

'I'll be here anyway. Doctor's orders,' Connie replied. 'I've been told to take it easy.'

'There's nothing wrong is there?' Danny asked.

'Men! You are all the same! I tell you I have to take it easy and you immediately think I'm on the way out. He said I have been overdoing it. We've been house hunting.'

'Hester throws a good party and, much as I'd like to come, I really feel I should go there,' Callum added.

'Callum...' Connie started, but Danny talked over her.

'No, he's right. I don't want to step on anyone's toes, especially Hester's. I should have known there would be a party, and I bet it's a good one. I invited Kate and her children here as a 'thank you' for sharing their Christmas with me, or I'd go to Hester's.'

'I can help out there, then!' Connie replied. 'We start here early and, when the kids are asleep, you, Callum and Kate can go on to Hester's to see the New Year in.'

Neither man argued. Callum was trying not to spit out the mouthful of coffee he had just taken.

'Have you found somewhere yet?' Danny asked, deliberately steering the conversation away from the party.

Callum disappeared into the bathroom, with the mug of coffee.

'We think so. We both like it,' Connie replied.

Callum reappeared with an empty cup, and resisted Danny's attempts to refill it for him. They talked for some time before Callum drove away leaving Connie to rest. She poured a mug of coffee but spat it back into the mug as soon as she tasted it.

'Yeuk! I think I should give you a lesson in coffee making, Canadian style,' she said, wiping her mouth.

'That bad?'

'Worse. How much did you put in there? No, don't tell me, I think I can work it out.'

She tipped the pot of coffee away and pushed the kettle on to the stove. Time for a lesson in coffee making.

New Year's eve arrived. With it came Kate and her children, Kate wearing the new dress Danny had bought her for Christmas. She looked very pretty in it, a contrast to how she looked when he first saw her. He had deliberately stayed away from the Walters' house, finding things to do, but it was hard, as he was happy when he was there.

They started celebrating as soon as Callum arrived, in order to put the children to bed and move on to Hester's party, but it was as if Red sensed that something was afoot and was having none of it. If they were moving on, so was he! Connie went to bed as soon as the girls were asleep, and they were forced to take Red with them to Hester's party, making sure they were there before midnight.

Captain Webb stayed at the cabin as it was likely to get very noisy in Turnround at midnight. It was one reason Danny had not bought party poppers for his party.

They mingled with the others at the party, with Danny speaking to the ones he knew, and, if Kate was there, she introduced him to those he did not know. When she said, 'Chief, this is Danny Turner,' his ears pricked up. This was the man Hester had mentioned when he had first arrived in Turnround. They shook hands, and Chief's hand was cold and limp.

'I have heard a lot about you, Mr Turner,' Chief said pleasantly.

'Call me Danny.'

'You have been a busy man since you arrived in Turnround, Danny.'

'I have certainly fallen on my feet, but it has been hard going Mr...?'

'Chief! Call me Chief. I prefer it that way.'

'Chief it is then,' Danny replied. 'Have you been talking to the others?'

'That, and listening on my radio. It fascinates me. I skip between channels for titbits of news, and to find out what is happening in town. I have a radio, so I can do it even when I'm working for Mother.'

'Is she here, your mother?' Danny asked.

'No! Not her scene. She was in bed by eight. Me, I was still serving gas until nine! No one wants to run out over a holiday, do they?'

'Ah, there yee are Danny!' Hamish called, and made a beeline for him. 'I did not introduce you to my friend last time, and felt the sharp side of her tongue for it. Come and meet her. Yee don't mind, do yee Chief?'

'Not at all, Mr McLaughland, be my guest,' Chief replied, and walked away.

Hamish steered Danny across to where Url sat.

'I know yee have met, but Danny, this is Url Jensen, a good friend of mine. Url, this is Danny Turner, the Englishman I have told yee aboot. Url has a place right by the river, a prettier spot yee couldn't imagine.'

Hamish was still sober, and Danny was surprised.

'Nice to meet you again, Url.'

'Nice to meet you again, Danny.' There was no accent. It was pure Canadian. 'Do you fish?'

'You bet he does! We caught loads of fish when we went,' the irrepressible Red said, appearing from nowhere.

'You'll have to try from the landing at my place, Danny. It has a good reputation, lots of big fish,' Url continued.

'Well, if I ever find myself with time on my hands, I'll take you up on that,' Danny replied.

Red stood there with his mouth half open, looking from one to the other.

'It's alright, Redman, the offer does extend to you if you are with Danny,' Url said, after a wicked pause.

'Thank you, Mrs Jensen. When can we go, Danny?' he asked immediately.

'I thought you weren't ever going fishing again,' Danny said.

'This is different. Everyone wants to fish from Mrs Jensen's place.'

'Mrs?' Danny asked, turning to Url.

'Mr Jensen passed away seven years ago, a wonderful man and sadly missed,' Url replied.

'My condolences, and apologies for being nosey.'

'I would have asked, were I you,' she replied.

'When are we going fishing?' Red repeated. 'I want to tell my friends.'

'Maybe after the wedding,' Danny replied.

'We are having a wedding, and I didn't know? I must be slipping,' Url replied.

'Yes, on January tenth at my cabin,' Danny explained. 'Connie and Callum are going to tie the knot. Did you know, Hamish?'

'Not a word, Danny!' Hamish replied.

'Then I think I might have just put my foot in it for mentioning it.'

'Mum's the word then, Danny,' Url said, and squeezed Danny's hand. 'We'll let them announce it when they are good and ready.'

Annette Foy appeared and dragged Red away. She was still full of go and wanted to play. Now alone, Danny mingled, talking to people as he met them. As midnight approached, an arm slipped through his.

'Hi! Remember me?' Kate said, with a winsome smile.

'How can I forget such a vision?'

'Flattery will get you everywhere!' Kate replied, and they kissed.

Seconds later it was midnight and the party exploded into life. There were party poppers popping, bangers going off, crackers being pulled, and guns firing. The loudest being Gaston's rifle. Then the cheering started and everybody was kissing everybody, followed by singing and dancing. Danny had missed this for so many years and he threw himself into it with total enthusiasm. At ten minutes past the witching hour, Callum borrowed Gaston's rifle and fired it until all were silent.

'I have an announcement!' he cried, well drunk. He fired the rifle twice more. 'Connie and I are getting wed on January the tenth at Danny Turner's cabin. Anyone who wishes us well is welcome, anyone who doesn't can stay away.'

That was his speech, and seconds later the party restarted. It continued into the early hours of the morning, and Danny danced with Kate for most of it. When the party broke up, Danny was just sober enough to ask about Red, but he was asleep in Annette's room in the spare bed. Kate could barely stand up. Hamish, who was stone cold sober, drove them home, and with the help of a slightly drunk Url, helped them into the cabin. They found the sleeping bag laid out for Danny, and were soon fast asleep. Kate in bed with Marie and Isobel, and Danny on the floor by the fire as Connie was asleep on the sofa. As soon as Danny lay down, Captain Webb moved over and curled up close to him. It would be a hard parting when it came, and it had to come.

Dawn meant nothing to Danny. The children were there, as was Connie, but it was hard to focus until after dinner time. Then, as his eyes began to focus, he started to move about. He took Captain Webb for his morning walk in the afternoon, just before it was dark, and Kate chose then to wake up and worry about Red. By the time he returned, she had phoned Hester twice to make sure Red was okay, and when Danny appeared he had to drive her in to get him. Red, of course, was fine, in fact better than Danny and Kate! Danny drove them home, then drove back to the cabin for an early night. Connie had cleaned up by the time he returned, and he kissed her good night and relayed the announcement about the wedding. She was happy, not as happy as if she had been there at the party, but it was all for the good!

His first Christmas in Canada over, Danny started preparing for the wedding. He had already had one party, and knew the drawbacks. He needed a floor in the room leading to the mine, and the mine needed lighting, with a solid wall to keep people where he wanted them as there was likely to be more people there than at the engagement party. Instead of planks, he wanted tables with table cloths! He wanted everything just right for Connie and Callum. The saw was put to good use again, and Callum brought in more wood, this time for free! As soon as he made a table and brought it into the mine, Connie covered it ready for the wedding. To her it was an important day. Danny was still required to work, but in the meantime, he managed to line the front part of the mine, put a floor in both rooms, and put a wall at the back of the mine shaft to stop people wandering. The wall was actually a painted tarpaulin, but it looked the part. With the mine door open, they had a lot of room, and the food could be stored in both rooms to keep it fresh.

Callum stayed away, and Danny knew how he felt. It is hard to stay away from someone you love. He stopped what he was doing and thought! Did he really love Kate? Yes, he did, but now what? He had caused her husband's death, indirectly, but he was the cause. There were children to consider, and he wanted children of his own. He worked on table after table, polishing each one until he was prepared to let Connie cover it. Connie of course was far from resting, it was her wedding.

Callum came on the fourth of January to collect Connie and take her to the hospital. Danny worked on, making a table, polishing it to keep spillages from staining it, then on to the next table until all were made. He sat there on the last table in front of the cabin thinking about a verandah. When he was older, he could see himself there on a chair, and next to him he could see Kate, the children grown up and long gone.

He remembered the letter to Lucy. 'I really must write that,' he thought, but still did nothing about it.

On the sixth, Danny visited Connie in the hospital. The cage was off, and a bandage covered the bad leg now. He gave her flowers and a box of chocolates.

She opened the chocolates straightaway.

'Want a chocky?' she asked.

'Don't mind if I do!' Danny replied. 'Might save a nurse from getting fat. What's the prognosis?'

'A day of physio, then I'm out of here on crutches, but I'm determined to be off the crutches by the time I walk up the aisle.'

'It's nice to see you smile again,' Danny commented.

'It's nice to want to, and it's all thanks to you.'

'Don't go all mushy on me or you'll have me blushing.'

'What you, dead shot Turner! Never.'

'Don't you believe all you hear. We all have our weaknesses.'

'Did you finish the tables?'

'Yes, it's all ready for you, and Hamish told me not to worry aboot the food.'

Connie laughed at Danny's impression of Hamish.

'I have an idea he is getting Hester to do something,' Danny continued. 'She did well last time, so I can't wait to see what she comes up with this time.'

Connie reached into the drawer next to her bed and pulled out a sheet of paper. She held it out for Danny to read. It was a list of food on headed notepaper. The heading was Maple Lodge.

'Does she do catering on the side, then?' he asked.

'She does all the dos round here, when we have one,

that is.'

'Well, you've certainly had your share of them recently.'

'All in a good cause. You think so anyway, or I wouldn't be here.'

'I'd do it again any time for you.'

'Don't worry, I won't do that again. Not for anyone.'

'I should hope not. I must admit it wasn't my favourite job. If I could have got out of it, I probably would have. It didn't help when I found another body at the bottom.'

'I didn't see anyone pass me,' Connie replied. 'But then I was unconscious for a long time. We must have been queuing up.'

Danny laughed.

'He'd been dead a while. He was under the ice.'

'No! Who was it?'

'I thought it might be Wilson, the mine owner, but I haven't found out yet. I get the feeling I might never know. I think it has something to do with the missing girls.'

'I'll talk to Callum. His Dad knows what's going on around here most of the time. I'll sweat it out of him!' Connie replied.

'It will be interesting if it was, because I got the impression from John Mulroon that he was their main suspect, in fact their only suspect.'

'It's so bad about those girls. I hope they catch the monster soon. Now let's talk about something nice.'

The talk turned to other things until Callum arrived, then Danny used that and Captain Webb as an excuse to leave, and the other two did not argue. His first stop was Maple lodge. He found Hester in the kitchen, cooking.

'I must owe you for all the food you cooked for my

party,' he said.

'All paid for by your new friends, me included!' Hester replied. 'I'm sorry if I gave you a hard time when you arrived. It must have been a big step for you at your age.'

From anyone but Hester, Danny might have been annoyed.

'And how! Coming to the back of beyond, then getting on a coach to come here.'

'It's a greyhound. If you live here, at least say things folk will understand. A coach is in charge of the baseball team,' she said with a smile, and she rarely smiled. 'If you want tea, you will have to make it yourself. I'm busy.'

'So I see. I've seen the list, so I know how busy you are going to be, but instead of tea it is time for a whisky after I have taken the Captain out.'

'That Red is something else,' Hester said, looking him straight in the eye. 'Fancy coming up with a name like that. I hope you will be a better father to him than his natural one.'

No beating about the bush with Hester.

'So do I,' Danny replied. 'Bye Hester.'

Back at his cabin, he took Captain Webb for a long walk in the forest, returning as darkness fell. He sat in his chair with a glass of whisky, but before he drank any he fell asleep. He woke when the glass fell to the floor, spilling the whisky over him. He flopped onto Connie's empty bed, and slept.

CHAPTER 11

THE day of the wedding arrived. All last minute preparations were either done or left undone. Danny used his chain saw to clear the trees and shrubs from the ground around the cabin for parking, and cleared the snow. He salted the ground to keep it clear, and cleared a patch of trees away from the cabin to make a place for Greg to land with the priest. Connie was there fussing over everything, just as Lucy had done before their wedding. She calmed down when Hester arrived. She had to. Danny helped Gaston unload, then drove to the Walters' house, to be away from the needless fussing.

If anything, Kate was worse. Complaining that she had nothing to wear, and that she should not have worn Danny's Christmas gift at the New Year's party so she could wear it now. Luckily, Hester had warned him what Kate was likely to say, and Danny produced a box from the Jeep. He had gone with Hester to buy it, to make sure the colour and length were right. Kate's eyes opened wide.

'I can't wear this. I'll look better than the bride!' she cried.

'You might think so, but you haven't seen the wedding dress. Believe me, it sure is something!'

It took ages, or at least seemed that way to Danny, for Kate to be ready to go. As Red was sitting behind the wheel of the Jeep, he showed him how to drive it, and Red managed to turn the Jeep round with a little help from Danny. By the time they drove back to the cabin, a crowd had gathered, waiting to see the bride. Kate went in to help Hester, so Danny and Red mingled with the guests who stood outside waiting. Danny knew most of them by now. The priest was there, but Greg Pomeroy had already left which surprised Danny, and annoyed Red who was hoping for a ride in his helicopter.

'Isn't Mr Pomeroy going to be at the wedding, Danny?' he asked.

'I thought he was staying. I'll go and ask Hester. You keep out of the way.'

Before he could move, he recognised Callum's lorry edging its way through the parked cars. Danny hurried inside, bumping into people as he went, trying to make sure Connie stayed out of sight, and found Hester.

'Where's Connie?' he asked. 'Callum has just arrived.'

'It is all under control, Danny. You go out and enjoy yourself,' Hester replied. 'We know what we are doing, don't we Kate.'

'And how!' Kate agreed. 'This is going to be a wedding to remember.'

'Now Scoot, Daniel Turner,' Hester scolded. 'You are getting under my feet.'

Danny wandered out at a more leisurely speed than he had gone in.

'Well?' Red asked.

'Well what?' Danny replied.

'Where is Mr Pomeroy?'

'I don't know. I just own the place. It seems I don't need to know what's going on.' He shrugged his shoulders. 'If you can't beat them, head for the bar.'

The bar was in the mine room, and the rear door was the only access at the moment. Callum was there talking to the priest. His suit was a twin of the one Danny wore.

'You're looking very smart,' Danny said when the priest started talking to someone else.

'I probably hired it from the same shop you did, Danny.'

'It wouldn`t surprise me, as you know the owner quite well!' Danny replied. 'How are you feeling?'

'Better than I was.' He held up a large glass of whisky, as yet untouched.

'Are you planning to get married laying down?'

'No. This is not for drinking. Just for holding until Hester sees it.'

Hester chose that moment to walk in. She took the glass from his raised hand and downed it in one gulp. Then gave him the empty glass back.

'Thanks, I needed that!' she said, and she shuddered as it slid down her throat. 'Now, get ready. The bride is about to arrive.'

Hester mustered everybody in front of the cabin and, to Danny's surprise, a band set up their equipment in the snow and started to play.

'They won't last long in this temperature,' Danny whispered to Gaston, who was already well oiled.

'You might be surprised just how long we can stand the cold, mon ami,' Gaston replied.

'I suppose it depends how much antifreeze they have

inside them!'

Gaston just smiled. Greg's helicopter appeared above the trees, circled the area then landed on the patch which Danny had cleared. Danny walked to his position and waited. Connie climbed out of the helicopter unaided, and walked very slowly to where Danny stood with his arm out ready to take hers.

The band started playing the wedding march as Danny and Connie walked arm in arm into the cabin, and through the lines of people until they reached Callum. The priest started the service and, when it was time, Danny passed her hand over to Callum and stood back out of the way. The priest's stentorian voice carried through the cabin and out to those who stood round the doorway. He droned on and on until he finally said, 'You may kiss the bride.' And it was all over.

The band set themselves up inside and started to play again as everybody took turns to congratulate the couple. Danny lined up patiently for his kiss. When Connie saw him, she walked over and kissed him.

'Thank you,' she said quietly. 'For everything.'

He kissed her.

'You are more than welcome. I hope the two of you will be very happy.'

She swept on in her long wedding gown, and the two newlyweds started to dance. They would not be dancing for long, but Connie had insisted on at least one dance. Danny felt an arm slip into his.

'Hi. Fancy a dance?' Kate asked.

'I might be a bit rusty.'

'These high heels have steel toe caps.'

'You might need them.'

They found a spot, but waited until Hamish and Url joined the newlyweds, then they started to dance. As they danced, life was changing. Red had cornered Greg and was having his first flight in a helicopter, and Danny was thinking he would like to get closer to this woman, a lot closer! The party stopped briefly when they all said goodbye to the newlyweds as they left for their honeymoon, then the party continued into the night until the band could no longer play due to alcohol abuse. Greg returned from taking the pair to the airport, and joined in the merrymaking. When all was quiet, Danny walked Kate to the door.

'Care for a stroll?' he asked.

Kate nodded.

'But it will have to be a quick one. I have to get the children to bed.'

They walked out under the stars, and Hester watched them go.

'One less to help with the clearing up, but good luck to you, Kate, you deserve it,' she said quietly to herself.

As they walked, the stars disappeared and it started snowing. They walked back quicker than they walked out. The children were already in Gaston's lorry by the time they returned, with Gaston asleep in the back. Hester sat behind the wheel, waiting. Kate climbed in and sat next to Red in the passenger seat.

'Thanks for a lovely evening,' Kate said, as she put on her seat belt. 'Come and see us when you have the time.'

'I will,' Danny replied, and meant it.

'Good night, Danny,' Hester said, with an unusually big smile. 'At least Gaston won't be complaining about my driving this time.'

They drove off, with Danny waving until they were out of sight, then he walked in out of the cold night air. It was funny that, when he was with Kate, it did not seem to be as cold! There were bodies everywhere, some still moving, some snoring. Captain Webb sat on the bed making sure it stayed clear.

'Well done, Captain Webb. Now, let's get some sleep.'

As soon as he lay down next to the wolf cub, his eyes closed and he fell asleep.

The smell of bacon cooking roused him, and he sought out the cook. Greg was at the stove. There were less bodies about now, but he still had trouble walking across the room.

'Good morning, Danny,' Greg said when he saw him.

'Morning Greg. How's the head?'

'Bad doesn't begin to describe it. That's the trouble with being the transport. By the time you start to party, everyone else is just passing out, and you have to hurry it which means you end up with the king of all hangovers.'

'Where did you take them?'

'She didn't even tell you?'

'Nope!'

'I left them at the airport. I think they were trying to make sure that they didn't have any pranks played on them, but I know Hamish left early in Callum's lorry with Url which is unusual for him, and the fact that he was stone cold sober.'

'I'll drive into Turnround later and find out.'

'I could take you in my helicopter?'

'No thanks, I'd rather walk.'

Greg opened his mouth to say something but stopped.

'I know! I'm being stubborn and probably stupid, seeing the way you make that thing fly, but I'll face my fear when I feel ready.'

'Did I say anything?'

'It's what you didn't say that counted.'

It was afternoon by the time Danny drove to Turnround. He found Hamish in his store, in a happy mood.

'You sound happy,' Danny observed.

'And why shouldn't I be? My bairn's just married the nicest girl in the county, and I am going to be a grandaddy. What could be better than that?'

'Your happiness has no relationship with the fact that you left early last night?' Danny asked.

'Maybe! Maybe not!' Hamish replied.

Danny tried to glean more information from Hamish, but for once Hamish was not talking, leaving Danny to guess what he had done when he left early, if anything! In the end he gave up and walked up to the office where Made was sorting through paperwork.

'This is all your fault,' he complained, when he saw it was Danny. 'A form for the requisition of a helicopter to take the boys to hospital, a form to go with the wolf pelts, another one for the stag. Three forms each for the deaths, including another requisition for a helicopter. One for the safe return of a lost child, with, I might add, the explanation for the delay in his return. Yet another requisition for a helicopter to rescue a girl from a cliff face. Another three forms for the discovery of Wilson's body. I'm going to be here all bloody week!'

'So it was Wilson?'

'Unofficially, yes. But they say they have more tests to

run on it to be sure. I think they are dragging their feet because they've crapped out. They had Wilson down as the man killing the little girls, but now they have to look for someone else.'

'Aren't there any other suspects?'

'No, not really. When the second winter passed, and they were nowhere nearer catching him, every male over sixteen had a blood test to try to find the bastard, but everyone who was tested, passed. Wilson didn't show for the tests, said he was too busy. Then he just up and left! Or so we thought anyway. When you found him, you really stirred things up.'

When he thought about Wilson's position under Suicide Falls, it set an alarm bell ringing in Danny's head but he still could not think why. He decided to say nothing for the moment, and left Made to his paperwork.

It was time to write that letter to Lucy. He sat in front of a blank sheet of paper for half an hour, then went for a walk in the forest with Captain Webb who actually started stalking things, but without any success.

'I will have to teach you how to catch your dinner before I can let you go back into the wilds, like your parents would have done if the poachers hadn't killed them, or you won't stand a chance out there.'

It was a long walk and took them past the Walters' back fence. Red was in the garden shovelling snow, and used Danny's arrival as an excuse to stop. He ran over to the fence.

'Hi Danny. Hi Captain Webb,' he shouted as he ran.

The wolf cub recognised Red and tried to jump the fence. In the end, Danny lifted him over. Kate appeared in the doorway when she heard Red call out.

'I'll put the kettle on. You'll be staying for tea!' It was not so much a question, more an order.

Danny did not argue. He climbed over the fence and followed Red up to the house. Walking that path, he knew there was the possibility of seeing Kate although he would not admit it. The letter forgotten, he settled at the table. He felt really comfortable there. Tea was made, then it was snacks, then an invite to stay for a meal, but as he was walking he wanted to get home before dark. He resisted the idea of staying the night, not because he did not want to, but because of what it might lead to. If he had been free to marry her, then he thought in these modern times anything that happened was okay, but now he felt he should go home. He left the way he came, waving as he went.

He thought he detected disappointment from Kate, but she hid it well. He sat in front of his fire after a good meal, and stared at the flames. No whisky tonight. He just sat there thinking what a good cabin he had built, but it was too small for a family of five. First a letter to Lucy, then plans to enlarge the cabin in the summer. He was dozing when his new telephone rang. It startled him, especially as he had told no one he had it, and also told no one the number. He picked up the receiver, ready to say the number as he would have done at home, but he couldn't remember it.

'Hello...' was all he managed to say.

'Hello Danny. This is Mrs Callum McLaughland here.'

'Hi Connie. How's the honeymoon going?'

'That Hamish is in for it when we get back!' Connie replied.

'Why? What did he do?'

'You weren't in on it, then?' She asked it as a question, but Danny heard her say to Callum, 'I told you Danny didn't know anything about it.'

'About what, for Christ's sake?' Danny replied.

There was a pause long enough for Danny to say.

'Come on, I know he left the party early but I couldn't get anything out of him.'

'He left early because he managed to find out where we were going and swopped our suitcases for duplicates, but without our clothes in. Don't ask me how he managed it, but he did.'

'What was in the suitcases, then?'

'Callum's was full of fig leaves, and mine was full of condoms!'

Danny laughed.

'You can stop laughing,' Connie ordered.

'Do I need to send clothes?'

'No, there was a letter in with the condoms. Apart from a poem which I won't read out, it just said to look under the bed. Our suitcases were there with five hundred dollars spending money in them. What I want to know is how he found out where we were going? We didn't tell anyone.'

'If you want to know what is going on round here, ask either Hamish or Hester!' Danny replied.

'You don't think Hester had any part in it?' Connie asked.

'I wouldn't suggest that for a minute. It would be more than my life is worth!'

'You do, then?'

'I didn't say that.'

'You didn't have to! Callum wants a word with you. I'll see you when I get back.'

Before Danny could say goodbye, Callum spoke.

'Danny.'

'Yes Callum, how's the fig leaf?'

'A bit itchy. Could you do me a favour?'

'Such as?'

'At midnight tonight, could you ring Dad's door bell? Not the front one, the one by the back door.'

'Then what?'

'Leg it would be a good idea!'

'Why?'

'I know what Pa is like. I rigged up something just in case I needed it.'

'Consider it done, old son,' Danny replied, a smile on his face. He would leg it, but not too far.

'Thanks. I have to go. Someone is waiting for me.'

'I wonder who that is? Don't bother with the condom!' The phone went dead, and Danny put the receiver back.

He looked at his watch, eleven o'clock. Time for a cup of tea before he left to carry out Callum's request.

At midnight, by his watch, Danny pushed the door bell by Hamish's back door. It usually went ding dong, but he did not wait to hear it. At first he was a bit disappointed when nothing happened, but, as he climbed into his Jeep, all hell broke loose. Alarms went off, bells rang, bangers were going off inside, and then a klaxon started to warm up. Danny drove away quickly. After all, he was just the messenger!

CHAPTER 12

SAMMY Tring sat watching television. It was early February, and she was waiting for her father to come home. She heard a car stop, but the front door did not open. She opened it to see what he was doing, but it was a mistake. Her last mistake! When her father returned home, her clothes were set out in front of the fire, and she was nowhere to be seen.

Once more, Danny had the office to himself while the others were called in to help with the search, but after his initial baptism of fire it was dead in Turnround and the park. He spent longer and longer over dinner at Hester's, and Kate took to calling in to see him before collecting the girls from school, although she still went home on the school bus. She was making sure they were on the school bus because of the man who was preying on little girls. Danny liked her visits but still had not written to Lucy.

The rest of the winter was much the same. Another girl went missing, and they looked for her in vain. None of the girls were found. Danny taught Captain Webb the value of approaching anything he was stalking from down wind and, apart from the first time when he had to shoot the rabbit before it made good its escape, he did not interfere. Captain Webb looked at the dead rabbit with disdain until Danny pulled it apart. Then Captain Webb recognised it as something to eat, and did just that.

Soon the snow started to fall off the trees, and the temperature started to rise, heralding the start of spring. Greg borrowed Danny's Jeep as his old banger was out of action and he needed to get to Lower Superior. Danny came home early on the school bus, and arranged for Callum to pick him up on his way through in the morning with his first load of logs.

Red came by in the evening on the pretext of exercising Harry, Connie's pony. He brought with him the offer of a meal at his Mum's, but Danny had to turn it down. With no transport, he would have to walk back in the dark and he did not want to do that. Staying the night meant he might miss Callum as he was expecting him to be at the end of his road. He sent his apologies and invited the whole family down on the Saturday for a meal to make up for it.

Red went home soon after, and Danny once more sat in front of a sheet of paper. This time he managed his address and 'Dear Lucy', but that was it. He went to bed early, and started down the Mine Road at five thirty a.m. to meet Callum at six on the Loggin Road.

Captain Webb was becoming quite a hunter by now and kept himself fed. He circled as they went, looking for prey. When they reached the Loggin Road, Captain Webb sniffed the air and crossed it. Danny was going to caution him, but it was early in the morning with no traffic about so he decided against it. Danny sat by his new sign which advertised the way to his mine, and watched him work his way about. Captain Webb pushed through some branches under a tree, disappeared, and reappeared almost immediately. He then walked along, sniffing the ground as he walked. After a few metres he stopped, sat down, and started a low mournful howl. Danny walked over to where he sat, and looked about but there was nothing visible. He walked to the tree, where the Captain had disappeared, and pulled up the lower branches. He saw nothing, but still pushed his head under them, and found a young girl, naked and curled up in the foetal position round the tree trunk. A light pink stain set Danny's heart pounding.

'Come on lass. This is no place to stay. Whatever's happened to you? Come on, I'll take you home.'

She did not respond, and Danny felt the hand which was away from her body and nearest him. It was soft but cold.

'You'll catch your death out here like this.'

He waited, but still the girl did not answer. He pushed under further with the intention of picking her up, but first he felt her neck for a pulse. His hand recoiled in horror. Her neck was frozen! For the first time in his life, Danny lost control. He thrust his way out from the tree and lurched away, from what he now knew was a crime scene, to throw up. The sickness gave way to intense anger. Captain Webb was still howling mournfully.

'Okay Captain, I've seen her. Now give it a rest!' he said.

He was upset, and the wolf sensed it. He stopped his wailing but remained where he was. Danny walked to the Loggin Road and, after hesitating, the Captain followed.

'Danny here, come on,' Danny said into his radio.

'You are an early bird. Over.' Made replied.

'I've just found a worm that I'd rather someone else

had found. She is about ten years old, naked, and most of her is frozen. Over.'

'I hear you. I'm on my way. I'll send the cavalry as well. Where are you? Over.'

'On the Loggin Road where the Mine Road joins it, over.'

'We'll be there, over and out.'

Danny sat by the sign again, but this time the Captain sat next to him. The wailing of sirens heralded the arrival of the cavalry. They cordoned off the crime scene in a big way. Danny walked over and showed them where the body lay, leaving Captain Webb by the sign. He was on his way back to the Loggin Road when he heard Hiram K call out.

'There's something over here, Sarge.'

Danny looked to where Hiram K stood.

'That's my breakfast,' he called over to Hiram K.

'Sorry!' Hiram K called back.

'It's not your fault, but I'd like to get my hands on the man who is responsible.'

'You are not alone,' Hiram K replied. 'I went through this last spring as well.'

'We are not here to gossip,' said a Mountie with lots of gold braid on his uniform. Danny took him to be in charge. 'Civilians should be kept away from the crime scene.'

Danny felt the hairs on the back of his neck rise, but he just walked away. He could see Callum's lorry approaching. Callum saw the Mounties, and stopped some distance away. Danny walked over to his lorry.

'What's going on, Danny?' he asked, when Danny reached his cab.

'I've just found one of the missing girls.'

'When you consider the area he's got to choose from,

it's right on your doorstep,' Callum replied.

Danny did not reply, but the comment did not go unheard. Captain Webb watched Danny walk over to Callum's lorry, then moved over and settled down beside him. With the area cordoned off, everyone seemed to be waiting. A pick-up arrived with two dogs barking madly in the back. The driver jumped out and let the dogs down on long reins. He immediately started them searching.

'What are they hoping to find with them?' Danny asked.

'The other three!' Callum replied.

'What, there?'

'Somewhere here. They were together last Spring when they found them, but it was later when they found them the previous year, and the animals had been at them.'

'The Captain could have found the rest for them. He found the first one.'

'This is our dirty linen, and you've already washed some for us.'

A cry from the man with the dogs brought the Mounties running to him.

'Number two!' Callum said angrily.

The dog handler moved on, and while the Mounties secured the area with the second body in it, he yelled again.

'Number three!' Callum said, almost spitting out the words. He punched the dashboard.

Danny said nothing. There was nothing to say. The searcher moved on and they waited for the fourth body to be found, but after an hour the man with the dogs was ready to quit.

'She can't be here, or my dogs would have found her,' he announced.

'They were together last time,' John Mulroon replied.

'Well, they ain't this time,' the dog handler snorted.

'Maybe your dogs are past their "sell by" date!' John retorted.

Danny listened as the argument raged. John wanting to search some more, and the dog handler wanting to quit. And although he had tried not to, he thought about the girl he found. There were no marks on her apart from the fact that she had been raped.

'Callum, there were no marks on her to show how she died,' he said suddenly.

'No, the cold does it. They don't last for long out here.'

'The first one might have - there was no snow. It didn't snow till later. She might have run off.'

'That's how he does it, just lets them run into the trees in the winter without any clothes on but he is not stupid. If she managed to hole up somewhere and get help, his goose is as good as cooked,' Callum replied.

'If he killed her and left her, she'd have been found, even by those dogs,' Danny added.

Then simultaneously they said.

'He must have buried her!'

They walked over side by side to where John Mulroon was still arguing with the dog handler. Captain Webb followed, and the dogs started to go wild.

'Keep that thing away from my dogs or I'll let them loose,' the dog handler warned.

'As the wolf is a protected species, I'd be forced to shoot both of them!' Danny replied evenly.

'This ain't the park. It ends at the Loggin Road,' he retorted.

'If you are right, I'd have made a terrible mistake, and I apologise in advance!' Danny replied, and levered a cartridge into the breech of his rifle.

'Knock it off, you two,' John said curtly. 'You, take your dogs away. They aren't any good anyway, and you're charging by the hour.'

They watched the dog handler as he dragged the dogs away.

'Now, what's your beef, Danny?' John asked.

'We think your man killed the first one, as there was no snow, and we think he buried her,' Danny replied.

The sergeant looked at both men for a moment.

'I get the feeling there is more,' he added.

'Let the Captain have a go. He might find her,' Danny said. He had no idea if Captain Webb could find the first girl, but he wanted to shut up the loudmouthed dog handler.

'Wait here,' John ordered, and walked over to the officer in charge.

'Do you think the Captain can find her?' Callum asked.

'The foxes back in England would dig up things we had buried if we didn't put pot plants on top of the grave. My wife was distraught when her first budgie we buried ended up as just a beak! A wolf is just a better version of a fox.'

'I hope you are right. He's coming back with the top brass.'

The officer in charge walked over, full of his own self-importance.

'If you think the cub can find her, I will not be the one to stop you looking. The Sergeant will oversee the search.' He walked away to his limousine.

'Well, it's up to you now, Danny,' John said, turning

his hands up in supplication.

'No! It's up to Captain Webb,' Callum corrected.

'You'll need these if you want to dig up anything,' the dog handler said derisively, and threw a pickaxe and shovel at Danny's feet.

'Find the missing girl, Captain Webb,' Danny said to the wolf cub's upturned face.

'Captain Webb!' the dog handler snorted. 'Now I've heard everything,' He walked to his pick-up where the dogs were still barking loudly.

Danny was worried that the barking might put the wolf cub off, but the Captain followed the now well-worn path to the crime scene. He passed the spot where Danny had lost his breakfast and, after a perfunctory sniff, walked on. He sniffed the air and the ground until he came to the spot where he had first sat and howled. He sat and howled again.

'Come on, Captain Webb, we need to find this last girl or we are both going to look stupid,' Danny urged.

In answer, the wolf stood up and started to paw the ground.

'Are you telling me this is what you were howling at in the first place? I hope you are right. Move out of the way and I'll start digging.'

Danny started scraping the snow away with the dog handler's tools. It was well packed down, and in the end he had to chop it with the shovel to loosen it. With the snow gone, Danny was left with frozen earth. Could Captain Webb smell a body through this? There was only one way to find out. He started to break the ground with the pickaxe. He wanted to do it another way, but it was the only way to shift the frozen soil. Bit by bit the ground yielded until they were through the frozen layer. When Danny tired, Callum took over, and when he tired, John took over and so on, until on one stroke the pickaxe blade came up with blood on it! The pickaxe was discarded, and all hands pawed at the loosened soil until the girl's hands were uncovered. They were tied behind her back, and she had been buried face down.

'We'll take it from here,' John announced, visibly shaken by the sight. 'Thank the good Captain for me with a piece of steak.'

Two Mounties cordoned off the grave as John walked over to the limousine. The dog handler had come to gloat at Danny's failure, but now he was impressed.

'Are you thinking of selling that wolf at all?' he asked.

Danny just looked at him in disbelief.

'Get me out of here, Callum. I need some fresh air.'

'I know I want a drink,' Callum replied, and the two walked away oblivious to what was going on around them.

When they were driving on the Loggin Road, Danny relaxed a little.

'Did you know any of them, Callum?' he asked.

'No, not know them. I did see their pictures in the paper. If you were right about her being the first one, her name was Sarah Talksloud, poor little thing. To die like that, and with her father doing life for murder somewhere!' Callum replied.

'I need a whisky,' Danny announced. 'In fact, I need lots of whisky after that.'

The lorry slithered to a stop in the slushy snow in front of Hamish's store and they walked in. The arrival of the Mounties and the search had taken some time, but it was still just before noon when they arrived at the store. Three bottles stood on the counter, each man's particular poison. Hamish stood there behind the counter.

'You heard then?' Callum asked.

'I heard, and these are on the hoos. There are four mothers who knew their bairns were dead, but now at least they can start to mourn. We will have our own wee wake.'

They sat and drank and talked until they fell asleep, no work was done, and nobody else came near.

Danny woke up on the floor of the store by the counter. Captain Webb lay next to him, watching.

'Good morning, Captain Webb. It's a big juicy piece of steak for you, courtesy of John Mulroon, and well you earned it! Sell you indeed!' Danny scoffed. 'What next?'

'Will you stop babbling?' Callum called from the other side of the counter. 'I am trying to sleep.'

'So am I,' Hamish added. 'I am waiting for the pain to go away.'

'The trouble is, I don't think the pain will go away,' Danny replied. 'All my life I have wanted a little girl or boy to call my own, and this callous bastard is killing them quicker than I could make them, even if my wife was willing! And what for? Ten minutes of pleasure before he discards them.'

'From what I have heard, he keeps them all night for his pleasure before he finishes with them,' Hamish corrected. 'What sort of man does that?'

'The worst sort!' Danny replied. 'But I'll get him. You just wait. I'll get him if it's the last thing I do.'

He stood up, waited until his head cleared, then walked outside. His Jeep stood where Greg said he would park it, and the keys were in the box under the seat. He drove home. Whether he was fit to drive never entered his head. He had a purpose.

Back at the mine, he made a notice board out of soft wood. He had seen police programmes, and they always had notice boards up with all the facts of the cases on it, whether important or not. When the board was made and stood on legs like an easel to make it moveable, he started writing notes and pinning them on the board. It was what he knew and what other people had told him. He had only one name to put up, and that was etched into his brain, Sarah Talksloud. He knew she was tied up and buried naked because he had helped dig her up. The snow was late and that was why she was buried.

According to Hamish, the perpetrator kept the girls all night before he killed them and, according to Callum, he just let them go with no clothes on, in freezing conditions. Leaving them to freeze to death. If that was true, this man deserved to die. Danny remembered the stain on the girl's lower thigh, and knew why he took them. He tried to imagine how the little girl felt when, after being so ill-used, she was left to run off into the forest to die. Alone and helpless. Then there was Sarah Talksloud. An absence of snow meant he had to kill her, or did he bury her alive? The thought was too much for him to bear, and he pushed it back as far in his mind as he could.

He drove to the library in Lower Superior to look through old newspaper reports of the killings. If that failed, he would go to the newspaper offices and look through their back copies. He wanted this man. If you could call him a man! If Made needed him, he had his radio.

He read the reports thoroughly and found out the names of the other girls involved, and the previous girls, but that was all. No modus operandi to help mothers protect their children. There was no other information apart from the fact that they were found dead. Danny understood the need to hold back some information but they could have at least told the readers how, when, and where he struck. He copied the pages to pin on his board and paid the girl for the use of the photocopier. The girl took the money and wrote out a receipt.

'The name is?' she asked.

'Turner,' Danny replied without a second thought.

She gave him the receipt and watched him walk out. When she was sure he had gone, she made a phone call.

Back at his cabin, Danny added the new information to his notice board. As he pinned up the sheets with the girls' pictures on it, the need to get his hands on this killer grew more and more intense.

Over the next few days, while going about his daily work, Danny chatted to anyone he could find, bringing the murders into the conversation somehow. When he gleaned new information, he noted it and added it to his board. Danny got the idea that they all knew more than they would let on, treating the case like a national secret, although they all wanted to tear the perpetrator apart with their bare hands. They all had a different name for him, but they all meant roughly the same.

To Danny, the board was still quite empty. He put up a label with Wilson on it. He knew he was not responsible for the latest deaths, but he still might have had a hand in the earlier ones. The latest deaths could be the work of a copy cat, but only if they new his modus operandi. Danny remembered Red saying he used to go to the mine when his father worked there, and drove to the Walters' house.

'Well, hello stranger,' Kate said when she saw him. 'I am sorry you were the one to find the girls this year. Not very nice, I suspect?'

Danny did not answer, as the girls chose that moment to arrive. They had heard the Jeep and came looking for Captain Webb. Marie was the eldest at nine, and soon to be this man's possible target. Danny wanted him caught before that happened. He sat at the table, watching the two girls with Captain Webb outside while Kate made him tea. The snow was all gone now, and it was starting to warm up.

'No Red?' he called into the kitchen.

'He's exercising the pony. Probably gone to see if you are alright as we haven't seen you for a while.' She said it as a complaint.

'I'm sorry! I've been a little tied up,' he replied, and waited until she was sitting opposite him, her with her coffee and him with his tea. 'I'm looking into these murders. I probably shouldn't, but I've made a lot of new friends here and I don't want to see them hurt like that.'

'If I had anything I could tell you, I would. I do have a vested interest you know.' She stood and watched the girls through the window. 'He could be watching them now, working out how he could take one from me.' She was close to tears.

He joined her. 'That's what I meant. Did you know they had Mike Wilson pencilled in as the killer?' he asked.

'What, Mike! I don't believe it for a moment. Now if it were boys, that would be different! That's why I never let

Red go up there without Seth. For all Seth's faults, he did love the children. Unfortunately, he loved a lot of other women as well.' She sat down again. 'I'd have left him years ago if I had had anywhere to go.'

The news that Kate thought Mike Wilson was interested in boys, surprised Danny.

'So, if Wilson was the other way inclined, how come they linked him with the murders?' Danny asked.

'He was the only one who didn't come in for a blood test, and all the rest passed,' Kate explained.

'And that was it?'

'Well, he was out there all alone most of the time.'

'Like I am now,' Danny pointed out. 'That makes me the next suspect.'

'No one knew Mike too well, except Seth, and we can't ask him.'

Red chose that moment to jump the back fence and ride up to the stable. He jumped off and led the pony inside.

'Red might know something,' Kate said quietly. 'I think he knew what Seth was up to, and tried to keep it from me.'

Danny finished his tea.

'You'll get more out of him about Wilson if I'm not about, but you will tread carefully, won't you?' she added.

Danny nodded, and walked up to the stable where Red was brushing the pony.

'You drove away as I reached the road, Danny,' Red said in between brushes. 'If I'd a known you were coming here, I'd a come straight back. What did the girl you found look like?'

The question came like a bolt out of the blue. Danny had tried not to think about the little girl, but he realised now that Red may have known her.

'What, the first one?'

'Yes, Sarah, the one you had to dig up. She was alright.'

Danny let his mind return to the tree, and the moment when he thrust his head under the branches.

'She had long blonde hair, about ten years old, and about four foot eight high at a guess, but it was hard to tell her height the way she was laying.'

'Was her hair in a ponytail held up by a red elastic thing?'

'No, her hair was free-flowing when I found her, but it might have been in a ponytail when she started out.'

'Oh, I remember now. She was taken from her bed, and they don't wear them things in bed, do they? That means it was probably Terri then.' He brushed harder. 'I liked her,' he added.

'She was taken from her bed?' Danny asked.

'Yeah. Her Mum had to go to work, and her Dad was due back half an hour after her Mum left. When her Dad got home, she was gone.'

'As I found her, I have decided to look into the killings in an effort to find out who is responsible, and stop him.'

'Can I help?' Red asked, expecting a straight 'no'.

'You have already but you can help fill in some more blanks on my notice board.'

'Grub up!' Kate called from the house.

'We can drive up to my cabin if you like. I have a few things for your Mum I forgot to bring. My mind has been on other things.'

'It's silly, really. I knew she was dead because the others were, last year, but it wasn't until you found her that I cried. It isn't fair. She was nice.'

'I know it's not. Life is rarely fair. Come on, or your food will get cold.'

Kate had laid a place for Danny without asking, but it was not until he smelled her cooking that he realised how hungry he was. After the meal, Danny relaxed for a while. He needed it. The talk which might prove useful could wait a few minutes. As Red was going to school, and children talk, he might have picked up some important information, or so Danny hoped.

CHAPTER 13

DANNY drove back to his cabin with Red. He was
hoping to jog his memory to see if he had heard
anything, and he could tell him which of the girls went to
the school at Turnround. He also wanted to ask Red about
Mike, but was uneasy as to how to ask him. He and Kate
were worried he might get upset. Danny parked and walked
inside, thinking he would leave Mike out of it, but he was
forgetting the board. Red walked straight up to it and
studied it.

'Why is Mike up here?' he asked.

'He didn't come in for a blood test, and that might have
cleared him.'

'I'm not surprised. Mike was scared of needles! Dad
made a joke out of it when Mike told him, and Mike got
the hump.'

'But it would have cleared him of suspicion.'

'If you knew Mike, you would know he wasn't
involved,' Red replied.

'How do you mean?' Danny asked.

Red did not answer.

'How do you mean?' Danny prompted, after a pause.

'I don't want to say,' Red retorted.

'Don't then! You are the last person I want to upset,' Danny replied. 'You're the one round here with the most reason to hate me.'

'I don't hate you. It's just...' He fell silent again.

Danny said nothing. He just waited. If Red wanted to tell him he would. He put the kettle on and started to clean the kitchen.

'Mike was bent,' Red said after a while.

'You mean, a homosexual?'

'Yes.'

'Your Mum said something like that.'

'Does she know what went on?' Red asked worriedly.

'No, I don't think so. Is it bad?'

'Yes.' Red fell silent again.

Danny waited, fearing the worst, and not sure if he really wanted to know.

'I guessed what they were doing. Dad made the same noises as he did when he was with Mum. The walls aren't very thick at home,' Red said after a while.

It took Danny a few seconds to realise what Red meant. He felt relief that it was not Red who was involved, but also realised how hard it must have been for Red to admit.

'You mean your father and Mike?'

'Yes!' Red's eyes overflowed with tears.

Danny reacted instinctively and held Red to him. He thought of saying he was glad it was not Red who was being used, but wondered if it might not upset him even more. He hugged him instead.

'Such a big burden for a little boy. They say a trouble shared is a trouble halved, and I won't tell a soul. We will keep your Dad's memory clean, but your Mum knew he was having some sort of affair. She thought it was with other women. She had an idea that Mike was different, and that's why she didn't let you go up there alone.'

'I was safe enough. I was more in the way than anything when I went, but Mike gave me money to keep out of the way when I was there so I liked to go at first. My Dad used to spend most of the money he got on booze and gambling, so the money Mike gave me kept us going. Mike had a computer, and I played on it when they went in to inspect the mine, but he only had three games. He said he was going to get another one, so one day when I was bored I followed them in to ask Mike if he had the new game yet, and heard what they were doing. I didn't know what to do. In the end, I just went back and played on the computer.'

Red made no effort to free himself from Danny's arms, but reached round Danny as far as his arms would go, and cuddled him back. Then he started crying harder.

'We'd come home from the mine where they'd been at it...' Red continued through his tears, 'And then he did it with Mum. I hated him for that.'

'Did you know that Mike was dead?'

Red stopped crying and looked up.

'No.'

'I found him when I dropped off the rope after rescuing Connie. I didn't say anything in case it upset you.'

'At least he can't tell anyone about it! I'm glad he's dead,' Red replied, regaining his composure.

They separated, and started going over other things on the board.

'I take it Terri went to your school?' Danny asked.

'Yes, the one in Turnround.'

'I've not seen it yet. I'll have to go and look at it to see if I get any ideas.'

Red read the list of victims.

'Marta went to my school as well, so did Katie, Sarah, and you know about Terri.'

'Where might the others go to school?'

'There is another school in Timberline, but I don't know of any others.'

'I'll have to go there as well. He must see his victims beforehand and find out where they live if he takes them from their homes. It must be a mother's worst nightmare, to put her daughter to bed and find her not there when she returns. I wonder if they were all taken the same way?'

'I can find out. They're all talking about it again at school now that they have been found.'

'If they are all left home alone, then he must go into it quite deeply. Maybe he spends the summer choosing his victims ready for winter.'

'What do I tell Ma?' Red asked.

'I just don't know Red, but sometimes not knowing can hurt more than knowing, other times ignorance is bliss!'

They started back to Red's house.

'It's okay if you want to date her,' Red said suddenly. Danny smiled.

'Kind of you to say so, but I have a wife back in England.'

'Why isn't she here?' Red asked, the disappointment clear to see on his face, and to hear in his voice.

'She didn't want to come.'

'You could, you know. Whatsit her.'

'What, divorce her?'

'Yes, that's it. Divorce her, then you could date my Mum.'

'I'm thinking about it. Believe me, I'm thinking about it.'

'Does that mean you like my Mum?'

'It does,' Danny replied, and Red smiled.

He stopped for tea and a bite to eat with Kate and, after the children were in bed, they talked. Kate tried to find out what Red had told Danny, but he only told her what Red and he had agreed she could know.

'When Danny returned to his cabin, he recognised the limousine which stood in front of it. He left Captain Webb sleeping on the passenger seat, nodded to the chauffeur as he walked past, and entered the cabin. The man sitting in Danny's armchair was none other than the officer who had been in charge when the girls were found.

'Please forgive the intrusion. You are Daniel Turner?' the officer said when he heard Danny walk in.

'I am,' Danny replied. 'And I do.'

'Thank you. A little bird tells me you have taken it on yourself to investigate our killings.'

'I'm sorry, I didn't catch your name,' Danny replied.

'So sorry. How remiss of me. Hugh Gosfar, Inspector Hugh Gosfar.' He spoke like an aristocrat.

The board with the names on was in plain sight.

'I thought a new set of eyes might shed some light on it.'

'Well, I shall make my position clear. I want no vigilante type action. If you find anything of importance, you will contact me or Sergeant Mulroon. Do you understand? I don't want anyone going off half-cocked because you think you know who killed their daughter. Do you understand?'

'I catch your drift.'

'Good! Now I have a function to attend. Good day.'

Danny followed him out and watched the limousine drive away. When he walked back into the cabin, he saw a thick file on the table. He opened it to see the body of a girl in roughly the same position as the girl he had found, who he now knew was Terri.

'This must be the file on the murders,' he said, although there was no one there to hear him. 'So he warns me off, then accidentally leaves it behind.'

He sat reading the file, noting anything he did not know, and adding it to the board as he read. It hurt to read about, and see photographs of, the girls, but it was necessary if he was going to have any chance of catching this beast. He read and reread the file until it hurt too much, then he closed it and took his notice board into the mine room out of sight, as some of the information was not supposed to be revealed. The thing that really made his blood boil was the autopsy of Sarah Talksloud. There was soil in her lungs, showing that she had been alive when she was buried and screaming for someone to help her. He slammed shut the door to the mine room.

'I'll get you, you bastard!' he hissed.

That night, he found sleep difficult, and at four in the morning he carried the notice board out of the mine room into the kitchen. He would have sat in the mine room and studied the board but it was too cold. He set it up in front of the fire and stirred the ashes to life before putting on more wood. Now he was ready, he sat looking at it, trying to build up a picture. The first girl was taken from outside a chip shop in Lower Superior where she had just bought some chips. She disappeared off the face of the earth until the snow thawed and they found her near the River Road.

He spread out his map and found the River Road. The road from the Loggin Road to Turnround, forked right just before Turnround to cross the river and carry on up to the Through Road. Where it forked, it was called the Bridge Road. Over the bridge, the road had a left turn which was the River Road and it ran up behind Urls Landing for several miles before it turned right and joined the Through Road. The girl was found halfway down the stretch of the River Road before it reached the river. A hunter found her under a tree. She died from hypothermia, not helped as she was naked. All the others, bar one, were taken from their homes in some way or another, and the clothes they were wearing at the time spread out in front of the fire. They were never seen again until the winter snows thawed and the countryside gave up its dead. Apart from the first girl, they all went to the schools in Turnround or Timberline.

So the first one was 'spur of the moment', and the others were planned and risk-free. Apart from the first girl, all the others were home alone, with the exception of Helen Richter who had a younger sister upstairs in bed, and she was left unharmed. Perhaps for later! According to the reports, there was no finger print evidence, but he used no protection during the act. The blood test should have found the guilty party if he was still about.

A knock on the door woke him with a start. He covered the board with the table cloth causing the salt and pepper to fly across the room. When he opened the door, the Inspector's chauffeur stood there.

'The Inspector left a file here by mistake,' the chauffeur announced.

'You are welcome to look for it. I had too much to do

to notice last night,' Danny lied.

The chauffeur walked in and saw it laying where the Inspector left it.

'I think that's it!'

'Take it then, it's not mine. Can I cook you some breakfast?' Danny asked.

The thought of the bacon and eggs that Danny was about to cook, tempted the chauffeur.

'I'd better not. My boss has a press conference about the murders, and he needs this with him,' he replied.

'Well, pop in when you are passing some time, and I'll cook you something.'

'I sure will,' the chauffeur replied, with a nod of his head, and left with the file.

Danny ate a good breakfast, then took a walk in the woods with Captain Webb. As he walked, he thought, and Captain Webb slowly drew away until he lead by some distance, but Danny was oblivious.

He was thinking about the killings and Mike Wilson. Wilson's name kept popping back even when he tried not to think about him. Why would he kill himself? He had financial trouble, but he was prepared for it and would have been able to earn a living cutting wood with the hidden saw mill. He was having sex, so that wasn't a problem unless he wanted Seth to leave Kate for him. Danny scratched his head. It was possible, but unlikely as it appeared he was paying Seth.

Suddenly in front of him was Wilson's landing place. There was no dip in the ground as he had been cut from the ice, the ice had since melted and the water was now level and tranquil. He knew where it was though, and compared its position in relation to the cliff face.

'You sure came over in a hurry, Mr Wilson.'

It raised a question in his mind, and he turned to go, his mind made up to look above, where Wilson had jumped. After a few metres, he remembered Captain Webb, and turned to find him following with a jack rabbit in his mouth.

'Well done, Captain Webb, you can have that when you are hungry.'

They returned to the cabin, and he put the rabbit in the mine before driving to the bridge. Danny started up the slope and Captain Webb followed, ever alert for another rabbit. The radio burped.

'Made here. Were you thinking of coming in to work today? Over.'

'Danny here. Sorry, I overslept. Over.'

'We are going to a press conference this morning, and I was hoping you could look after the shop. Over.'

'Is that the press conference about the little girls? Over.'

'Do you know everything that goes on?! Over.'

Danny looked along the trail, and the signs were just starting to be visible. He did not want to turn back.

'Not everything. I am out with the wolf. Have I got time for breakfast before I come in? Over.'

'I have no problem with that. I'll get Hamish to sit in for you, but don't be too long. He'll only get grouchy, over.'

'I'll see you when you get back, over and out.'

He walked on and encountered the first sign and picket fence. Both were securely fixed in place, as were the next three. Of the three which covered the spot where Mike had jumped from, the picket fences were loose but the signs were nailed to the trees. He looked at the sign right next to the jumping spot, and saw it was not level. It struck him that if you put up a sign, unless you didn't care what people thought of your work you would put it up level. He levered it off and found four nail holes instead of two. It had been removed and refitted, but why? He walked back to the sign he had passed, and found that was the same. If the one the other side was the same, someone walking from the track where Harry was tied would not know it was the edge if all the three signs were removed as well as the picket fences. Someone running would land just about where Mike had landed, especially if he was running for his life! Maybe he knew who it was?

He followed the path directly away from the edge looking for signs of a fight or a chase, and what he found was a lot better. An empty cartridge case. He smelled the open end, it had been there a while. He walked on and found another two. Someone could have been chasing him, firing at him. He thought about the signs. 'No, firing to miss so you ran over the cliff. I reckon you were murdered by my killer, and that might just help me find him.'

By the time Danny walked into the office, closely followed by Captain Webb, Hamish was indeed grouchy. He also wanted to go to the press conference.

'And where have yee been, may I ask?' he chided.

'Suicide Falls. I'm working on a theory. Any problem with that?'

'None at all if it helps to put this killer in my gunsight!' Hamish replied, aiming his anger at the killer.

He stood up, and Danny flopped into the chair he had just vacated.

'Between you and me, I think Mike Wilson was

murdered,' he said from the chair.

'Yee mean he was thrown over? It would take a strong man to do that.'

'I have a theory which might cover it, but I'll tell you more when I figure it all out. When Made comes back, I'll walk down to the school and have a look round. I might look in on the clinic as well.'

'If yee go now, yee will catch Greta all alone in the clinic. The others are bound to be at the press conference. The clinic opened this morning for the summer.'

'You're not going to get all testy on me again if I'm gone a while, are you?'

'Just make sure yee are back before Made.'

Danny walked down to the school. All was quiet as the children were in class. As he approached the school, he could see a sign for the clinic. It was part of the school buildings, but the entrance was outside the school area. He walked in and found a girl, all alone, reading a book.

'You must be Greta?' He said it as a question but it was more rhetorical as he was expecting her to be Greta.

'And with an accent like that, you must be the new ranger from England I've been hearing about,' the girl replied.

'All good I hope?'

'Mostly.'

'Daniel Turner at your service.'

'What can I do for you, Daniel? You don't look like you need to be booked in for our de-wrinkling course or our pre-natal and anti-natal classes.'

'I understand that the clinic was asked to help when all the blood tests were carried out?'

'We were, and it was murder!' Greta replied.

'I have a question about blood tests.'

'Fire away.'

'If I had a friend who was petrified of needles to such an extent that he would do anything rather than face one, is there anyway you could help him?'

'That's easy. If it's a man, he could give a sperm sample. Of course if it was somebody as big and strong as yourself, special help could be given to help you supply one!'

'That I can understand, but would my wife?'

'Probably not!' Greta answered, suitably crestfallen.

'I take it you could go behind a screen to do it?'

'Oh yes, or a doctor could push button B from behind and make you shoot your lot, but it's not as much fun as my way.'

'That I could believe. Thank you for your time.'

'You are welcome. It's a bit boring until the old biddies start coming in and causing havoc.' She returned to her book, and Danny returned to the office to relieve Hamish.

An idea was forming in his head about the death of Mike Wilson, but it was a long way from becoming more than an idea. He sat in the office alone, thinking about his idea and finding it more ludicrous as he did so, until Made stamped into the office. He was in a foul mood.

'Trod in something?' Danny asked.

'No! It was a farce. They gave us no more information than we had.'

Danny looked at Made.

'I didn't realise you had a daughter as well.'

'She is nine tomorrow, and the youngest one taken was nine,' Made replied indignantly.

'What do you know about the abductions, then?'

'Practically nothing. That's what hurts!'

'I can give you enough information to protect your daughter, but you must keep it to yourself,' Danny replied evenly.

Made looked up in surprise.

'What can you know that I don't? Dammit, I live here!'

'So do I now, and I have a vested interest in catching this perverted git,' Danny replied.

'I'm sorry, Danny. That came out all wrong. I just don't want her to end up freezing to death under a tree after he's finished with her.'

'I can understand that. If she were mine, I would feel the same way. Now listen carefully, and don't repeat it unless it is for the same reason I am telling you.'

Danny outlined the killer's modus operandi, and pointed out that when Made and Rosie's shifts overlapped, they could be a target. Made listened without comment until Danny finished talking.

'Barry chose well when he chose you,' he said.

'I'm glad you think so. Just make sure you look after your little girl.'

'We will. She will never be left alone again.'

'If you need me to come in so you can stay home until Rosie gets there, just let me know.'

'You'll hear. Now you can go home, if that was where you were headed,' he added with a sly grin.

'Probably. I need to think, and it is hard to think in the right company.'

'That bad, eh?'

'Do you think there is a chance?'

'From what I hear, there is,' Made replied, and sat in

212

the chair Danny had just vacated.

Danny left the office to find Hamish waiting for him.

'Buy a poor Scot a drink?' he asked.

Danny looked up and smiled.

'You just said the magic words,' he replied, and they walked into the store.

As usual the door was unlocked and the sign read 'open'. Captain Webb followed them, but settled down outside to wait. A note lay on the counter, and Danny managed to read the name Selwyn off the bottom before Hamish tucked it into his pocket. Danny knew no one named Selwyn, and stored the name for later questions. He sat there and drank two whiskies, but although his heart was in it, his mind was far away.

'Are yee going to talk to me, or shall I read a book?' Hamish asked to break a long period of silence.

'Sorry, I was miles away.'

'I hope it was a hanging.'

'I never thought about that. Do you still have capital punishment over here?' His mind returned to the death of Sarah Talksloud. If ever there was a crime which deserved the death penalty, that was it!

'Nay laddie. They stopped that a while back, but there is a good chance he'll be shot when they find him. Yee could manage that after dispatching Abe Dupont, if he tried to run away that is.'

Danny smiled his 'if only you knew' smile and poured another whisky.

'What have I said? Surely yee think he deserves to die.'

Danny weighed the 'tell him' or 'not to tell him' question, and the 'tell him' won.

'Yee mean yee were aiming at his leg and shot him through his heart?' Hamish asked.

'Yup!'

Hamish poured another drink, and halfway through he started to laugh.

'Hawkeye indeed!' he said through his laughter.

'John Mulroon thought it was a good idea not to broadcast it,' Danny explained.

'I can see why,' Hamish said with tears running down his cheeks.

Danny started laughing, but the vision of a little girl, her hands tied, struggling as someone pushed her in a hole and started covering her with soil, stopped his laughter.

'This won't do. I have things to find out. Nice talking with you Hamish. Who is Selwyn?'

'Just a friend.'

'Should I consider him? Did he give a blood sample?'

'Here in this very store to Dr Amos,' Hamish replied.

'Do we have two doctors then?' He remembered Callum calling the other, Dr Shoesmith.

'Dr Amos does the old ladies, the ones who want to be pretty again. There were so many people to test, he was roped in, much against his will as there was little money in it compared with what he charges the old dears!'

'Money, money, money!' Danny complained. 'I'll see you later.'

Danny walked back to the clinic when he saw the lights were still on. Captain Webb followed him in. Greta was still reading her book.

'Still busy then?' Danny asked.

She looked up.

'Rushed off my little feet, but I'll find time to help you,' she replied.

'When does Dr Amos come up here?'

'You don't mess about do you, straight for the jugular,' she replied, putting her book down and pulling a slip of paper from the rack next to her.

'This is his summer schedule, but you don't look very wrinkled to me.'

Danny took the slip of paper.

'I want to ask him about my stretch marks.'

'You had a baby then?' she asked.

'Just the one.' Danny pointed at the floor next to the counter.

Greta leaned over to look.

'That's a wolf!' she cried, and jumped back. 'Don't they eat people?'

'Not the Captain. He's only just worked his way up to jack rabbits.'

He tucked the slip of paper into his coat pocket and walked out, holding the door open for the Captain. He was feeling hungry, but instead of driving home he walked to Hester's to eat something he did not have to cook for a change. He knew food would be ready, or near it, and he was prepared to wait. When she saw him, Hester called to Annette to bring out another plate for Danny, and she ran out to see him, plate in hand.

'Hi Danny,' she said, and gave him the plate instead of putting it on the table.

'Hello Annette, just what I wanted,' he replied, looking at the plate.

Hester took it and set a place for him at the table. Annette ran off to make some tea. She had been practising. With the place set, Hester gestured to him to sit. Danny walked over and sat down.

'Nice to see you Danny. Any progress with your investigation?' she asked.

'Does everybody know about it then?' he asked.

'Most,' Gaston replied from the other side of the table.

Next to him sat Bob Trueman, who drove the school bus and knew all the local children who had been killed. Soon the three were deep in conversation, trying to catch up on any goings on they might have missed. Captain Webb was looked after well with his own bowl and Annette for company, and he was soon asleep on the floor.

It was late when Danny drove back to his cabin. He propped the leaflet on the coat rack by the door. The coat rack was the communal present from the other rangers when Danny built his cabin. It was the place for any non-urgent things. After a cup of tea he went to bed, but the draft from the bedroom door caused the note to fall into the boxed umbrella stand underneath the coat rack.

CHAPTER 14

DANNY climbed out of bed in the morning, and walked into the forest with Captain Webb with no thoughts of pieces of paper. The wolf still needed looking after even though it could now catch its own food. Sometimes, more escaped than was eaten, and Danny knew he would have to show him how to hunt somehow, but that could wait. After the walk came breakfast and the drive to the office. The wolf was left in the mine room. Danny figured, rightly or wrongly, that it would stop him getting too friendly with other people. The less he was friendly with people, the more chance of letting him back into the wilds. He knew he must let him go when he was old enough, but until then he had to teach him what he needed to know.

The days in the office became less tedious as summer arrived, but with Danny making little headway in his search for the killer. It was less important now as he only killed in the winter, letting the weather do his dirty work for him. He took the time to walk down to the school, and had driven to the school in Timberline to look for shady characters. There was always a Mountie present, who took the number of his Jeep when he stopped for too long.

Made arrived to relieve him of his office duties one sunny morning. The other rangers were out looking for two pony trekkers who were late returning. Danny chose to walk down to the school again, and found Chief sitting in his mother's car talking to three young girls through the high mesh fence which surrounded the playground. The car was a convertible and not cheap.

'Good morning, Ranger Turner. How are you today?' Chief asked.

'Just taking a constitutional, Chief, and you?'

'I'm waiting for Ma to be made to look like Miss World again, or at least to be conned out of her money only to be told she looks like the next Miss World!' Chief replied.

A bell clanged, and the girls hurried away.

'Expensive, is it then?'

'And how. She has it done eight times a year, the silly old trout!'

'I take it you don't approve?'

'Do you know how many hours I spend behind the till at the gas station?' he asked.

'No.'

'Twelve hours a day, seven days a week. That's why I tried for your job, just to get out of there. She's too mean to hire anyone to stand in to give me time off except when she has this done. This is my holiday.'

'Isn't there any other work about?'

'Yes, but not for the money I earn. She has to pay me the minimum wage and overtime, so I don't do too bad but it would be nice to have a day off occasionally. I end up in the local for a beer, or drive to Lower Superior of an evening to have a beer in there.

An old woman appeared in the clinic doorway.

'Jeremy!' she called loudly, and backed up the call by waving her walking stick.

'Time to go. It was nice talking to someone over six for a change.'

'I am surprised the Mountie didn't come over to see you?' Danny added, nodding in the direction of the Mountie who sat in a patrol car.

'Perky did stop for a chat the first time he saw me, but now he just waves as he drives by. I'll have to go or the old cow will throw an eppy!'

Chief drove off, and Danny waved. He continued on his way, thinking as he walked.

'Eight times a year, four too many, and the poor sod doesn't have time to breathe, let alone spend the night with his victim.'

He walked a full circle, turning left on to the Main Road and ending back at the office, an idea floating about in his brain. The three girls had made him think, girls as young as that are likely to talk to anyone, and might let slip things that could cost a sister her life. He made a note on his pad to check which dead girls had sisters and which did not. It was a dead-end idea he decided as there was no way he could ask a six-year-old who had lost a sister if she had talked to anyone before her sister was murdered.

'Haven't you got a home to go to?' Made asked when Danny walked in and flopped down in a vacant chair.

The door opened and Phil Porter walked in.

'No sign of them by the lake,' he announced.

'Carrick's on his way in. He found the two trekkers,' Made replied. 'They were just lost.'

'Townies, I bet,' Phil replied. 'Hi Danny. How are things?'

'Not bad, Phil. What's it like out there?'

'Hot and sunny.'

'I think I'll get me some of that then while it's still here. I could do with a bit of fresh air. I'll see you two later.'

On his way out, he passed Carrick.

'Did you point them in the right direction?' he asked.

'Yep. I'd a put a squib up where the sun don't shine if I had my way!' Carrick replied.

'That would have sorted them out.'

'And it would have made me feel better after traipsing all the way out there after them.'

'At least you found them. Phil just came back from the lake area after a fruitless search. He'll be after you with the squib.'

Danny drove off with a wave and headed for his cabin. He let the wolf out the side door, and then read through the notes on his board. The obituary notices told him which girls had younger brothers or sisters. Two had younger sisters, but when he read through his note from the police report, neither of them had been talking to anyone before the abduction. They rarely saw anyone near the playground in the winter as it was too cold.

He followed the wolf out the side door, and started up the trail which lead to Kate's, but stopped before he reached their back fence in a clearing. Captain Webb was trying to catch anything that moved, without success, although he nearly had a squirrel which ventured to the ground. Danny had not seen the wolf creeping up on the squirrel.

'You're getting better all the time, Captain Webb,' he

said, and threw him a chew. It was made for dogs, and was probably packed with everything the wolf should avoid but they were his favourites.

'At least you're not talking to yourself,' a voice answered. 'You had me worried for a moment.'

Danny looked round to see Kate on the edge of the clearing, and patted the grass next to him.

'There's room for two,' he said, inviting her to sit with him.

She sat next to him and they talked. It was two hours before they moved again, and Danny had felt urges, not only to kiss her but to do more. He resisted them all, after all her husband died only last winter, and he did not want to appear callous or pushy. Lucy had been the pushy one.

'Lucy! I will write that letter,' he thought. When they parted, Danny watched her until she jumped the fence with one hand resting on it and disappeared into the garden. He walked back to the cabin, sat at the table, and wrote the letter to Lucy. There, it was done. He stood up, sealed the envelope and left it ready for posting on the coat rack by the door.

He made a mug of tea, carried the notice board in, and sat looking at it in deep thought. He had ideas about Mike Wilson's death. If someone had taken him up there and made sure he had no idea where he was, making sure also that the signs and fence were nowhere to be seen, he could chase him and Mike would end up where he landed, instead of close in to the base. It must be a local man to know his way about, but why did he want Mike out of the way? To keep him as a suspect, or maybe he somehow managed to put Mike's sample in as his own and he needed Mike out

of the way to escape being found out. It was not possible
with a blood sample, but a sperm sample might be switched.
To sort out the blood samples from the sperm samples
would cut down the list of suspects, but there might still
be a lot. Danny sat back thinking, and an idea came which
had him leaping out of the chair. If they cross checked all
the samples with Mike's, that would lead directly to the
killer, if he was right.

He drove to Lower Superior and parked in the Mounties'
car park. He walked in and asked for John Mulroon.

'What can I do you for Danny?' he asked when Danny
was shown into his office.

'Inspector Gosfar came to see me and warned me not
to go off half-cocked if I had an idea. Well I have an idea
I would like to run by you to see if it holds water.'

'Fire away. I am all ears.'

Danny sat down opposite him.

'I think your killer also killed Mike Wilson.'

'I thought he jumped over the Falls?'

'I think he was chased over, and that's why he was so
far from the base.'

'Sounds plausible. Have you any way to prove it?'

'I found that the signs had been removed and renailed
to the trees, and the little fences were loose. He could have
easily taken them away, chased Mike over after disorienting
him somehow, then put them back. I followed the track
back and found these.'

He pulled out the cartridge cases and stood them on the
table.

'I think before he was killed, Mike was forced to give a
sperm sample, and the killer passed it off as his own.'

'I can see what you are getting at, but how the hell do you force a man to give a sperm sample, and surely the doctors would have noticed something?' John replied.

'As far as I can make out they were rushed off their feet, and Dr Amos' heart was not fully in his work then.'

'You're right there! They had to do two or three of his again when he botched it up, but they were all blood samples.'

'As to giving a sperm sample, I have found out there is a way to do it without getting a stiffy, but it is only a theory. I thought that if you cross check all the samples with Mike's, the one that matches is the killer!'

John leant back in his chair.

'Well, we are certainly no closer to catching the son of a bitch, and it is a long shot with a lot of ifs, but I for one am willing to give it a go. I'll have to run it past the Inspector before I can go ahead but I'll keep you informed.'

They shook hands again, and Danny drove home a happier man. If his idea panned out they would know who the killer was quite soon. And that would be before winter. He walked in and greeted Captain Webb cheerily. The door slammed, and the letter to Lucy joined the list from the clinic in the bottom of the umbrella stand. Danny did not notice. He was in a good mood. He sat in his armchair after feeding the wolf, and drank a whisky. It was followed by another and another until he decided to go to bed. He hoped for news in the morning.

Morning found him in the office, but there was no news, only people asking directions or asking for maps to the area. He served them politely, even the fishermen who needed frozen bait. By the end of the day, with no news, he was disappointed, but he would wait and not phone John.

It was a week later, with no news, before John drove up to his cabin. Danny was out of the cabin and opening the door to the police car before it had stopped.

'Any news?' he asked expectantly.

'Yes and no,' John replied.

'That doesn't sound too good,' Danny said, and followed him into the cabin.

'I thought the idea was sound enough, but people have rights. Anyone who wanted to, could come in and collect their sample after they were cleared to make sure it was destroyed. It's one of the rules of the game.'

'But surely no one bothered to do that.'

'With all the villains we have round here,' John replied. 'They think if we keep their samples we can pin anything we like on them. There was a queue to collect the things.'

'Surely you had records?'

'Of course we kept records, but that is another rule of the game. They are destroyed after one month of the test if they are in the clear. But you haven't heard the worst. This is the killer, or the one that lets a killer get away! We can't make them do it again!'

Danny looked at the list. The names were numbered and the last number of the people who gave sperm samples was one hundred and three.

'Can I take a copy of this?' Danny asked.

'You can keep that. I brought it for you, but I doubt if anything more will happen. We have sent out a letter to everyone on that list asking them to give another sample, but we also have to put in a leaflet explaining their rights, so don't hold your breath!'

'Coffee?' Danny asked.

'Some people call me brave, others call me mad, but I'm not that mad!'

'Connie gave me some lessons in making it after I nearly killed Callum.'

'It was Callum who warned me not to try it, but I'll give it a go.'

For the first time, someone drank Danny's coffee without spitting it out. They talked for a while, then John drove away.

When John had gone, Danny pinned the new list to the board. He looked down the list for a Selwyn, but was surprised to find Chief on the list. It was a name you could not easily miss! There was no Selwyn as he was a blood sample. There were too many loose ends for Danny. He liked to have all the facts and figures. It was a bit like swimming with one hand tied. What he had to do now was to wait and see if anyone volunteered to give another sample. He assumed Chief would as soon as he could find the time.

A month later, with no news from John Mulroon, Danny lost his patience. They were well into summer, and soon the winter would come - not the time to be female, ten years old and alone! He drove to the office in Turnround to see Made, but the office was empty, not what he wanted. He sat and waited impatiently until Made arrived. He wanted time off to go and see John Mulroon, but he did not want to ask. Made walked in, nodded, and flopped in a chair which promptly broke under him. He landed on top of the chair on the floor, cursing, and flung the bits across the room when he stood up.

'Who's in a bad mood?' Danny asked.

'It'll soon be fall, then winter, and he'll be at it again!' Made retorted. 'And what are you doing? Sitting there! That's what you are doing!'

'I could go and see John Mulroon. We have something on-going, but I haven't heard anything yet,' Danny replied.

'Well, go and see him then!'

Danny was out the door in a flash, and driving to Lower Superior. He was buzzed straight through, and sat in the chair opposite John who was on the phone. At last John put the receiver down.

'What can I do for you?' he asked.

'I just wondered what the response was to your letters,' Danny replied.

'Better than expected. It seems the local villains want him caught, or at least prove that they aren't him,' John explained. 'I have had two thirds of the names cleared from the list.' He gave Danny a copy of the new list to replace the old one.

'At this rate we might have him before winter!' Danny said hopefully.

'At least it might come down to a small enough figure for us to keep an eye on. I would dearly like to meet him. And, for that matter, save another little girl suffering at his hands.'

'I shot the wrong man when I arrived.'

'Abe Dupont needed shooting, but even he looks like a saint compared with this other son of a bitch,' John added.

'It is certainly easier to pick out the bad guy when he is shooting at you,' Danny replied. 'Let me know if any more come forward.'

'Will do. Thanks for the idea. If you have any more, let

me know.'

'I will.'

Danny drove home and compared the lists. One name that stood out was Jeremy Julian Joliff.

'Looks like the old battle-axe is keeping him busy. Maybe he'll find time when she has her face done next,' Danny said out loud. Captain Webb was the only one there, and he just opened one eye for a few seconds before closing it again.

Remembering Chief's mother's face brought the list into mind. It was not on the board, so he started to look for it - shuffling papers and looking under the table. His search was interrupted by the phone, only the second time it had rung. He picked up the receiver.

'Danny, it's Connie!' Her voice was tremulous.

'Hi, Connie. What's up?'

'I think it's on the way.'

'What is?'

'The baby!'

'But it's early.'

'You tell IT not me. I tried Hester, but she's gassing on the phone!'

'Okay, don't panic. I'll send Made over to get Hester, and I'll get there myself a.s.a.p. I'll call Callum as well. Remember, deep breathing.'

He slammed the phone down, called the office, and sent Made over for Hester, then jumped into his Jeep and roared down the road. As he drove, he called Callum on the radio.

'Calling the Big Bad Wolf, come on and now!' he said urgently.

He repeated the call over and over until he was greeted

by a loud YEE HAR.

'Connie is about to drop her load, over!' Danny said before Callum could say anything.

'What, now? Over.'

'Yes, right now. Can I tell her you're on your way? Over.'

'That's a big ten four. I'm burning rubber! Over.'

'Was that a yes? Over.'

'That was, over and out. Hang on. Where will I find her?'

'From what she said, in your house, in your bed. I'll find out for sure when I get there, over.'

Danny drove to Callum and Connie's cottage, on the Loggin Road. Callum had wanted it not for the pretty cottage, but for the parking, and for the back garden which sloped up from the house and would eventually make an excellent ski slope for their son or daughter, once it was cleared. He slewed to a halt, and was in the house before the engine had stopped. Connie lay on the bed, which was very wet.

'I take it your waters broke?' he asked.

'And how! I nearly called a plumber.'

'How long are the contractions?'

Danny had covered childbirth in his first aid classes, but it was a long time ago, and he was playing it by ear.

'I don`t know,' Connie replied irritably. 'Should I?' she added, now a little concerned.

'I'll time them. You just relax as much as you can and remember your pre-natal classes.'

Danny treated it as though it was old hat, keeping her calm and reassuring her, but he was pleased when he saw Hester walk in. She took charge, giving orders to everyone, whether it was for hot water or just for them to get out.

Made arrived with Kate, and Danny was free to get some fresh air. By the time Callum arrived, he was the father of a healthy, although premature, boy. Cigars were handed out, even to Danny who did not smoke. All from Hamish, showing no Scottish streak unless he was planning to bill everyone for them later. The paramedics arrived to take Connie and her son to hospital. Callum went along, and Danny offered to collect him later from the hospital.

When everyone had gone, Danny drove back to his cabin. It had been an interesting day. A day to remember. He wondered if he would have been as calm as that if it had been his baby? Would he have stayed as calm if it had started coming before Hester had arrived? He sat looking at the cold grate, and started to unwind, but Captain Webb had other ideas. He had been cooped up all day and he wanted out! Danny climbed wearily to his feet, and they walked out into the quarry. He had thought of just opening the door and sitting down again but the wolf was still only a cub, without the knowledge to survive yet, although he was quickly reaching his full height according to the book he had bought.

Once in the open, Danny's tiredness disappeared. He liked being out here. He walked further than he expected, and it was late when they returned. He poured a whisky and looked at the new list. It reminded him about the slip of paper from the clinic. He searched for it without luck. If he had been at home with Lucy, he would have looked in the bin assuming she had thrown it away, but he was the only one here bar Captain Webb.

'Have you seen the list, Captain Webb?' he asked.

The wolf just grunted and rolled on to his back. It

reminded him of Lucy and the letter. She had yet to reply, even to say what a low-down rat he was. He could not remember when he posted it, but he did remember writing it! He kept an eye on the time, and at ten o'clock drove in to collect Callum. Hamish was there with Url. They had both looked in on the baby as it lay in its incubator. They were taking no chances after Connie's failed suicide attempt. Callum was reluctant to leave, but the nurses insisted and Danny drove him home. He was too tired to look for the list again, and went to bed.

In the morning, he stopped in to see Hamish.

'Yee just caught me, Danny. I'm off to the hospital to see Connie.'

'How are they?'

'Fine. They are keeping a close eye on them in light of past goings-on, but they say if things progress as they are they will be home by the end of the week.'

'When did I post my letter to England?'

'Yee haven't posted a letter in months! I was beginning to think yee had forgotten how to write. If I relied on yee're post for a living, I'd be a skeleton by now.'

'Then what did I do with it?'

'That I don't know. I'll see yee when I get back if yee want to talk aboot it some more,' Hamish replied, and climbed into his car.

'Give my love to Connie,' Danny called.

'I will.'

Hamish drove away, and Danny walked to the office in time to meet Made coming out.

'There is a God!' Made announced. 'I have just the job for you! Two fishermen are overdue. Go out and find them.

230

They were headed for the lake, but the idea was to fish their way back down the river until they reached their car. They usually drink themselves stupid and, if they don't fall in the river and drown, we find them flat out nearby. It caused so much bother they were banned from taking booze with them, but now they are met where they want to fish by someone with booze at an inflated price and they buy it. Just look for their tackle!'

'I'll go straight from here. It will save going home again,' Danny answered. 'When I find them, I'll call in.'

'You can stock up in the store and put it on our tab,' Made added. He hesitated as though he was going to say more, but decided against it and walked back into the office.

Danny packed his bags with the necessaries and started out half an hour later. He walked to the river and, keeping it on his right, followed it into the forest. He kept looking at the river in case one of the fishermen floated by. One glance at the river made him take a second glance, then a longer look. It was not a fisherman, but he thought he could see a streak of red in the water.

He took his rifle from the case on his back, and levered a cartridge into the breech, not wanting to be caught with his pants down. He rounded the next bend slowly, making sure he did not walk into trouble. In the river, was a man, his hooded top snagged on a dead branch which jutted into the water. He was out of Danny's reach and, with his face under the flow and a stream of blood from a wound, Danny was not going out on a limb, literally!

'Danny here, come on.'

'Yo Danny. What's cooking? Over.'

'Is that you, Carrick? Over.'

'In the flesh. What can I do for you? Over.'

'I have what I think is a dead fisherman, about a mile downstream from Black Rock Flats. He's too far out for me to retrieve, but his head is under the water and he's not moving. Can you send a party out to get him while I find his mate? Over.'

'Flaming fishermen! Will do. Watch yourself, it might have been a bear or worse. Over.'

'What can be worse than a bear? I've seen one close up, and I was quite happy for it to be dead. Over.'

'You'll know it when you see it, Danny. Hang a balloon on the nearest tree so we can find him. Over.'

'Is that why we carry them? You live and learn, over and out.'

Danny blew up a ballon, tied it to a tree and walked on, his eyes peeled and his ears flapping, but he saw and heard nothing. When he reached the cave side of Black Rock Flats, he stopped. Should he go round the front or go above and look down to see if it was safe? He chose safety first, and walked up the slope to get a bird's-eye view to make sure nothing was down there. The sight which greeted him was not pleasant. The other fisherman was there, and covered in blood. His own blood!

'Danny here, Carrick, come on.'

'It's Made. What's the score? Over.'

'Two-nil to something big, I'd say. The second fisherman is lying on the Flats covered in what I assume is his own blood. Over.'

'Where are you? Over,' Made asked.

'On top, looking down at him, over.'

'Stay where you are, and that is an order! We're on our

way in the helicopter, and whatever did it might still be down there. Over.'

'What if he's still alive? I could just go down for a look. I do have a rifle. Over.'

'So did they! Over and out!'

It went against the grain to just sit and wait. He crawled to the edge and looked at the man through his binoculars. He could see the rise and fall of the man's chest. He was still alive!

'Sorry Made, I just can't sit here and let him die.'

He walked back down the slope and followed the path to the river, keeping as quiet as possible, with every nerve taut. He crept round the rock at the bottom, making sure nothing was there or creeping up behind him. He saw nothing but the injured man, and walked carefully over to him. Blood was leaking out of his many wounds. He started to staunch the blood flow, laying torn flesh back over bones when it was necessary, and bandaging over the top. Suddenly, the fisherman's hand gripped Danny, causing a spurt of blood from the wound on his arm.

'Careful, you've lost a fair bit of blood,' Danny warned.

'A wolf!' the fisherman cried. 'A big, black, evil-looking wolf!'

'A wolf did this?'

'Yes, a big, black one. A big, black...'

The fisherman shuddered and died. Danny saw no point in trying to resuscitate him. He was beyond saving. Instead, he cast about for tracks until he saw fresh tracks going away from the area. Satisfied that he was alone, he put his back against the rock with his rifle ready and waited for Made to arrive. He heard the helicopter arrive, but did not see it.

'Where are you Danny?' a voice called from above.

'Down here!' Danny called, knowing he was in the mire.

Made soon appeared round the corner, and walked over to him. He was flanked by Carrick, Greg, and a man Danny did not know.

'I told you not to come down here. Didn't I tell you not to come down here?!' Made ranted. 'What if the thing that did this, came back?'

'I could see him breathing. What else was I supposed to do?' Danny argued.

'Obey my order would have been good! He looks dead enough now, so it didn't do you or him any good, did it?'

'But it might have done.'

'Probably a bear,' Carrick said in the pause.

'It was a wolf, a big, black wolf,' Danny corrected.

'It couldn't have been,' Made retorted.

'That's what he said before he died!' Danny nodded towards the dead fisherman. 'A big, evil-looking, black wolf to be exact!'

'Do you think it's Scar, Made?' Carrick asked.

'I thought he died in that bloody fire. We'll have to find him before he kills any more tourists. You guard him while I organise it. The Mounties will want in on this.'

'Who's Scar?' Danny asked.

'A big, black, ugly looking wolf, and if it was him, look out! He's killed before, and he'll keep killing until we get him,' Made replied, and walked off, heading for the helicopter.

Soon, Mounties arrived, and the same two dogs which had been used to find the girls. They began searching. When it grew dark, they camped, and the helicopter went off for supplies, including tea bags and milk. The next morning, at first light, they started again until the dogs picked up his trail. They howled and bayed as they pulled their handler along until they came to the Loggin Road and the end of the park.

'He's gone back into the mountains,' the dog handler observed.

'I reckon!' John Mulroon replied. 'Damn him. One day I am going to put a bullet right between its evil eyes.'

'There are men who reckon they already have,' the dog handler retorted. 'But he ain't dead yet! Not by a long shot!'

The search was abandoned, and everyone went home for a well-earned rest. Notices were posted, warning of a black wolf, and Danny had to keep Captain Webb close by him in case some trigger-happy tourist shot him by mistake.

CHAPTER 15

DANNY remembered the letter to Lucy, and started to look for it. If he did not post it, then it had to be somewhere in the cabin. He looked methodically until, clutching at straws, he looked in the umbrella stand and found it, along with the slip of paper from the clinic. It all came back now. The standing of the slip and the letter on the umbrella stand for attention later, in this case, much later. He slipped the letter into his pocket for posting, and read the paper from the clinic. It only had eight days on it. Two in Turnround, two in Timberline and the other four were at a place called Pine ridge. He spread the map out and found Pine Ridge. It was too far away for anyone living in Turnround. It struck him as odd, but when he checked, they were all summer dates.

'There must be another list for winter!' he moaned. 'I'll have to stop by and get it when I have time.'

With the incursion of the black wolf, the rangers were now out on patrols, in pairs, to be seen to care. The visitors' income kept the park running - no visitors, no park. With his days kept busy and a young wolf to bring up, Danny found the time slipping by and he was powerless to do anything about it. When he found time to go into the office one morning, he found Made sitting there long-faced.

'Why so glum?' Danny asked.

'I thought you would have caught the bastard by now, but winter is just round the corner and he is still at large, and about to start his sick perversion again!' Made replied.

'I haven't given up. I have just not had the time to look into things. We have a list which is getting shorter, and I hope to cut it down again when I go to Lower Superior next,' Danny explained.

'Go now. You haven't taken any holiday yet, and you are likely to lose it unless my boss is in a good mood when you ask.'

'I'm on holiday then,' Danny replied. 'Unless I'm needed to fill in for any overlaps?'

'Not yet, but soon.'

Danny drove to Lower Superior, and was buzzed through to John's office.

'Any news?' he asked, still standing.

John shook his head.

'Well, apart from these two. They died and we were able to get a DNA sample from them.' He gave Danny a list of two names. 'No one knows we took them,' he added, tapping his nose. 'They were clear and can be crossed off.'

'Twenty eight left. That's a lot of suspects to keep an eye on.'

'And we don't know if we are barking up the right tree,' John added.

'No, it's only a theory to fit what I know. I suppose it is out of the question to follow all the suspects?' Danny asked.

'You suppose right! One of them is the mayor, and he controls our budget. He said that to give another sample

237

might give his opposition some ammunition.'

'Politics before life. Tell me about it. Do I get to vote next time?'

'I suppose so.'

'Then I will vote for someone else!' He turned and walked out, an angry man.

His next call was to the library to read up on the other attacks by the black wolf. Better to know the enemy you might have to face. Afterwards he drove back to the clinic in Turnround. Greta was reading a book as usual.

She put it down when she saw who it was.

'Good afternoon, Daniel. How can I help you?'

Danny held out the list.

'This list stops at the end of October. Can you give me the winter list?'

She pulled a leaflet out of its box and gave it to him.

'Is that all I can do for you?' she asked, clearly disappointed.

'For the moment, yes thanks. Bye.'

He drove home and, after feeding Captain Webb, he carried the board into the cabin. He often stood looking at it, but this time he crossed off two names and pinned up the two lists. The latest list had only four dates on it, all starting at nine a.m., and finishing at eight p.m. A footnote warned, 'anyone being treated after six p.m.', should stay the night. He did not understand it, but took note of the first date late in November.

He also thought he should pop in and see Chief. The sooner he gave another sample, the sooner he could be crossed off, and Danny needed to get rid of a lot of names!

In the morning, after walking Captain Webb and trying

to instill some hunting instincts in him, Danny drove to the newspaper office to look through old copies to see if he could glean any more information. He was not looking for things related to the killings. He had the list of names, and wanted to know if they were somewhere else when one of the murders took place. It was hard going, but by the end of the week, three more names were crossed off. One was on his honeymoon in Singapore, and two were in gaol. That still left twenty-five names.

When Danny arrived for work after his week off, there were two letters waiting for him. At first he thought one might be a reply from Lucy, but his letter to her was still in his pocket! One was a scented letter, and the other three rangers were all there waiting for him to come in. It caused a lot of comment when he picked it up. He opened it, read it, and pushed it into his pocket.

'A woman friend?' Carrick asked

'In a way,' he replied, but said no more, leaving them not knowing who it was from, and walked over to the store.

On his way, he looked at the other letter. It was a child's writing. He opened it and read the handwritten note.

Dear Danny
         You are cordially invited to my birthday party on the 25th of October, presents are optional.
         Red

He wrote a reply to the first letter in the store, to be away from prying eyes, and sealed it in an envelope. Then he wrote a reply to Red's letter. He remembered the letter to Lucy and dropped that on the counter as well.

239

'Yee don't post a letter for two months, and then there's three at once!' Hamish commented. 'I don't know if the service can stand it!'

'A bit like London buses.'

'And Glasgee buses!' Hamish added. 'I should know. I lived there for ten years.'

He looked at the three addresses.

'Are yee coming then?' he asked.

'As I'm down as one of the Godfathers, it looks like I have to. Trust Connie to send it in a scented envelope. Or do you think that was Callum's idea?'

'I wouldna put it past him,' Hamish replied, a big smile on his face. 'Drew a few remarks, did it?'

'A few!' Danny looked up suspiciously at Hamish. 'I wouldna put it past yee tay think aboot it either,' he added, trying to mimic Hamish.

'As if I would do anything like that,' Hamish replied, with an even bigger smile.

'Yes, as if! It's a shame there isn't a church in Turnround to save all that travelling.'

'We have a church.'

'Where? How come I have never seen it?'

'If yee walk up past the office and round the corner, yee'll see it, but it doesn't look much nowadays. The bishop at Lower Superior thought the expense of keeping a priest here full time was unwarranted, so in his wisdom he took the priest away. The idea was to send him up when he was needed, but he overlooked one thing. The local villains! They took the lead from the roof at first, then they took the tiles. Chester Petersen found it when he came to read his sermon at the weekend. He's our lay preacher.'

'A very religious man!' Danny snorted.

'I'll admit he religiously spends her money, but I have no complaint against the man since he dropped the case against Connie and gave her the horse to boot!'

'It's a pony,' Danny corrected, as he had been corrected, and used it to change the subject. 'How long will it take for the letter to England to arrive?'

'I would allow two weeks to be sure, unless yee want it to go by airmail?'

'No, the boat will do. I don't trust planes.'

It was Hamish's turn to snort.

'I can see I am going to have to take yee in hand!'

Danny held up both hands, palms forward in supplication.

'I know you think it is stupid, but that is up to me, isn't it?' he replied.

'Yee and yee're new friends!' Hamish added.

'I can see you are not going to let go of this, so I'm off! If I don't see you before, I'll see you at the christening.'

'Talking of christenings, are yee going to have a go in our "name the baby" competition?' Hamish asked.

'How much?'

'One dollar, but it is in a good cause.'

'Don't tell me, a new roof for the church?'

'That, and our own priest to live there. The two go hand in hand or it is a waste of time putting on the new roof,' Hamish replied. 'It is hard to understand their thinking really. When the plate was passed round, it came back well filled, but it all went to the bishop and he still takes away the priest!'

Danny thought about Callum and Connie, and wrote two names down in the space provided, then walked off to see the deserted church. The road past the office was overgrown, and it was obvious that no vehicle had driven up it for a long time. When he turned the corner and pushed through the shrubbery, he found a quaint old church with rotting timbers on the roof.

He looked at it from where he stood, then started to walk round it. He was surprised by a path which led from the trees to the side door of the church on the other side. It had obviously been used. He walked to the door and opened it. A flickering light caught his eye, and he walked in, only to hear another door slam. There was no wind to make it slam, and Danny walked through, past a burning candle to the door and looked outside. Footprints led away from the church, and he followed them until they just seemed to stop. He returned to the church and looked inside. The candle on the altar still flickered. Someone had come from the forest to light a candle. He let it burn and went in search of Hamish. When he eventually found him, he was eating at Hester's.

'There was someone in the church when I went in there, Hamish,' he announced.

'I bet you didn't see him,' Hester replied, before Hamish could.

'No, just a slamming door, footprints which stopped at the edge of the forest, and a lit candle.'

'That'll be Klondyke Bill,' Hester explained. 'Today is the first of November. He lights a candle in there every first of November, but for the life of me I never found out why! Are you eating Danny?'

'What's on the menu?' he asked.

'Menu indeed! Stew, stew, or more stew!'

'I'll have some stew then, please.'

'A good choice, I'm sure,' Gaston said from the doorway. 'I'll try some too, Hester.'

He sat at the table to wait, and Annette brought out a teapot on a tray, already covered with a tea cosy.

'Thank you, Annette.'

'It's okay. Mum told me to bring it,' she replied. 'Not that I didn't want to, mind.'

After a good meal, Danny walked back with Hamish.

'I'll have to add this Klondyke Bill to my list. Things are getting worse instead of better,' he complained.

'No, he's been cleared. That's Selwyn,' Hamish replied, and walked off to his store.

Danny followed to look for a christening present for Connie's baby, and a birthday present for Red, but as he put his choice of christening present on the counter, with a camera for Red, Hamish pointed to a list on the wall. There were twenty presents all ticked off, including his choice!

'I take it the camera is not for the baby?'

'No, for Red's birthday. Anything in here that they might have missed?' he asked.

'Nary a thing,' Hamish replied. 'That baby is going to have a lot of friends.'

'Can you copy that list? I'll drive into Timberline or Lower Superior and have a look there.'

Hamish unpinned the list and photocopied it. Danny tucked it into his pocket and drove off. Timberline was a waste of time, and Lower Superior was not a lot better. In the end, he bought a rocking horse. It was too big now, but he would grow to fit it, and he was tired of tramping round the shops. On his way back, he dropped it off at their cottage and stopped for a mug of tea with Connie.

'I hear your coffee is improving?' Connie said, when she sat opposite him. 'John Mulroon dropped off something from the Mounties for baby.'

Until it was named, she was going to call it baby, then choose his names and see who was nearest. The list of names might even influence them in their choice.

'I've paid my dollar,' Danny said, holding up his folded ticket. 'He looks like a Fothergill Maclaughland to me.'

'It certainly has a ring to it,' Connie replied with a laugh. 'I hear you are looking into these killings?'

'The grapevine works well round here, so at least the killer will know I am on his trail.'

'You think it is someone local?'

'I am not allowed to say anything which might cause a lynch mob or vigilantes.'

Connie sighed.

'It looks like college is out of the question now,' she moaned.

'Why? I don't think you will have any trouble finding a baby sitter round here.'

'It's not that. I thought that when it was born, I would hate it, but I don't, I adore it! He's so beautiful, and Callum is over the moon.'

'Are you planning to tell him who the father is?'

'As far as I am concerned, he is the father and that is an end of it,' Connie replied stubbornly.

'People who bury their head in the sand are likely to get their backside bit,' Danny warned.

Connie gave Danny a sharp look, but before she could speak, the baby started crying.

'I'll leave you to it,' Danny said, and headed for the door while Connie went in to see why her son was crying.

Danny was not a great lover of arguments. He stopped outside long enough to inspect the slope behind the cottage which Callum was planning to turn into a ski slope. Skiing was something Danny had yet to try.

The day of the christening came, and the boy was named Conrad Callum Mclaughland. Danny was amazed. He had never won a competition in his life, but they were his choice of names. He thought of a name which started with C and was unusual. The prize money was halved between him and the church fund, and he was surprised by the amount he was given. He thought of giving it to the church, but as Petersen was the lay preacher, he dismissed the idea. In the end, he split it in two and gave half to Kate when he went to Red's birthday party, despite her objections. The other half he gave personally to Trailer Collins' widow. She had three children to bring up on her own now.

On the eighth of November, the first snow fell. Not like the blizzard he had been greeted with last year, just a thin coating of snow on the ground as it snowed steadily all day. Danny drove to Turnround to take over from Made who wanted to go home before Rosie left for work. Marcus was there, but he was taking no chances until the killer was caught. Danny walked into the office after stamping the snow off his boots.

'Anything going on, Made?'

'Not a thing. It's as quiet as the grave.'

'Will I have time to call into the clinic on the twentieth to see Chief?'

'Go to the garage. The clinic is closed for the winter,'

Made replied, as he threw on his coat. 'He's always at the garage.'

When Made had gone, Danny settled down to wait, and as he waited he started to think. Had he missed the fact that the clinic closed for the winter, or was it Dr Amos' clinic they were talking about? If he had the note here, he could phone the number on it to see just where the clinic moved to during the winter, for the vain old ladies to have their faces lifted, stretched or whatever they had done. He had to wait now until Phil came in to take over from him. The phone did not ring and the only visitor was Hamish with some teabags. When Phil did arrive, Danny tarried long enough to be polite, then he was on his way home. He took note of the number on the paper and dialled it.

'St Margaret's Hospital. How may I be of assistance?' a woman's voice answered.

'I am trying to contact Dr Amos' clinic,' Danny replied.

'Dr Amos holds his clinic here during the winter. If you tell me where you are, I will tell you what dates have been put aside for your area.'

'No, I already have that information, thank you.'

Danny replaced the receiver. Now he understood the overnight bit. Most of Dr Amos' patients were well past their sell by dates, and a drive home straight after might kill them, thus killing the goose which lays his golden egg. Plus, he probably charged well for the overnight stay, thereby making even more money. No wonder Chief had not repeated his sample yet. He sat in front of his blazing log fire, a mug of tea in his hand, and started thinking about Kate. He could always drop in to see them even though it was late in the day. He knew he would always be welcome, but he ruled out the idea. He went to bed at ten o'clock after walking Captain Webb. Soon it would be time to take him back to where he found him to make his own way in the world.

At two o'clock in the morning, he woke and, try as he might, something would not let him sleep. He eventually gave up and walked into the mine room. It was cold but he hardly noticed. The note was pinned to the board with four dates on it. If Margaret Joliff stayed overnight in hospital, what did Chief do? He could hardly sleep in their car. He wrote Jeremy Julian Joliff on a card and pinned it on the board as a possible suspect. He could not rule out anyone until they were cleared. Chief was local and, if the dates coincided with the visits to the hospital, it would leave him alone and in Lower Superior where the first girl was taken from. If he checked with the hospital, and the dates did not coincide, then he would take Chief's name down again. Was it possible he took the first girl as a protest against his overbearing mother, but when they did not catch him he started to plan his next victims? Danny yawned. It was all ifs and buts. If he took his idea to the police, he would probably lose some friends as they all liked Chief. When he got back into bed, he fell asleep straight away.

Morning found him sitting in the office, waiting for Made to come in. More snow had fallen overnight, and winter was well and truly here. Made stamped the snow off his boots and walked in.

'Any news?' he asked.

'No, and as they say, no news is good news.'

'My Jeep needs filling up, so I thought, as you wanted to see Chief, you could kill two birds with one stone,' Made suggested.

'I'll do it now just in case it gets busy round here.'

'Don't hold your breath,' Made replied.

Danny drove to the filling station in Made's Jeep and filled it up. Normally he would sign and they would pass pleasantries before he went, but this time he thought he might say more.

'Morning Chief. I see you are still tied to your till. Had any chance to give another sample yet?'

'Not yet, Danny. You know Ma likes to work me to death, but then I don't suppose many have come forward with the people round here?'

'Quite a few have as I understand it. The sooner you do, the shorter the list will become. Maybe you can do it when you take your mother to the hospital on the twentieth?'

'You never know! I have to go to the good doctor's winter venue which is the hospital. It's the only time I get to drive my toy in daylight. Ma doesn't like to travel after dark.' He pointed to a camper van parked on the forecourt. 'They even let me sleep in it in the hospital car park if I want.'

Danny sat in the Jeep thinking. If he could find out the past winter dates, it would either clear Chief or put his name at the top of the list. If he was the one, the twentieth would see the end of another young girl. He drove to the hospital but they were not very helpful. Doctor patient confidentiality stopped them looking at her notes, and no one knew the dates for last year. He drove to the police station and sought out John Mulroon, a good friend of Chief.

'I am trying to find out when Dr Amos held his winter clinics for this area last winter, but no one can find out,' he announced.

'Important, is it?' John asked.

'Just part of the picture I am building, and you never know how important a piece of a jigsaw is until you fit it!'

'See Greta in the clinic. She never throws anything away, puts them in the cellar just in case she can re-use them.'

'The clinic is shut until summer.'

'I'll give you her address. It's only just round the corner from the clinic. Do you think there is a connection? Winter is here, and I would like not to have to go searching in freezing conditions for any more little bodies.'

'Only ifs and buts, I'm afraid. As soon as I have something tangible, you will be the first to know.'

Danny's radio burped.

'Where the hell is my sodding Jeep! Over,' Made yelled.

'Just on my way back with it, over,' Danny replied. 'I'll be in touch,' he said to John as he hurried out.

When he stopped in front of the office, Made was waiting for him.

'Did you have to refine it yourself?' he asked. 'Hell, there's only half a tank left! I hope it was important, more important than me being late for my lunch.'

Danny climbed out.

'Won't know for sure until later, sorry.'

'Well, you get the office for the rest of the day for your trouble,' Made replied. 'I'll get some food sent over.'

He roared off up the square, throwing snow out behind him. Danny walked in and sat down. Back to boredom. Gaston's lorry pulled up across the square, and Danny saw Kate step down in her red cape. Ten minutes later she walked over carrying a basket.

'See anything you like, Danny?' she asked, coquettishly, from the doorway.

'That depends on what is in the basket,' Danny replied.

'I'll be taking the basket back in a moment,' she warned.

'In that case. Yes, I see somebody wrapped in red who I admire greatly,' he replied.

'That's better.' She walked in and closed the door. 'Hester told me you had to work through lunch so I thought I'd keep you company.'

'A welcome sight indeed. I'm sorry I haven't been around for a while.'

They ate the food, talking in between mouthfuls, then Kate made drinks, tea for him and coffee for her. One thing led to another, and when talk turned to the New Year dance and their first kiss, they decided to refresh their memories. Soon, kissing led to petting and heavy petting, until they moved into the rear office and made love on the desk. Papers were strewn everywhere, but they did not care. With passion spent, they dressed, and Danny started to clear up. Kate helped for a while, but she had to make sure she caught a ride back with the children on Bob's school bus. As she walked past Hester's, Hester held up her hand with the thumb pointing up, then turned it to point down. Kate held up both hands with the thumbs up!

During the rest of the afternoon, Danny finished tidying the office and sat back at the desk. Then a plume of smoke caught his attention and made him walk outside. The school was empty now as the bus had long since gone so where was the smoke coming from. He donned his snow shoes, picked up his radio, and walked down to investigate, only to see smoke and flames pouring from the clinic.

'Damn!' he hissed.

Before he could do anything, Greta arrived.

'I've called the firefighters, but it looks pretty bad, doesn't it?' she asked.

'It does, I'm afraid,' Danny answered.

Made roared up in his Jeep.

'Anyone inside?' he asked.

'Shouldn't be,' Greta answered.

'Then we wait for the fire brigade,' Made replied. 'No point in risking life just for property.'

Danny stood watching. The flames were fierce and, although he wanted to see a list, he did not fancy going in there or going against Made's orders. As he watched it burn, he wondered, was it an accident or was it deliberate?

'I might have caused that, indirectly,' he said quietly to Made.

Made led him away out of earshot of the gathering crowd.

'How do you mean?' he asked.

'It's still ifs and buts, but I might have trod on the right toes this time. We won't know until we find out if it was arson.'

'I think I have the right to know,' Made replied angrily. 'I am your boss, and I do have a daughter who is at risk!'

'I can help a bit. If I am right, and I may not be! Then a little girl is going to meet her maker after spending an evening with the killer on the twentieth, so you make sure you stay home with her that night!'

'What are you going to do about it?'

'That depends. Can I have the twentieth off?'

'You've got it.'

'Then I shall be keeping an eye on my suspect. If a girl

does go missing, I will be there to stop him, I hope. If he's not the one, I will just be wasting my time! I'll need a different Jeep.'

'Take one from Hamish's, and leave yours in there out of sight. Just make sure you get the bastard!'

'I hope it's that easy.'

They watched as the firefighters tackled the fire. They were more concerned for the school than the clinic, which they thought was already beyond saving. The hoses soon had it under control, but Danny realised that he was not likely to find his list in the remnants of the flooded cellar. The two of them returned to the office, and Made walked into his office at the back.

'What's been going on?' Made asked, walking back out of his office.

'How do you mean?' Danny asked in reply.

'My desk is tidy! My desk is never tidy, so what's been going on?'

'I was bored so I tidied up a little,' Danny lied.

'Did Kate help?' he asked with a little mischievous grin, and closed the door.

Danny smiled.

'I might have known, in this place,' he said, more to himself than to Made, but then raised his voice. 'I'm surprised we didn't have an audience.'

'It depends whether you turned off the surveillance tape,' Made replied, through the closed door.

'You might be able to sell it. It's got a good view of the inside of my hat!' Danny replied.

On the morning of the twentieth, Danny was up by five a.m. and drove to the garage, intent on following Chief to the hospital. He was in a four by four borrowed from Callum. As he rarely drove it, it would not be quickly recognised.

When he arrived, the camper was gone and Danny's heart sank. Had he been outguessed? He went to the hospital and drove round the car park. There were no campers there. Was he early, or was he late? Too late! He decided to ask about Margaret Joliff as if he was a friend. The news was bad, she was in her room waiting for treatment. Apparently they had misread the appointment time, and she was well early. She would be staying the night.

This meant Chief was free to roam until the morning, and if he was the killer he had someone in his sights. Danny felt sick. It was possible that Chief was back to open the garage, and not the killer, or he might even have a girlfriend somewhere waiting for him. In fact, he could be anywhere doing anything to anyone, and Danny could do nothing to stop him. He had the map with him, which showed where the girls had been left each time. The first one over the river, the rest close to the park. There was one area which had not yet been used. It was a large area but surely the Mounties had worked that one out. It could be staked out in some way but the killer would also know that.

He sat and thought for a long time before he turned towards Turnround. The garage was open when he drove by, with no sign of the camper. If I was the killer, where would I put the next victims? He drove home and mulled it over, drinking mugs of tea and munching biscuits.

By nightfall he had come to a decision. The same place he had put the first one, to rub their noses in it. If he drove round the area of the River Road up Bridge Road, along the Through Road and back down the River Road, he might see something if he was lucky. The snow would be the key thing. If it snowed and covered today's tracks, then stopped, he could see when something had gone down the road and investigate, but since when was the Canadian weather kind! It was the drowning man clutching at a straw but he was going to try it.

At midnight, he parked on the Through Road in sight of the junction of the Bridge Road. Any vehicle which passed would be followed discreetly to see where it went and what it did, if anything.

At one in the morning, it started to snow, by two it had stopped. He was surprised by the number of cars on this road. He followed each one as far as the River Road, and when they passed it, as they all did, he returned to his waiting point.

By four in the morning, he was cold and feeling very foolish. A camper passed him, and he followed it. The camper drove by the River Road but there were tracks going down it! He turned down the road and followed the tracks until they pulled in to the side of the road. Danny investigated by torch light, but the sign in the snow showed why the man had stopped, even to the point of writing his name 'TOM' in the snow.

He drove in a circle, down to the Bridge Road, intending to drive up to the Through Road, but he could plainly see the camper's tracks going across the bridge, with another set of tracks leading up the Bridge Road. He followed them. At the top, they turned right, travelled to the River Road and turned into it. As he drove it started to snow again.

'Not yet, dammit!' he cursed.

Captain Webb lifted his head and opened one eye before snuggling down again in the pile of blankets. They were well prepared. The tracks stopped again but in a different place. Danny climbed out with his torch to see what this one had written, but he could see snow shoe tracks going into the forest. They were overlaid with the returning tracks which were not as deep, meaning that the person was carrying something or someone. Danny's heart froze.

He clipped on his snow shoes, threw one of the blankets over his shoulder and followed the tracks. Where they ended, a set of prints made by small bare feet started. He followed them to a tree, where they had sought shelter and warmth. After a moment's hesitation, he pulled the branches away. Under the tree was a naked red-headed girl curled up in the same position as the first girl he had found. This time though, the little girl turned her head and looked at him pleadingly. It was Annette Foy! He scooped her up and wrapped her in the blanket he had over his shoulder, and carried her to the four by four. At least the four by four was faster than his Jeep.

Before he drove away, he pressed the small counter to zero it, then he drove to the hospital; only stopping to read the mileage at the bridge. As he drove, he was working out what to do. First he had to make sure she did not die. Secondly, he had to keep this quiet in case she could not name her attacker, and that way they would know where the next one would be dumped. It meant that he could not tell anyone, but he must find a way to tell Hester. It would be too monstrous to do otherwise! He had no radio with him, as Chief listened to the police on his radio. This had to be kept off the radio and, to do that, he needed the

Mountie who had given him the file to read. Should he point the finger at Chief, or could this be coincidence? If he pointed the finger and got it wrong, it was not going to help anyone. He pulled into the car park, looking for Chief's camper, but it was not there. He stopped in front of the entrance and carried her inside. As he walked, and nurses came over, he was barking orders.

'I want an isolation ward, and no one must know she is here!'

He put her on a trolley and the nurses took over. She was wheeled away. Danny pinned the duty doctor to a wall.

'She can identify the killer if you can save her. God help her if you can't! However, we know where he is going to put the next victim, but only if he doesn't find out that she has been found.'

'I get the point, now let me do my job! I'll leave you to phone the Mounties. There is a phone in there you can use.' He pointed to a nearby office.

Danny sat in the office. He was trembling. How did he tell the Mounties without letting the cat out of the bag? He waited for an answer and asked for John Mulroon.

'He is not available,' the Mountie on the other end replied. 'Can I help?'

'No! I very much doubt it. Can I speak to Inspector Gosfar?'

The phone went dead for a minute.

'Gosfar speaking.'

'Danny Turner here. I have just found a hit and run victim, who is hurt badly but still alive. Can you come down here personally?'

'I am a bit busy at present. Another little girl has gone

missing and I am co-ordinating the search.'

'The victim has red hair, and I think you need to come,' Danny insisted.

There was a pause.

'Do you know this person?'

'Yes, quite well.'

'I hope I am putting two and two together and not making six!' he replied, and the phone went dead.

Seven minutes later, Inspector Gosfar walked in. Danny steered him to an empty room.

'It is imperative that this does not go out over any radios,' Danny urged.

'What doesn't go out over the radio?'

'I found Annette Foy this morning and she is still alive!' She is in a bad way, but if she pulls through she might be able to finger her attacker.'

'You have been watching too many gangster movies, Mr Turner. What if she cannot finger her attacker?'

'We will know where he is going to dump the next victim, and I think I can give you a date as well.'

'Good work. Barry chose well, but what about Mrs Foy?'

'I'll find a way to tell her and keep it quiet. I don't know how yet, but I hope something will come to me.'

'Why no radios?'

'I have no proof yet, but if it is the man I think it is, he scans the radio while you are searching, probably enjoying their struggle and their pain.'

'I can leave the search to take its course, then call it off. Believe me, anything they say will come right from the heart! You go and see Mrs Foy, and I'll make sure I stop up all the leaks at this end.'

Danny walked to the door.

'Well done, Daniel Turner!' the Inspector called out.

Danny turned back.

'If I am right, I could have saved her from his attentions all night. I could shoot myself for that,' he replied.

'I'd rather you didn't, you are far too useful,' the Inspector called after him.

Danny drove back to Turnround in the four by four without seeing Chief's camper. There he found a very distraught Hester Foy.

'She's all I got!' Hester said over and over again.

Rosie Brickman was there with her. The rest were out searching. He knew he had to keep it from Rosie, and that was bad enough.

'Can you show me her room? It might help,' Danny said quietly.

'I can do that,' Rosie replied quickly. 'She has been through enough.'

'No Rosie, only Hester has the information I need,' Danny argued. 'Come on Hester. It might help me find her.'

Hester walked woodenly to the back room which served as Annette's bedroom. Danny closed the door and whispered in her ear.

'I've found her, and she is alive, but I need to keep it a secret from everyone.'

'She's al...' Hester started to repeat, but loudly, and Danny had to stifle the rest.

'Yes, but I need you to whisper.'

'Where is she?' Hester whispered.

'St Margaret's Hospital in Lower Superior, but you can't just go and see her. It has to be kept a secret until we find out if she can identify her attacker. Have you a relative we can go to, who can make out you don't want to see anyone because you are too upset?'

'I have a sister in Fort Thompson I can go to. She will keep our secret.'

'If Annette did not see who it was, or can't remember anything, we will at least know where the next one will be left. If he finds out, he'll just put them somewhere else and my luck will have been for nothing.'

'What do I do?'

'Be really upset and I'll drive you to your sister's now. That way you can be at the hospital fairly soon.'

'Upset! I can be upset! Thank you Danny.'

Hester gave a command performance, so much so that Rosie turned on Danny for upsetting her more. Hester then insisted that Danny drove her to her sister's immediately.

Later, after a quick talk with her sister, Hester drove to the hospital to be with Annette, making sure she was not seen going in.

As he drove home, Danny reflected on the killer's latest choice. Was this personal as she was a friend? He parked by the store, collected his Jeep, and drove home for a well-earned rest. It was just his luck that as he drove there, it was decided that he should be called out to help with the search, and he had to be seen to search diligently!

When he finally returned home, he found his duvet missing! He scratched his head, pulled Connie's duvet out of his bulging cupboard, threw it on the bed with no cover on it, and crawled into his bed. For what was left of the night, he slept like a log!

CHAPTER 16

DANNY was woken from a deep sleep in the morning by a hammering on his front door. He looked at his watch and it was only six thirty.

'Not again, I've only just got to bed!' he thought, and stumbled out of bed. Captain Webb had more sense and stayed put.

When he opened the door, two Mounties stood there. He did not know either of them.

'Daniel Turner?' one asked.

'That's me.'

'We need you to accompany us to the station.'

'What the hell for?'

'All in good time. Can you put some clothes on, please?'

Danny dressed, and he was taken to the police station, but to an office he had never been to before.

'Please sit,' the officer behind the desk ordered.

Danny sat.

'Interview started at seven twenty hours on the twenty first of November. Present are Chief Inspector Blunt, Inspector Harris, and Sergeant Dubois. You are Daniel Turner of the mine works Turnround?'

'I am.' Danny was bemused. He did not understand what was going on.

'Where were you between the hours of six p.m. yesterday evening and six a.m. the next morning?'

There were two other officers present, and the tape was running. The wall beside him had a large glass mirror which might well be two-way, with an unknown number of people listening. There was no way he could tell the truth and keep it quiet. Obviously Inspector Gosfar was as good as his word, and even these did not know about Annette.

'I was out and about,' Danny replied. 'Why?'

'I'll ask the questions, thank you. Where were you out and about?'

'I can't answer that with all these ears listening. What is this all about?'

'Did you know that another little girl is missing?'

'Yes. I ought to. I only finished searching for her three hours ago!'

'You should have searched where you dumped her so we could give her a decent burial,' Inspector Harris retorted. 'You should be taken out and shot!'

'Inspector Harris is leaving the room,' Chief Inspector Blunt said haughtily. 'I will talk to you later.'

'One down,' Danny thought.

'I need to know where you were last night,' the Chief Inspector said, raising his voice.

Danny thought for a moment. If he told him where he was, and Annette died or could not point out her attacker, then the area might be searched, which would put the killer off. He might put the next one somewhere else, and that was not an option.

'I took my wolf for a walk round Timberline,' he answered evenly.

'A wolf is a wild animal, not a pet.'

'I know that, and I hope to return him to the wild before next winter, when he is big enough,' Danny replied, less evenly.

'Sergeant, inform the relevant people and get them to collect this animal. The sooner it is in kennels, the better,' the Chief Inspector said haughtily.

'I think I need to make a phone call now,' Danny snapped. He was very close to punching this man's lights out, and that would be more than frowned upon. 'And I mean now.'

'This interview suspended at seven thirty-five hours.' He turned off the tape. 'Take Mr Turner to a telephone, and then lock him up.'

Danny telephoned Kate.

'Hello Kate, it's Danny. Listen carefully. I have been locked up in connection with Annette's disappearance. Tell Hamish, and get Red to collect Captain Webb now, or it will be too late.'

'Are they mad?' she asked.

'Yes, quite mad, I think!'

'Is there anything else I can do?' Kate asked.

Danny considered asking her to ring Inspector Gosfar, but what could he say if he was asked about Danny's whereabouts by his superiors? Best play it by ear as long as the wolf was in safe hands.

'Bake me a cake with a file in it,' he joked.

'It's not funny,' Kate replied. 'You are the only one who might catch him, and you can't do that in prison.'

'I know, but there is not a lot I can do about it at the moment. Now get things moving or it will be too late!'

'Bye Danny. Love you,' Kate said, and the phone went dead.

Danny was locked in a cell to ponder his next move.

Red was despatched to Danny's cabin on Harry. He sat watching from the trees as animal welfare officers looked in the cabin and surrounding area for the wolf standing next to him.

'Come on, Captain Webb, time to go, I think,' Red whispered, and he rode away with the wolf following.

Kate phoned Hamish who nearly exploded. He took the details and ran over to the office. Made listened intently before he spoke.

'He needs a lawyer first. Do you know a good one?' he asked.

'Aye, I do.'

'Use that phone and call him,' Made ordered. 'I'll drive in and see him if they'll let me. He was working on something last night, and he is not likely to have an alibi.'

'What can yee do?'

'I put store in my gut feelings, and I don't think for one moment that he has anything to do with Annette's disappearance, so I'll say he was with me.'

'Is that wise?'

'Since when have I done anything wise?'

Hamish paused to think for a while.

'Don't milk it!' Made warned.

'Yee married Rosie.'

'I still don't know yet if that was wise,' Made replied. 'Now get on the phone.' He walked to the door. 'It looks like you are in charge again, but this time I'm paying you!'

'Yee know I won't accept it, yee charlatan!'

Made winked before he closed the door. While Made left for the police station, Hamish was left in charge of the on-going search for Annette Foy. Every able-bodied man and several women were out searching, but they held out little hope of finding her.

Made drove straight to the police station where a crowd of reporters had already gathered outside like a flock of vultures. He walked up to the desk and waited until the Mountie on duty there had finished what he was writing.

'How can I help?' he asked politely.

Made did not know him, and he thought he knew all of them. This one must be here to help out with the search.

'I'm Made Brickman, and I'm here to see Daniel Turner,' Made announced.

'Are you his lawyer?'

'No! I'm his boss!'

'Take a seat over there, and I'll see what I can do,' the Mountie said, indicating a row of seats.

Made sat, but waiting was not his strong point. At regular intervals, he returned to the desk to see what was going on, and each time was fobbed off with the same answer. Just wait. When an hour had passed, he walked up and slammed his fist on the desk.

'I want to see someone in charge!' he said through clenched teeth. 'And don't tell me to sit down again. I'm standing here until I see someone.'

The Mountie phoned through, and an Inspector walked to the outer office. Made instinctively disliked him.

'What is all the noise about?' he asked.

'I have been waiting to see Daniel Turner for over an hour now,' Made almost shouted.

The doors opened and a young, confident-looking man walked in.

'Graham Gorton to see Mr Turner,' he announced.

'Are you his lawyer?' the Mountie asked.

'Yes I am, and I want to see him now,' Graham replied.

'Come this way, Mr Gorton,' the Inspector said, turning away from Made. 'I will show you in, and I will let you know when Mr Gorton is finished with your employee, Mr Brickman.'

Made returned to his seat to wait, but this time in a happier frame of mind. At least he knew something was being done.

Graham was shown into Danny's cell. He held out his hand, and Danny took it as soon as he recognised him. He was the same lawyer who had defended Connie.

'I hope you can help,' Danny said sadly.

'So do I. The first thing is to get you out of here without delay, but bear with me as I haven't had a chance to go over their case.'

Graham sat and read the file.

'According to the Chief Inspector, Wilson killed the other girls, and this is a copycat murder of which you are the chief suspect.'

'Well, he got one word right, but I am not at liberty to tell you which,' Danny replied.

'Why not?'

Danny sighed.

'I had it all worked out, but now it is in tatters. To clear myself I will probably cause more girls to be killed, and I can't do that!

'If you can't help me, I can't help you,' Graham replied. 'Where were you last night?'

'That I can't answer, and I know all about client confidentiality. It's just not worth the risk,' Danny replied. 'How long can they hold me before they have to charge me?'

'That depends. If they apply for an extension, you could be here most of the week,' Graham replied. 'But looking at the evidence at hand, I think they will charge you before too long. Then you are here indefinitely.'

'What about bail?'

'Unlikely, to say the least.'

'If they found her, a blood test would clear me,' Danny retorted.

'That I do not doubt, but that would be after the snow thaws,' Graham warned. 'Instead, you could tell me where you were and what you were doing.'

'There's no chance of that at this time,' Danny said evenly.

'You are worse than she was,' Graham complained. 'It is hard to do my best when my hands are tied.'

'I know, but it is an on-going situation and from what I can gather, it is in good hands.'

'That doesn't help you.'

'I will say my piece sometime in December, if my memory serves me correctly. I will only start talking then because I have to, and until then my lips are sealed.'

'That does not make any sense,' Graham cried. 'Did you kill this girl?'

'No!'

'Did you abduct her?'

'No!'

'Then why won't you speak? You know I am bound by client confidentiality.'

'It is difficult. One word out of place and it could all go pear-shaped. Then it would all have been for nothing.'

'So you are willing to rot here in this cell until December?'

'That is about the size of it.'

'Well I must admit I don't understand, but you are my client and I will go along with whatever you say. Made Brickman is out there waiting to see someone. Can he help?'

'Only if he thinks I am innocent.'

'Why would he be here otherwise?'

Danny smiled.

'You see what's about, don't you?' Danny said seriously.

'Most of the time. What did you say to Petersen to make him back off?'

'Client confidentiality?'

'Of course.'

I was going to tell his wife who the father of Connie's baby was.'

It took a minute for Graham to put two and two together.

'And it worked,' he admitted. 'If only I had had that information.'

'I didn't! I was just guessing!'

'A good guess. Can I raise a file on it for later, just in case?'

'I take it I get a bill?'

'Of course.'

'Raise your file. I don't mind staying in here for a while, but I want to be out when our man strikes next.'

'I'll see what I can do. Now, I expect they want an

interview, but remember, last time you thought you didn't say much. This time you do nothing but nod or shake your head if I give you the go-ahead.'

'You're the boss.'

Danny sat at the table with the tape running while the Chief Inspector asked questions, and Graham fielded them without involving him. According to the Mounties, the MO was different, but they were not saying in what way. Danny opened his mouth and closed it so many times, he had a jaw ache by the time he was taken back to his cell. Nothing had been divulged, but he was still in the cell. Graham had long since gone. Danny was alone. The cell door swung open.

'I hear you like a little chess?' Hugh Gosfar said.

'Some moves take a long time,' Danny moaned.

'All in a good cause,' Hugh replied, and set up the chess board. 'She is out of danger, but she remembers nothing of the attack, blanked it out completely. Probably for the best, and I do not propose to try and dig into her mind for information.'

'Which means I am stuck in here.'

'Maybe not. I met Made Brickman outside. He was cooling off, and he swears you were with him during that night, drinking!'

'He said that?'

Hugh Gosfar nodded.

'If he sticks to it, you will soon be out of here, but we will have to steer clear of the reporters or you will be on the front page.'

'Is Hester still with her?'

'Yes, but they are going to move her to a private nursing home fairly soon to make security easier.'

They played chess as they talked.

'What was the different MO?' Danny asked.

'The girl went out to fill the salt cellars. She was told to do it earlier, and obviously failed to do so, although she complained that she had done it. She never came back!'

'Then it must be him! She knew him, but why would she go with him?'

'Who?'

Danny made his next move before speaking.

'The killer. You were the one who said not to go off half-cocked and cause vigilante action.'

'Would it cause vigilante action?'

'No! Not many people would believe me.'

'Who would?'

Danny thought for a moment.

'Barry Jaimeson would! He tu...'

'He tu... what?'

'Nice try, but I am the only one who will know my suspicions until I have proof.'

'Check mate,' Hugh said slyly.

Danny looked at the board and knew he was right.

'You obviously knew, or guessed, when he would strike, and got the area right where he would put her. Do you know the next date?' Hugh asked.

'It's on the board in my cabin.'

'No, it's on the board in the Chief Inspector's office, but I can hardly take it out. You might want to know that a picture of Annette Foy, naked, was on your board as the first victim this year.'

'I underestimated him,' Danny said, as he set up the chess pieces. 'I won't do that again.'

'Surely we must find enough evidence if we pulled him in?' Hugh asked.

'Only the blood test, and he doesn't have to give one again, maybe if I accidentally hit him with my fist and you used your handkerchief to wipe away the blood we could get one?'

'A judge would throw that out immediately,' Hugh replied. 'They have more rights than the children they kill!'

'Any suggestions?'

'Try the pawn gambit.'

'What, so you can win again?'

'No, so you can make a game of it!'

Danny sat looking at the board, all set up and ready to play.

'Will I get my board back?'

'No, but I can supply copies of all the information on it.'

'I will need a copy of everything.'

'How did the picture of the latest victim get on the board?'

'My door is never locked, and he knows where I live! Do I need to say more?'

'So he knows?'

'Yes! That's why he burnt down the clinic. The dates there might have proved his guilt.'

'Greta Goodchild's house was burnt as well.'

'Is she all right?'

'No! She was in it at the time!'

'He's covering his tracks,' Danny sighed. 'He may stop killing.'

'No chance!' a voice replied from the doorway.

Danny looked up to see Barry Jaimeson.

'He has a taste for it! It's a bit like being an alcoholic. You get the urge, and that's it!' Barry added.

'Hello Barry,' Danny greeted him. 'What brings you to such an out of the way place?'

'I am here to do a profile on the killer, to help the Mounties get their man.'

'I always thought they did,' Danny replied.

'This one is causing them a bit of embarrassment,' Barry replied. 'But I hear you are helping them out.'

'From where I am sitting, it doesn't feel like it,' Danny grunted.

'Wheels are turning. The Inspector here has seen to that, but so far I do not know why.'

'And that is just how I want it,' Danny responded.

'I'm glad to hear it,' Barry replied. 'The other possibility was that the Inspector had lost his marbles!'

'The Chief Inspector thinks I have,' Hugh Gosfar replied. 'Any ideas to get Danny out? He's not much use in here!'

'Help is on hand. I saw Made Brickman outside. He was outside to cool off, and mad as hell. He's been trying to see you for over two hours. He's just been taken in to make a statement.'

'Who's minding the shop?' Danny asked.

'Hamish, as usual,' Barry replied. Made is going to make a statement that you were with him when Annette was taken.'

Danny looked up from the chess board.

'His idea!' Barry said, holding his hands up palm first. 'To be honest, I couldn't think of a better way but what reason would stop you from saying that in the first place?'

All three thought about it for a while, but no ideas came to mind. The chess continued, with Barry giving Danny advice, whether he wanted it or not.

'We could have been arranging a surprise for someone,' Danny said, holding a bishop in mid-air.

'And you were willing to go to prison to keep it quiet?' Hugh asked.

'You could have been so drunk you couldn't remember!' Barry suggested.

'Are you talking from experience?' Danny asked.

Barry smiled.

'Maybe,' he admitted.

'You could say you were waiting for your lawyer before you answered, and he told you to say nothing until he had all the facts,' Hugh added.

'That is just what he did say,' Danny replied. 'It's the best suggestion yet. At least it won't sink without trace as soon as it hits the water!'

'Do I get to know what is going on?' Barry asked.

Hugh looked at Danny, and Danny looked at him. There was a short pause before Danny spoke.

'What do you think?'

'Need to know only, is what we decided, Danny,' Hugh replied. 'But if you think it might help? I know you have a high opinion of Barry.'

'I'll tell you if I decide it is for the best, but not while I'm in here. You know the old saying, walls have ears!' Danny said decisively.

During the afternoon, Hugh Gosfar left, but Barry stayed and took over the chess from him. Graham Gorton arrived later in the day in response to a call from Chief Inspector

Blunt. Made had made a statement, and Danny was released, but there was a large crowd of people outside, some reporters, others wanting to get at the killer. Danny moved from the cell to an office to wait for the crowd to dissipate. Barry stayed and played more chess until they were both sick of the game.

Barry drove away from the police station, with Danny as his passenger, at two in the morning. It had taken that long for the crowd to go. Only a few reporters remained. Several flashes lit up the car as they drove away, but Danny was down out of sight.

'Don't they ever sleep,' Danny complained.

'No, they don't,' Barry replied. 'Do I get to know?'

'Did you know I was looking into the affair after I found the little girls?'

'When I arrived, I was shown your board.'

'Well, I had a hunch and followed it. It nearly didn't pay off but I found Annette before she died, and got her to hospital in time for them to save her.'

Barry whistled softly.

'She is alive? Can she point the finger?'

'No, but we know where the next one will be dumped, and we can nab him there when he drops her off. I hope to come up with a plan to stop him before things get that far, but to do that I will have to enlist the help of the Mounties, and that will be the hard bit.'

'Do I get to know the suspect's name?'

'Yes, but it is not for repeating. I have little or no proof, but if something should happen to me, someone else should know my thoughts. I think it is Jeremy Julian Joliff.'

'Well, I thought he was a loose cannon when I ruled

him out of this job, but I can see why you aren't going about telling everyone. He has a lot of friends, and his mother has a lot of clout! If you are mistaken, your name will be mud.'

'So what's new? I'll probably be in the papers tomorrow as Jack the Ripper, Canadian style!'

'No, no name has been released. I saw to that, but how did the picture of the latest victim get on your board. It certainly made a few hairs bristle in the station!'

'He must have put it there. He probably assumed I was out searching for Annette, and put it there early in the morning.'

'Bumping you off might be in his timetable as well, but then again he might be treating it as a game. Cat and mouse, but which one is which? I hear you built yourself a cabin.'

'Yes, in the quarry, surrounded by forest, just how I like it. Have you anywhere to stay?'

'I'm in a hotel. Expenses you know, but I will take a look at your handiwork.'

'The turning is about a mile along the road.'

As they approached the turning, there was a group of reporters with cameras at the ready. Barry drove straight past.

'Someone's leaked your name to the press,' Barry said. 'They are going to be everywhere. I'll take you back to my hotel.'

'No thanks. Just drop me off round the next bend. I can walk through the trees to my cabin.'

'I have some snowshoes in the boot, just in case I need to walk anywhere. You'd better use them.'

Barry stopped out of sight of the reporters, and Danny slipped the snowshoes on. With a wave of his hand, he was gone in case anyone drove by. He walked through the trees by moonlight making sure he was not seen. He approached the entrance to the quarry quietly, but there was no one about. He hurried to the cabin, and for once dropped the wooden bar, which served as a lock, in place. He did the same with the back door and went to bed. He did not want any nosy reporters disturbing his beauty sleep!

In the morning, Danny left without cooking breakfast. There were reporters about. He could see them, so he slipped past them and headed for Kate's. He needed some peace and quiet. As he neared the Walters' house, he started to think. 'What if they thought he had done it? What if they rejected him?'

His pace slowed, and he determined to turn back, but in front of him stood Red with Captain Webb.

'They're a right load of dick heads if you ask me!' Red declared. 'Mum was livid. It's a good job she couldn't get to the police station, she would have got herself arrested!'

As he got closer to Red, he could see he had been crying. He was crying for Annette and, although Danny knew she was alive, he could not tell him. He wanted to, but if word got out, the killer would either find her and kill her, or stop killing and go to ground hoping she could not remember anything. He climbed the fence and walked with Red up to the house. When Kate saw him she threw her arms round him and started to cry.

'Was it bad?' she asked when her tears had stopped.

'Bad enough, and now the cabin is surrounded by reporters.'

'You are welcome to stay here for as long as it takes,' she replied immediately.

'You can have my bed,' Red offered. 'I can sleep on the couch.'

Danny looked at the length of the couch.

'Thanks, I'll take you up on that,' he replied.

'Red can sleep anywhere, even at school,' Kate added.

'I didn't get much sleep, remember? I was listening to the police on our radio. I was hoping they would find her but they didn't, and now they've called off the search!' Red replied heatedly.

It was as if someone was turning a knife in Danny's stomach, but Danny just stood there and said nothing. When this was all over and they found out that he knew Annette was alive and did not tell them, they might not want to know him any more. If that were the case, he would go home and let them keep their sodding country!

'I take it you can drink a mug of tea?' Kate asked, bringing him back to the present.

'No thanks, I'll drink what the natives drink.'

'You want coffee?' Kate asked.

'Yes. Make it black and strong!'

He took a mouthful of the strong black coffee, with the entire Walters family watching.

'Needs some sugar, I reckon.' Danny put in two heaped spoonfuls of sugar, stirred it well, and tried again. 'Not bad! I can see why you drink it. It sure has a kick!'

CHAPTER 17

DANNY was still there a week later. He had only two callers, one was Callum with his post, a letter from England. The other was Inspector Gosfar. He needed the location of the spot where Annette had been found, but he only asked that when they were out of the house in the garden. Red was hostile towards the Inspector, and Kate had to rebuke him although she felt the same. When Danny got in the police car, Red was suspicious immediately, and ran to the car.

'Is he arresting you again?' he asked angrily, ready to 'have a go'.

'No, Mr Turner is helping us with our enquiries. No one thinks he is involved, but he is a very clever man and we would like his help,' the Inspector replied. He was going to mention a blood test, which would have cleared him, but if Red was clever he might put two and two together. It was obvious that Danny was not involved in the other deaths, so the only way a blood test could clear his name was if they had Annette's body. A press announcement about Danny, destined to get rid of the reporters from Danny's cabin, was quashed by Hugh Gosfar with the help of the Chief Inspector for the same reason. He had confided only enough information to the Chief Inspector to get his backing. Kate arrived a few seconds later in the same mood as Red.

'Where are you taking him?' she asked.

'To get me more clothes,' Danny replied. 'It's alright when you need a police escort for that! I won't be long.'

Red looked at Danny, but said nothing. The Inspector drove away and they watched until he was out of sight.

A mile down the road, another car started to follow them. It stayed with them when they turned onto the Bridge Road and again when they turned onto the Through Road. Danny saw the car but said nothing as it had two men in it. When they turned into the River Road it followed.

'I see you brought some help,' he said, when it became obvious that they were following them.

'I need someone to keep tabs on the place. We still have a radio silence about Annette and this place will go on the list. One will stay and the other will drive to get the rest of the unit.'

'How many are coming?' Danny asked.

'Ten altogether. I don't know how big the area is we are going to be watching.'

'You soon will. We are almost there.'

'A copy of your file is on the back seat.'

Danny looked down to see a thick file held together with an elastic band. He lifted it over the seat and opened it. The first thing he saw was a picture of Annette Foy, naked. Her hands were tied and she was laying on his missing duvet! The picture was taken in such a way as to just show the duvet and the victim.

'No wonder they were after my blood!' he declared.

'How do you mean?'

'That's my duvet she is lying on! It was missing when I returned that night to sleep.'

'No one told me,' Hugh Gosfar replied. 'He is trying to set you up. It was fortunate you found her.'

'It's a shame she can't point him out. Slow down, we are close to it.'

The terrain was different now, a snow plough had been through, and the side of the road was piled with snow. It was difficult to spot the exact place where he had found Annette.

'Damn. The snow plough has made it hard work,' Danny moaned. 'If it wasn't for the Mounties, I would have been here the next day.'

'Are you saying you can't find it?' Hugh asked.

'No, I can find it. Drive to the bridge, but leave your men here. We'll be coming back.'

Hugh stopped, and one of the men walked to his car.

'Wait here Jones, we'll be back.'

'Drive to the bridge. It was exactly 2.4 kilometres to the bridge when I drove off.'

They turned at the bridge, measured the distance back and stopped. Danny climbed out of the car and scrambled up the snow.

'This is the place. He carried her into the trees there, and dumped her about a hundred metres in.'

They donned snowshoes and walked into the trees, Danny looked under three trees, and under the last one there was a blood stain.

'This is where I found her.'

'Good! Jones, you suit up and stake this place out until the unit gets here. Wilson, you go to Mr Turner's cabin and get him anything he wants from it. Bring it back with you and we'll rendezvous on the Loggin Road.'

'Yes Inspector,' Wilson replied. Jones was already suiting up, to stay out here too long was to freeze to death unless you were well prepared!

Danny looked through the file for the slip with the dates he wanted, but found an A4 photocopy instead. He took the sheet out, then handed the file to the man by the window.

'Put this file back in my cabin, please,' Danny said. 'I don't really want pictures of dead girls falling on the floor when the children are about. Put it out of sight somewhere.'

'Yes, Mr Turner,' Wilson replied.

Danny and Hugh sat in the car for a while, and Danny looked at the dates.

'The next date should be the sixteenth of December, if I'm right,' he said, and put the folded paper in his pocket.

'I will have this place staked out around the clock from now on, just in case. I really want to meet this animal,' Hugh said, and wrote the date in his diary.

'On the afternoon of the fifteenth, I will tell you who I think is the killer, and I will want him followed to make sure another little girl doesn't go through the same experience as Annette. But they won't like it, believe me!'

When he had his clothes, Hugh drove Danny back to Kate's. Hugh stopped long enough for Danny to get out then drove away. He had things to do.

'Everything okay?' Kate said, when he walked in.

'Fine.' He sat down, and his letter was laid in front of him. He opened it and read it.

It was a long letter, covering Lucy's thoughts of him going with other women while she was still wed to him, and what she thought about husband stealers. The last bit read, 'It is obvious that as you are far away, your wedding vows mean nothing, so have it your way. I shall find myself someone who wants me for who I am, not for the children I might bear!' He read it several times. It was the same old Lucy. Now she was in town, he could picture her out dancing every night, but still trying to make him feel bad. The last line gave her away, 'Mother passed away last January.' If she written when it had happened, he would have tried to make it to the funeral, but she had not bothered.

'Bad news?' Kate asked.

'Might be good news, but I won't know for a while.'

'Is it from your wife?'

'Yes, I wrote to her. I told her I was sparking. I hope that was alright?'

'Is that a quaint old English saying?' she asked with a smile, then looked at the three faces nearby and all were smiling. 'It seems to be alright,' she replied.

'I'm sorry it is a shitty beginning.'

The children laughed.

'So am I. Just do what you have to do, to put this sick person in prison where he belongs.

Another week passed, and he remained with Kate and the children. As the date grew closer, he started pacing more and more. The Mounties finally released a statement removing Danny from their list of suspects, but without saying why. He walked back to his cabin through the trees and made another board. He found the file and pinned everything on it except Annette's picture. He felt happy knowing something the killer did not.

'You think you are so clever, you little shit, but I'll get you!' He had been mulling over what to say to the Mounties, but it was not going to be easy. He drove his Jeep back to Kate's. There was no reason to stay there now, but he was happy there and he could keep an eye on the girls.

The day before the killer was due to strike again, Danny took Kate to one side.

'Look after the girls, Kate, he will soon strike again.'

'They've been sleeping with me a lot since Seth died.'

'I hope to change that soon.'

Danny meant it would be safe for them to sleep in their own beds when he caught the killer, but the wicked smile on Kate's face told him she had taken it another way.

'Oh you will, will you? We'll see.'

'I meant... Oh never mind, just look after the girls. He is making this personal now, so it is likely that they might be his next target!'

'Over his dead body.' She patted their old rifle. 'It may have a broken stock but it still roars! You sound like you know who it is?'

'I haven't any proof, and to alert him would be to lose him. He isn't stupid.'

'Just you be careful and come back home,' she said, and closed the door behind him.

Danny stood outside the door. Home! Did she mean here? He climbed into his Jeep and drove to Lower Superior. When he passed the turn-off to his cabin, the junction was deserted. The reporters were nowhere to be seen. He expected it to be a stormy meeting, not so much with Hugh as with John who was one of Chief's friends. When he suggested Chief was the killer, with no tangible evidence to back it up, only a coincidence with one date, all hell might break loose but it had to be done! If not to catch Chief, then to clear his name. If he was wrong, he could always return to England, but if he did nothing and another girl was taken, he would never forgive himself. The police station was swarming with reporters, and he had to fight his way through them to get inside. He headed for John Mulroon's desk. It was only fair, he thought, that John should be told first. He was intercepted by Inspector Gosfar.

'Good morning, Danny. I hope you have come to divulge a name today?' Hugh asked.

'I have, but I thought John should know first.'

'You will be able to tell him about it as soon as we know what is going on. Come with me, please.'

They walked into the Chief Inspector's office.

'Good morning, Mr Turner,' the Chief Inspector said politely. 'Do take a seat. I understand from Inspector Gosfar that you have something to tell us.'

'How much does he know?' Danny asked, looking at Hugh.

'Need to know only!' Hugh replied. 'But now I think he needs to know. We are going to need a lot of man power if we are going to follow someone. I take it that is the idea, and pick him up when he has his next victim?'

Danny nodded.

'The night you wanted to know about Chief Inspector, I was not with Made getting drunk. I had tried to follow someone on slightly more than a hunch, but he was already gone. I tried to guess where the killer might dump his next victim. One area stood out like a sore thumb and I ruled that out. I chose the area where he left his first victim, and spent the night watching and following potential vehicles. When I returned to the spot where I had chosen to wait, after following one vehicle, I saw a set of tracks made by another vehicle, a set of tracks that I had not followed. I found deep snowshoe tracks leading away from the vehicle, and shallow ones returning. I followed the tracks and found Annette Foy. She was alive, so I hurried to St Margaret's Hospital with her and bound them to silence about her arrival. I then contacted Inspector Gosfar, and he took it from there.'

The Chief Inspector's eyes opened wide when he heard Annette was still alive, but he waited until Danny had stopped speaking.

'I take it she has not been able to name her abductor?' the Chief Inspector asked when Danny fell silent.

'No sir,' Hugh Gosfar replied. 'A complete blank.'

'And you have kept this under wraps up till now?'

'Yes sir. Complete radio silence about it. In fact, the only person who was told, who was not present when she was brought in, was Ms Foy, the girl's mother.'

The Chief Inspector looked from one to the other.

'Well, I think congratulations are in order. We obviously know where the next victim will be left, and I suppose it has been staked out by that special team you brought in, Hugh?'

'Yes sir.'

'I do have to okay things like that you know. As you are here with this ground-breaking news today, I get the feeling that you think the next kidnap is imminent?'

Danny nodded.

'Tomorrow night, if I am right,' he advised.

'Let us pray you are,' the Chief Inspector replied. 'Do you have this killer's name?'

'Jeremy Julian Joliff.'

'Margaret Joliff's boy!' the Chief Inspector said in surprise.

'Yes, and I would like the chance to talk to Sergeant Mulroon about it before anything is said,' Danny replied.

'I am not surprised and, I think, a wise move. We will give you a few minutes before we come for a briefing. It will give Hugh a chance to fill me in on all the facts.'

Danny went in search of John Mulroon, but his desk was unmanned.

'He's in Inspector Gosfar's room,' Hiram K called from the other side of the room.

'Thanks.'

Danny stood in the open doorway.

'Come in, Danny,' John said when he saw him. 'To what do I owe this pleasure? If it's to lodge a wrongful arrest complaint, I'll write it up now! I don't know what brought that about!'

'I think it was the Chief Mountie pulling strings via a Chief Inspector, or that was what I was told, but that is not why I'm here and I don't think you will call it pleasure when I've said my piece.'

John sat down.

'Serious, eh? Let's hear it then.'

Danny closed the door and sat down.

'You know I have been looking into this case ever since I found that little girl?' Danny started.

'It's common knowledge. In fact, some were surprised

when another girl went missing! They all thought you'd catch this creep where we had failed.'

'I nearly did. I was going to follow him on the day Annette disappeared, but he left in the night.'

'Who were you going to follow?'

'Chief!'

'What!' John jumped up, and the chair he was sitting on went flying. 'He happens to be a friend of mine.'

'I know, but if you will hear me out...'

'Why the hell should I?' John roared. 'I've known him a lot longer than you, and I definitely don't think he is the killer.'

'Because if you don't,' Danny continued, 'There is going to be another little girl curling up naked under a spruce to die, thinking that the world has it in for her, and she'll be right!'

John picked up the chair and sat on it.

'I'll hear you out, but only out of friendship, and I don't say I'll go along with it.'

Danny took a deep breath.

'I've been looking for a link with someone who is still on our list, and who has the freedom to be our killer, which originally ruled Chief out because he works until late and is then under the thumb of his mother.'

'That I know!'

'It wasn't until I found out that his mother had to go to the hospital in Lower Superior for her treatment in the winter, and the fact that he slept in his camper, that I saw him as a possible suspect. He is still on the list for another test. When he took her this year for the first time in the winter, I was going to follow him but he left in the night before I arrived. It was still dark when I arrived, and his mother doesn't like to ride in the dark.'

'That I also know!'

'I drove to the hospital to make sure he stayed there all night, but he was gone when I got there, and his mother was in a room because she was way too early! It seems they mistook the time of her appointment.'

'That doesn't make him a killer.'

'No, but Annette was taken the same night during dinner.'

'But where's your proof?' John asked. 'I can't go accusing people of something as serious as this without evidence, and I won't go accusing Chief without a lot of corroborative evidence.'

'I don't want you to accuse him,' Danny declared. 'He is taking his mother to hospital tomorrow, and all I want to do is follow him without him knowing.'

'You've got a nerve! I'll admit you've done well since you've been here, and if it was anyone else I'd do it, but Chief? I've watched him grow up. He did break free from his mother's influence once, and started working for Mike Wilson, but that didn't last long. He was soon back working for the old cow again.'

'I wonder if that had anything to do with it?' Danny replied.

'You wondered what had anything to do with it?'

'How old was he when he started working for Mike Wilson?'

'Eighteen, why?'

'Wilson was an active homosexual. I wonder if he took advantage of Chief when he was working there?'

'Not only have you accused one of my friends of being a killer, in fact the worst kind of killer and with very little proof, now you say he is bent!' The chair flew on to the floor for a second time as John jumped to his feet again.

'Gentlemen, please!'

John turned to see the Chief Inspector in the doorway. He stood to attention, but it was obvious he was unhappy. The Chief Inspector walked in, followed by Hugh Gosfar who closed the door.

'The whole station can hear you! Can we have some decorum?' the Chief Inspector added.

'Have you any idea what Mr Turner has just told me sir?' John asked.

'I am the Chief Inspector. If I didn't know, I would not be doing my job very well,' the Chief Inspector replied. 'What I fail to understand is your attitude. I know Mr Joliff is a personal friend, but are you afraid that if you have him followed he will kidnap, rape and torture a little girl prior to leaving her to die alone in the frozen wilderness?'

'No sir! At no time!' John snapped.

'Then if you do have him tailed, you will clear his name without him even knowing and we can cross another name off the list of suspects. Is that not what friends are for?'

John remained at attention without answering.

'Personally, I think it is worth a try, especially as the little girl was taken on the night Mr Turner had anticipated, and also because...' The Chief Inspector lowered his voice. 'Mr Turner, after trying to guess where she might be left, spent the night searching for camper van tracks and by following one set and the snowshoe prints which lead away from it, he found the girl, alive!'

John looked from one to the other.

'Annette Foy is alive?' he asked, his voice now lowered.

'Yes. She is with her mother in a private clinic, but as you know these things never run as you want them to. Far from her saying, 'It was him!', and pointing the finger, she has blacked out the traumatic events of that night. From what the doctors say, it is for the best, and we are not going to try and dig any of it up, not while we have this chance anyway. All she does remember is her mother telling her off for not filling the salt cellars as she was told to do, and her saying she had done it. If she was right, then this man not only knew her well enough to know that filling the salt cellars was her task, he must also have emptied them to make sure she had to go out and fill them again, where he lay in wait. I want this man! Now, do I have to go out of the area to find someone who can follow him professionally!'

'No, Chief Inspector, we'll do it! That way we can prove his innocence,' John replied.

'Good,' the Chief Inspector replied.

'I hope you do prove his innocence, John,' Danny added.

'I will send the lads out to hire a couple of cars,' John declared. 'Chief knows everything we have.'

'Good, then they will not have radios,' the Chief Inspector replied. 'No radios are to be used during this surveillance operation because the subject frequently listens to the police band.'

'How do we stay in contact?' John asked.

'Telephone,' Danny replied. 'There are several pay phones in the hospital and, if you are right, Chief will just stay in the car park or opt for a meal somewhere.'

'The girl is our secret,' the Chief Inspector stressed. 'The last thing we want is for the killer to know that we found her. As you know, he leaves them all...'

'Of course you know where he is going to leave the next one,' John declared, interrupting the Chief Inspector.

'Quite so, but the idea is to catch the man when he has just taken the girl, not after he discards her! We have a team staking out the area where Annette Foy was left but it is a big area and even he might not find the right place next time. Mr Turner had trouble finding it again.'

'When do we start?' John asked, now anxious to clear his friend's name.

'If I am right, he will strike tomorrow night. Last time I tried to follow him and he went out early,' Danny said. 'He might have been avoiding me, or just needed more time to get back to take Annette.'

'Only if it was him,' John pointed out.

'As you say,' Danny replied. 'I thought it might be an idea to make him think I was out of the picture again.'

'How do you mean?' the Chief Inspector asked.

'As he likes to listen to the police bands, you could send out a radio message for your men to arrest me again on sight in connection with the murders.'

'You'll have the reporters all over you like flies,' John warned.

'Not for long if I'm right, and if I'm wrong, you'll run me out of town,' Danny replied.

'Well, I am confident you will need your running spikes when Chief drives back with his mother,' John declared. 'He is bound to find out sooner or later, but not from me I might add.' He opened the door. 'Find Pinky and Perky, and get them in here.'

Ten minutes later, two men walked into the office.

'In the canteen again Floyd? No wonder your car keeps

breaking down,' John said, patting the fat man's belly.

The two men were Peter Floyd, nicknamed Pinky after the group, and Perkis Washington who, when he was partnered with Pinky, was quickly called Perky!

'You're joking, Sarge! I lost two stone last week,' Pinky replied.

John leant sideways and looked Pinky up and down.

'I know where they went. They're hiding behind you!'

'Very funny, Sarge...' He saw the Chief Inspector and the Inspector standing there and tried to straighten up his bulky frame. 'Sir.' Perkis was more alert and had seen them straight away. He stood stiff and straight.

'The Sergeant has a difficult task for you which must be done in complete secrecy, assuming you want to remain Mounties! Do you catch my drift?' the Chief Inspector asked.

'Yes sir!' they answered together.

'Good! I will leave you to instruct them Inspector Gosfar, as you have been the figurehead in the investigation so far. I will take Mr Turner's statement. Follow me Mr Turner. We will use interview room two.'

Danny followed, knowing that his future was either going to end, or he was going to be hailed a hero. If he was wrong, he would move on, but it would be hard leaving Kate. They walked straight through the interview room into the Chief Inspector's office. The Chief Inspector sat down and motioned Danny to do the same, as he pushed a button on the intercom.

'Coffee please, Madeline. What is your poison, Mr Turner?'

'Coffee please, black with two sugars.'

'Make that two coffees, please.' He relaxed in his chair.

'I suppose you are wondering why I am going along with all this?'

'To catch a killer, I suppose?' Danny replied.

'Now that we have a suspect, I am sure if we pulled his camper to pieces we would find enough evidence to convict him, assuming you are right. But I want him bang to rights! No plea bargaining down to a lesser charge. I want first degree murder, first degree rape, and first degree kidnapping. This has cost a lot of young lives, and we have looked, believe me we have looked. I hope you are right about Mr Joliff, despite his being well known and well liked around here. The killer has been like the invisible man. God help us if he is not our culprit!'

'We will know tomorrow night, or evening, if he sticks to his new MO, which is why I came in today. He has to drop his mother off at St Margaret's sometime, and if a car or cars are waiting to follow him from there, we should be able to stop him if he snatches another girl. He stepped over the line when he left that photograph of Annette Foy on the board in my cabin.'

'We must wait until he commits himself, but why not follow him from home?' the Chief Inspector asked.

'If he spots them, he might just sit it out. He is starting to enjoy the cat and mouse game, as well as the thrill of the kill...' Danny stopped speaking. 'He must have seen the list I am working to, on my board!'

'But his mother will still go on the same date, surely?'

Danny pulled the list out of his pocket. It was only a photocopy, and hard to tell if it had been altered.

'We need the original list to make sure he did not alter it,' Danny cried.

The Chief Inspector picked up the phone, and almost instantly Hugh Gosfar walked in.

'Right again, Mr Turner. I would say that was a five changed to a six.' He said holding the paper out for the Chief Inspector.

Danny was third in line, and he too thought it had been altered.

'By the time we were ready to spring into action, it would have already been done,' he declared.

The Chief Inspector phoned the hospital.

'I wonder if I could speak to Margaret Joliff, please. Yes, a friend. She hasn't. Okay, I'll phone you later.' He put the receiver down. 'She is due in today, but she has not arrived yet. Hugh, get things going for tonight, and make sure they get there before he leaves the hospital car park.'

'Yes sir.' Hugh left at speed. He knew there was no time to waste.

'Damn! I hope we can get there before he leaves the hospital,' Danny said angrily. 'I was stupid. I should have realised sooner!'

'At least he only changed it by one day,' the Chief Inspector replied. 'Two days, and we might be out searching for his next victim.'

'He probably did it to wind me up, but I don't understand why he did not drop his mother off earlier. He'd be away now to do his dirty deed.'

'Maybe the old girl was playing up. I hear she is no angel.'

'You can say that again! Still, this time she did us a favour if she is putting her foot down. On the other hand, his intended victim might be nearby and, with me out of the way, he feels home and dry.'

'Only time will tell,' the Chief Inspector replied, as the coffee arrived.

Hugh Gosfar found Pinky and Perky in the canteen again.

'We have moved it forwards to tonight! Get yourselves to the garage, get a car, and get to the hospital before your subject leaves the car park. Do I make myself clear?'

'Yes sir!' Perkis replied. Pinky still had a mouthful of food and could not answer.

'And remember what you were told. No radio. You do not discuss this with anyone and make sure you are not spotted. You ask to talk to me or the Chief Inspector, no one else! Is that clear?'

'Yes sir!' This time Pinky was able to speak.

'Well don't just sit there. Get moving! Your target is already on his way.'

'What about a mobile phone, sir?' Perky asked.

'A good idea, but we do not have one to hand. Do you have one?'

'I'll stop off at home and get it.'

They scrambled out of the canteen, knocking over chairs in their hurry, and ran for the door.

'And get out of those uniforms!' Hugh shouted after them. 'Or he'll see you a mile away.'

CHAPTER 18

THE two Mounties changed, then drove off at speed. First they had to get a car, then collect the mobile phone before they could go to the hospital, and they had to be there before Chief left the hospital car park. They drove to the garage, and had to take the only car there, then they drove to Perky's house for the phone.

In his haste, he had trouble unlocking the door, and his wife opened it to see who was there. He pushed past her but the mobile phone was not where he kept it.

'Where's the phone?' he almost shouted.

'In the hall,' she replied sleepily.

'No, not that one!'

'Oh, the mobile's flat. I tried to use it just now,' she replied, stifling a yawn.

'Why didn't you put it on to charge?' he asked, already heading for the door.

'You always do that,' she replied indifferently.

He slammed the door and ran to where Pinky had the car ticking over, trying to warm it up.

'The mobile phone is flat,' he said disgustedly as he climbed in. 'You'd think she'd have the gumption to put it on to charge. I swear I'll kill that woman one day! She rings someone on it, just so she can talk from the bath.'

'I know who is going to be walking over to the phone box then,' Pinky replied as he put his foot on the gas.

When they arrived at the hospital, there was no sign of Chief's camper. They parked in a corner of the main car park to discuss their options. If they walked over and enquired after Margaret Joliff, Chief might find out and be tipped off, but they needed to know if he had arrived yet, or if he was still on his way. They decided to find out, and Perky, being slimmer and less noticeable, climbed out.

He was half way across the car park when he saw Chief's camper turn into the hospital car park. He pulled his lapels over his face and carried on walking. He thought it would be more suspicious to turn back. Once over there, he stood in a phone booth and waited, pretending to phone someone. Margaret Joliff walked in, but Chief remained in the camper. When the doors closed behind her, Chief drove into the car park and parked. Perky phoned the station.

'He's just arrived. I'll ring if there are any developments,' he said quietly.

'I'll be right by the phone,' Hugh Gosfar replied.

Perky chose a route back to their car which gave him most cover, but did not try to hide and arouse suspicion.

'That was close,' Pinky said when Perky returned. 'Just remember! I do not want to go back to walking the beat!'

'Me neither,' Perky added, and they settled down to wait in the cold with the engine turned off.

Back at the police station, Danny was as nervous as a man about to become a father. He walked up and down to the annoyance of the others. When the phone call came in, and they said they were watching Chief and his camper, he settled down.

'Thank God for that!' the Chief Inspector cried. 'I thought you were going to wear out my carpet.'

'Sorry, I thought they were too late, and I hate to think of another little girl going through it!' Danny replied.

'I can understand that, but now they have him in sight he cannot do anything without us knowing,' the Chief Inspector assured him.

At six o'clock, the camper moved off.

'Shit! Get it started!' Pinky yelled as he wrapped up his sandwich.

Perky turned the key, and the battery gave a low growl before it fell silent.

'Trust us to get the duff one!' Perky cried. 'Do we wait for him to come back? He's probably only getting gas or beer.'

'Are you kidding?' Pinky replied. 'I have three years left and, from what the C.I. said, we could be walking the beat! Can you honestly see me back walking the beat?'

'Then get out and give us a shove!' Perky hissed. 'There is a clear bit over there, we might get some grip.'

Pinky jumped out and pushed the car to the salted area of the car park. There they did get some grip and, with Pinky's bulk pushing, the car roared into life. They raced off trying to catch up with Chief's camper, who by now had a good start. But Chief was in no hurry. He was trundling along and they soon caught up with his camper.

'There it is!' Pinky said between mouthfuls. 'He's not in any hurry!'

'I bet it's beer,' Perky replied.

'Don't get too close,' Pinky warned.

'At least it will give Chief something to talk about at the next party. He's always wanted to be involved,' Perky replied. 'Chief, our serial killer!'

He slowed to the leisurely pace of the camper, and followed at a distance until it swung into a motel car park.

'I thought he liked his camper!' Pinky cried. 'He's going to stay in a motel. I'll be sure to mention that to him next time I see him.'

'And we are going to have to sleep out here while he sleeps in the motel in comfort,' Perky complained. 'I'll go and phone in. There is a kiosk over there.'

He walked toward the phone kiosk, keeping out of sight as he walked, but when he could see it, Chief was there to make a phone call. Chief tried the phone, then walked into the motel. Perky waited until Chief was out of sight, then walked to the kiosk, but the wire had been cut. Perky walked back to the car.

'The kiosk has been vandalised,' Perky complained. 'Chief has gone into the motel.'

'Well, you can't use the one in there,' Pinky replied. 'That's for sure. There is a phone up the road we can use.'

'Shouldn't someone stay on watch?' Perky asked.

'What, and freeze our balls off!' Pinky replied. 'He's here for the night. He'll be here when we get back.'

They drove off to phone in. It was only two kilometres up the road, in the foyer of a hotel. Pinky sat in the car keeping the engine running while Perky phoned in.

'He's stopped at the Valley Motel,' he said. 'What now?'

'Watch to make sure he stays put. I'll be here all night.' Hugh Gosfar replied.

'Yes sir.'

He walked back to the car.

'We have to watch him all night,' he announced.

'It's that or walking the beat again,' Pinky replied, and drove them back to the motel.

When they reached the motel, there was an empty space where the camper had been parked. Pinky skidded to a halt, and a lorry had to swerve round him, honking loudly as it did so. At the crossroads, the lorry let another lorry across in front of him, thus obliterating all tracks. The lorry drove on to finish the job.

'Where's the camper?' Perky asked.

'How should I know?' Pinky replied.

'What do you reckon? Go back to the hospital and see if he is there?' Perky asked.

'Yep, we can use the canteen,' Pinky answered.

A shout from the motel caught their attention. A man was outside, shouting.

'What do you think? Chief not pay for the call?' Pinky said, and chuckled at his joke.

'I'll go and find out,' Perky replied. 'He looks a bit distraught to me.' He pinned his badge on, so it was clearly visible, and struggled through the snow to the shouting man. 'Is there a problem?'

'My daughter is missing, and the phone line has been cut to both the phones,' the man replied. 'Do you have a radio?'

'No radio, but there is a phone up the road. I'll call for assistance.'

When he was out of earshot he said. 'Shit, now we're for it!'

He walked back to the car.

'Pinky, get inside and play at being a policeman,' Perky ordered. 'His daughter has just been kidnapped.'

Pinky's jaw dropped.

'Oh my God!' He hauled himself out of the seat and struggled through the snow to the waiting man.

'Let us go and look for her in case she is still about, but try not to disturb anything,' he said, ushering the man inside.

Perky drove back to the hotel.

'When we got back to the motel, the proprietor's daughter was missing and the camper was gone,' Perky announced.

'What do you mean? When you got back?' Hugh Gosfar yelled.

By now, John Mulroon had joined Danny and the Inspector. The Chief Inspector was in his office. They both looked at the Inspector expectantly.

'We had to use a phone up the road. The one outside the motel had been vandalised,' Perky replied.

'You didn't think to leave a man on watch?'

'I thought of it, but Pinky was against it.'

'You could have stayed. Try and see which way Chief went.'

'Too late for that. A couple of sixteen wheelers went through just after we got back. He could be anywhere.'

'Get back to the motel and wait for me.'

'Yes sir.'

Hugh put the receiver back in its cradle.

'They used a phone up the road to call in, both of them! When they got back, Chief was gone and so was the proprietor's daughter,' he declared. 'The tracks have been wiped out by lorries, so they have no idea where Chief is.'

'He might be back at the hospital,' John suggested.

'Yes, and pigs might fly!' Danny said derisively, a little annoyed by John's 'it can't be him' attitude.

'Take a turn round the car park, Sergeant, on your way to the Valley Motel,' Hugh ordered.

Danny stood up, ready to go with John.

'This is a police matter!' John said, and walked out.

'You can come in my car, Mr Turner, but first I will have to tell the Chief Inspector.'

He explained the events, as they had occurred, to the Chief Inspector, holding the receiver away from his ear to stop himself being deafened.

'That is one angry man!' he said, after the Chief Inspector had slammed down the phone at his end.

'I'm not over the moon about it myself!' Danny replied. 'If they had done their job properly, Chief would be under lock and key by now, and the girl back home.'

'Assuming he has her. He might have come along, found both phones not working, and driven off again quite innocently. The killer might have been there keeping the girl quiet until Chief left, and then made off with her.'

'It's possible, but my money is on Chief being the killer!'

They walked outside and the snow was falling again.

'Makes it a bit tricky now,' Hugh said. 'He will be listening in if you are right, so we have to use the radio as normal and be heard to search, but the search should be for the camper, without letting him know. If we find the camper, we might get the girl back unharmed.'

The chauffeur drove them to the motel, and Hugh walked inside. Danny sat in the car. Inside, Hugh saw the girl's clothes spread in front of the fire, the killer's trademark. The Chief Inspector walked in.

'Damn bad thing, this,' he complained.

'It's our man,' Hugh replied. 'I will order a search over the radio, but it is better to find that camper before he goes too far, sir.'

'Yes, he will expect a search as usual, but we can send cars out to look for the camper,' the Chief Inspector replied. 'This snow will cover his tracks very quickly. He might be parked up, but covered in snow, and they drive right by it. This has not been a good evening's work for the R.C.M.P!'

'It could still be a coincidence, sir.'

'It could, but the most important thing is to find this girl as soon as possible. I have sent the two idiots who lost him to look in the hospital car park, just in case. If we find the camper, we go in as though she is in there.' He pointed to the photograph of a young girl with long blonde hair and blue eyes. 'Get copies of that and get it circulated. In fact, do everything we usually do, as well as looking for the camper. Draft in all the help you want.'

'Yes, sir.'

By now the proprietor of the motel was in tears. He had read the papers, and knew he might never see his daughter alive again. His wife had died two years earlier, and now he was to lose his daughter.

Danny sat in the car thinking. He needed to get to the place where he had found Annette. He wanted to make sure there were no foul ups at the other end, but he knew that John was not about to take him. Hugh climbed in beside him and used the car radio to issue orders. While he was talking, an engineer arrived to reconnect the phones. Hugh was careful not to let anything slip as he spoke on the radio. The area they had staked out was now their only real hope. When everything was arranged, and people were mustered to search, without being told it was a waste of time, Hugh turned to Danny.

'This should have been avoided,' he said with feeling. It was the first time he had shown any feeling in his voice.

'That little girl is going to have a bad night,' Danny said with as much feeling. 'And I am damn well not going to sit on my backside and do nothing! Whatever you say or do, I am going to be there to make sure nothing goes wrong at the other end.'

'I have no argument with that, but we will need better clothes than these if we are going to join the stakeout,' the Inspector replied.

The chauffeur drove to Danny's cabin, and he changed into warmer clothing. Not white, as Hugh had, but he planned to stay well out of sight. At midnight, they drove to the bridge, turned left once they were over it, onto the River Road and continued until the corner where the road left the river. The chauffeur followed a track by the river, and parked alongside three other vehicles. One was John Mulroon's car. They climbed out, and Hugh opened the trunk which contained several guns.

'As you haven't brought your rifle, you might want to borrow something of mine,' Hugh offered.

Danny looked, and chose a blanket, the type used to keep in body heat.

'This will do,' he said, and tucked it under his arm.

'No gun?'

'If he is carrying a girl, I don't think he will carry a rifle as well. Besides, the rest will have guns.'

'We have spread the men out in case he cannot find the exact spot again. I am not taking any chances with this.' Hugh chose a rifle and hooked it over his shoulder. 'I hope he resists!'

They walked through the trees to the place where Annette was left, expecting to be challenged, but only John Mulroon was there.

'I moved the others up a bit to give us more coverage sir,' John announced.

'Without my say so?'

'This is personal, sir. If it turns out to be Chief, I want to be the one to take him down.'

'We do have to think of this little girl,' the Inspector replied.

'I know, sir.'

'Very well. I will go further up, but I will arrange for a paramedic unit to be out here with their radio off!'

'Yes sir!'

Hugh walked back to his car.

'You can go too!' John ordered.

'No way, Hosea. Shoot me if you like, but I am making sure this little girl does not suffer any more than she has already,' Danny replied.

'Then don't get in my way, Danny.'

'I won't, and I won't make a move until the girl is freed,' Danny replied. 'After that, seconds count out here.'

They both chose a place to hide. Danny behind the tree where Annette had chosen to die, and John nearer the road, but he was in a snow suit. When he lay down, he was almost invisible. They waited silently, both angry, and both ready for anything that might happen, or so they hoped.

Red was asleep when he heard a scratching at the front door. He walked bleary-eyed into the lounge to find Captain Webb scratching at the door.

'Do you want to go out, Captain Webb?' he asked, stifling a yawn.

Kate had drummed into him not to leave the door unlocked even though the girls were sleeping in with her. He unlocked the door and the wolf walked out. Red locked the door and sat in the armchair next to the fire, the one they usually moved to make way for the Christmas tree. He had not gone tree hunting yet. He was hoping to do that with Danny nearer Christmas. He stirred the fire into life, threw on some more wood, and settled down to wait for the wolf to return. He snuggled up in the chair as the fire crackled into life, bathing him with its warmth. He was soon asleep.

Danny watched a lorry as it trundled along. It stopped and a woman climbed out. She struggled through the snow to get behind a tree on the same side of the road they were hiding on, where she dropped her lower clothes to relieve herself, her white bottom shining in the moonlight.

'If only I had a camera,' Danny thought.

The woman, oblivious to those watching her, struggled back to the lorry and it moved off. A camper appeared, and Danny stiffened, but it drove by without stopping, although it was hard to tell the shape in the snow, even in the moonlight. Another camper approached. This time it stopped. Danny watched as a hooded figure climbed out and donned snow shoes. Then the figure picked up a white bundle and walked towards him. As he grew nearer, he could see that the bundle was a small, naked girl. He felt his hackles rise, and cursed himself for not having a rifle to shoot this son of a bitch dead. The hooded figure walked nearer and nearer until he stood the girl on the ground, with the snow reaching above her knees.

'Well, you can go!' the hooded figure said quietly.

The girl did not move, just shivered.

'Scat or I'll start doing it again.'

Now she ran! It was not easy in deep snow and as soon as she was near enough Danny stepped out and scooped her up in the blanket, tucking her feet in to stop her from getting frostbite. The hooded figure saw him and started for his camper.

That was when John stepped out into his path.

'Okay you bastard, time to pay the piper!' John hissed, his rifle held loosely, but ready.

The hooded figure removed the hood.

'Well, hello John. How nice to see you,' Chief said politely.

CHAPTER 19

SERGEANT John Mulroon took an involuntary step back in astonishment. He was visibly shaken. All those years of friendship, and he really hadn't known him at all.

'Chief! It is you! How could you? I mean... do that to little girls?' he spluttered. 'Danny said it was you, but I wouldn't let myself believe it.'

'Oh, believe it, John. You ought to try it. They are so sweet, and ready to do anything to stay alive.'

'Shut your foul mouth!' John hissed, his mood changing immediately. 'I'm taking you in.'

'Why should I?' Chief asked. 'You are only going to arrest me. I'm unarmed, and I'm sure Mother will find a way to get me off. Then I can move on and start up somewhere else.'

John walked forward and pushed the barrel of his rifle into Chief's stomach.

'Shut up, or I'll save the taxpayers the cost of a trial,' he warned.

Chief took a step back, but as he did so he put his left snow shoe on his right snow shoe, holding the catch, which secured it to his boot, open.

'Surely not. Not you! Straight as a die Mulroon. Or are you? I bet you've already tried it with your daughter.'

John pulled the gun back to hit him with it. Chief had been trying to bate him and, as John pulled the rifle back, Chief used the now free right boot to kick John hard between the legs. John doubled up in pain, and Chief took his gun.

'I thought that would get you going! I've been reading a book on psychology, and I might even take a course on it when they finally catch me. I'll have more time when I am in prison.'

He levered a bullet into the breech, and put his snow shoe back on.

'Now it seems I have a bit of clearing up to do. You must have found Annette, Danny. That was clever of you. She wouldn't normally be my type, but I knew you liked her. She was so gullible. I crept in before dinner and emptied the salt pots, and took the rest of the salt.

When she came out, with Hester yelling at her because she was told to do it earlier, I was waiting. When she couldn't find any salt, I told her there was some in my camper. I said, "Come on and I'll give it to you," but it wasn't salt I gave her.'

'You bastard! I'll make you pay,' John said, still on his knees in the snow.

Danny stood there, holding the girl. 'Surely someone is on their way,' he thought. 'What's up, Chief? Didn't you like Mike's attentions?' he asked, to gain time. 'I bet you lead him on! Did you tease him? I expect he got fed up with it!'

'No, it wasn't like that,' Chief replied. 'There was a

job going so I applied for it as the money was good, but he just wanted me there. He spiked my drink and spent the next two hours up my arse. I could feel what he was doing but I couldn't do anything about it. I never went back to work there, but it's not the sort of thing you go around telling people about, is it?

When they started doing the tests, I went back there and he thought I'd come round to his way of thinking and it was going to be a long-term relationship. I made him use a rubber when he did it, and when I thought I had enough of his sperm, I took him up onto Suicide Falls blindfolded. I'd already prepared it by removing the signs and the fences, so I undid his blindfold and told him he had until I counted to twenty, then I was going to start shooting. He ran for his life, straight over the Falls. I was too late to see him hit the ground, and that annoyed me. I wonder what he was thinking as he flew through the air.' All the time he was talking, the rifle was pointing at John without wavering.

Danny detected movement to his left. Two people, wearing snow suits, were moving toward Chief, but they did not have snow shoes on, and a charge would probably end in their deaths. If they fired from there John might get hit, or Chief might shoot John and him. They needed time to close in.

'Is that what started you off then?' he asked.

'No. It was Ma, the old cow! When old Ferguson retired from the Force, they had a big do for him, but Ma wouldn't let me go, because I had to take her to the hospital the next day! I was mad as hell!

'When I dropped her off I had a couple of beers just to

spite her, but it wouldn't go away. In the end, I went in for some chips, and this girl was in there, in a tutu. You know, one of them dancing dresses, in the middle of winter! All leg she was. I thought I would snatch her and have some fun, but she got straight into a car outside. Well I suppose you would, dressed like that in the middle of winter. I followed them a little way, then I saw another girl walking along the road. She was all wrapped up against the weather, and all alone. I waited up the road she had just walked down and grabbed her when she came back. Then I drove to a place I know and we ate the food she had bought. Very frightened she was, did everything I told her.

'I had no intentions of hurting her. I just thought they would send me to a hospital for a while if they found me, but after we did it I must have fallen asleep. When I woke, she'd legged it, but I was asleep on her clothes so she took my curtains to wear. I followed her footprints in the snow, and it must have been hard work for her as she struggled along. When I finally caught up with her, she was dead from the cold! I took back my curtains, and took her boots off her. She looked silly, naked and wearing boots.

'I drove away from there in a hurry and parked in the hospital park. It wasn't until the next morning I realised I hadn't used a rubber when I did it, and I did it a few times. I was sick with worry, and the next night I went back there to see if I could cut her open or something, but I couldn't find her body under the snow. When they finally found her, I was so sick with worry that Ma even called Doc Shoesmith and he gave me a week off.'

All the time he was speaking, the two men in white were closing in.

'After the first one, I got a taste for it. I started chatting up girls at the school in the summer, and taking notes. I used to say things like, "it must be awkward if you get locked out if your parents are out." They usually told me a lot, even where the spare key was kept sometimes. Or, "does your Mum work as well?" I kept a book and chose my victims from it at random, except for Annette. She was a special. After the first one it got easier and easier.'

'What about her?' Danny nodded to the girl in his arms. 'She can't go to Timberline or Turnround school.'

'No, she was a free gift. I picked up the local paper, and there she was with her father. They were doing a piece on how he coped after his wife died. He ran the place on his own, and always walked round to make sure everyone was happy at the same time every night! Leaving that little beauty there all alone for a minimum of twenty minutes, sometimes more. I just drove in and took her.'

Danny could see that Chief was getting tired of talking.

'You'll have to kill Annette!' he warned, 'Or your freedom will be short lived.'

'So you found her alive, did you? I don't believe it! I'd be locked up by now if she'd talked. She's either dead and you are lying, or she hasn't said anything yet.'

Chief stopped to think. 'I did wonder why Hester went to her sister's, and refuses to talk to anyone! Maybe I should take a looksee at the hospital. They know me there. In fact one of the nurses has this pretty little daughter. She's next on my list. She showed me her picture. Now, enough talk! If I do this right, they will think one of you is the killer, and the other one a hero trying to save little Suzy there. Good old Danny can't be the killer because he came along

311

too late, but you were here for all the killings, John!'

John climbed to his feet. The rifle followed his every movement.

'Don't try anything stupid, John. You know I am a crack shot, unlike Danny there who shoots at legs and hits hearts!'

Chief smiled at the sharp look Danny gave John.

'Yes, it was him,' Chief declared. 'A couple of whiskies on his nights off, and I can sit back and catch up on all the local news.'

'You two-faced bastard,' John yelled. 'I'll kill you with my bare hands.'

He lunged at Chief who repelled him with the rifle barrel. As he lunged, Danny tried to run behind a tree, Chief swung the rifle and put it to his shoulder ready to fire at Danny.

'Goodbye, you English pain in the arse! Maybe I'll get the job this time!'

The branches in front of him parted, and a wolf sprang at him. Again he used the barrel to hit the wolf. The wolf yelped in pain but the wolf's impetus unbalanced Chief, knocking him over and knocking the rifle out of his hands. He pushed the wolf off him, but before he could regain the weapon, two other rifles were held up to his head where he lay.

'Just give me a reason to shoot Chief,' Made snarled.

'I don't need no more reason,' Hamish declared, and he fired.

Made managed to knock Hamish's rifle away as he fired, and the bullet parted Chief's hair. Made returned his rifle to Chief's face.

'Don't lower yourself to his level, Hamish,' Made

312

warned, ready to deflect another attempt, but Hamish did not try again.

Danny turned to walk back, but as he neared Chief the girl was visibly upset.

'Okay, we won't go there until they take him away,' he assured her.

Made unzipped his suit and pulled out his radio.

'We have him. Send in the paramedics and the paddy wagon,' he said triumphantly.

Seconds later, a siren sounded, then another. Paramedics came running, if you could call it that in deep snow without snow shoes. Danny walked round the place where Chief was laying to meet them, and ended up carrying Suzy to the ambulance. As soon as she was in safe hands and on her way to hospital, Danny walked to where the wolf sat, his paw held up in the air.

'What are you doing here, Captain Webb?' Danny said, and stroked his head. Danny examined the wolf's paw.

'Thank you for saving my life. I guess we are even now, but it will take more than my skill to fix that paw,' he said gently.

Meanwhile, John snapped the handcuffs on Chief with great pleasure.

'Try them for size,' he taunted.

'We are going to take this murdering git to the police station. Will yee come with us?' Hamish asked.

'No thanks, Hamish. I'd rather walk than ride with that scum! How come you were here anyway?' Danny asked. 'Did everyone know about this stakeout?'

'I had a phone call from the Inspector a wee while ago saying yee might need some help, and he did tell us to be inconspicuous,' Hamish replied, then added, 'I do hope he makes a run for it.'

Danny watched them as they piled into the paddy wagon and drove away.

'Well, it's just you and me, Captain Webb, and we are a long way from home,' Danny said, walking toward the road.

Captain Webb limped after him, but by the whimper and his limp, it was obvious that the paw was hurting him a lot. Danny looked back and stopped.

'You could have said you couldn't walk, Captain Webb,' Danny scolded. 'I am never going to be able to carry you to the cabin from here.'

His mind ran through the possibilities. Url's house was not far away. If he could rouse her, he could at least have some warmth. If not, he would have to wait there until morning. He picked up the wolf and headed for the road where the snow was less deep. Hugh Gosfar's limousine pulled up in front of him. The window hummed as it opened.

'Is he injured?' Hugh asked.

'Yes, he damaged a paw saving my life.'

'Get in. I know a man who will treat him.'

'What, at this time in the morning?' Danny asked, looking at his watch. It was five in the morning.

'He's probably been up an hour by now,' Hugh answered. 'He is a medicine man.'

'Why would he help me?'

'He is not helping you. He is helping the wolf, and he will do it because I ask him to. You see, when I joined the Mounties, I changed my name! After all, 'He Who Goes Far', would never have made it to Inspector. It just goes to show that my father was indeed a man of great vision.'

Danny slid Captain Webb on the back seat next to Hugh Gosfar, and climbed in next to him. The chauffeur obviously knew the way because in five minutes they were parked outside the medicine man's house, complete with Teepee in the front garden. Danny followed the Inspector into the house, carrying Captain Webb.

'I am honoured, He Who Goes Far,' the medicine man said when he saw the Inspector.

'The honour is all mine, Tall Trees. I have a friend who needs your help.'

Tall Trees looked across at Danny and Captain Webb.

'Bring him through,' he said, as though it were an everyday event.

Danny followed, but stopped when the medicine man donned a white coat.

'What's up, Danny? Haven't you seen a vet before?' Hugh asked.

'Not one who smiles when he is treating something at five in the morning.'

'My people bring their animals in now as I have to open my surgery in Timberline at eight in the morning,' the vet explained. He examined the damaged paw.

'I'll strap it up, but you will have to keep him off it for a few weeks,' the vet advised.

'What's he done?' Danny asked, expecting the worst.

'Torn a few ligaments, I think. Bring him back in a week and I will take another look at him. Between five and six a.m. is good for me.'

He bandaged the paw, and Captain Webb limped outside.

'Red will be worried about you in the morning,' Danny said as they walked to the limousine.

315

The chauffeur drove to Danny's cabin.

'Can I offer you gents a share in a bottle of whisky? I feel like celebrating.'

Hugh looked at his watch.

'Why not, I think we all deserve to celebrate,' he replied. 'Come on, Humphrey, you can have a little one as well. Don't bother to lock the car. Not out here.'

'You never know who is about out here,' Danny declared.

He was thinking of the woman as she squatted behind the tree, blissfully unaware of the eyes that watched her, but quite happy in the knowledge that she was out of sight of the lorry driver. He started to laugh.

'No sir, you never know!'